A Summer of Castles

A Secret in Ruins

Also by Rachel Walkley

The Women of Heachley Hall
The Last Thing She Said
Beyond the Yew Tree

A Summer of Castles

Rachel Walkley

Spare Time Press

Published by Spare Time Press
Copyright © 2022 Rachel Walkley
All Rights Reserved
ISBN: 978-1-8383289-4-8

PROLOGUE

An extract from the Memoirs of Professor David
Carmichael, Emeritus Professor of Art History,
Charnwood University.

WINTER IS A TEDIOUS TIME OF YEAR when days shrink into mere interludes in the night. January of 2003 was no exception. It was in the midst of this relentless gloom that I received an unexpected telephone call.

'I need photographs.'

The abruptness was typical. There was no expectation that either of us would be able to fulfil the request. I'm a terrible photographer. The significant details were relayed in staccato bullet points. The urgency was somewhat alarming, although sadly expected. The nature of the request was certainly bizarre. However, I confess I was intrigued.

The improbable project was worthy of a dismissive head shake and I nearly backed out. However, occasional eccentric challenges were welcomed, especially in colder months when my students lost all enthusiasm and slept late into the mornings. So regardless of my mounting reservations and the insistence that I was under no obligation, I accepted my fate. The repayment of my debt was overdue.

I anticipated problems in abundance, mostly practical, for who would want to traipse from one remote place to another in the rain and wind, armed with a camera. England wasn't a sun-drenched country at any time of the year.

'Have faith,' came the wishful reply.

I recall we both chuckled at that comeback. That wonderful, deep-throated laugh is something I keep safely locked in my memories as it always brings back recollections of that distant summer I recounted in the earlier chapters of this loosely constructed memoir. Memories that are both delightful and painful.

And the voice rattled on, breathlessly, like an old wheeze box.

I had to interject. 'And this other matter—'

I shan't forget the cutting response, the secrecy. 'Leave that to me. I can handle that myself. This is harder. Somewhat unlikely, too.'

The brash smile wasn't visible, but I felt it all the same as if my friend was there in the room. When we talked or wrote to each other, I imagined an occupied armchair by the bookshelves, the reluctant opining, the quiet musing. The closed eyes and nodding head.

I did as asked, and continued to do so until I was no longer needed. And to this day I kept my role a secret from friends and colleagues; only my wife knows my involvement. Now, as I write it down, the events that unfolded seem unimaginable, almost surreal.

The specific requirements were sent separately in an email, and I dogmatically worked my way through the list. I needed a young and energetic candidate prepared to work unpaid and left to their own devices for extended periods, which might be haphazard. It should have been an ideal project for an eager student, but I wasn't permitted to engage one of mine, and certainly nobody professionally trained who might go off on a tangent. The list was sacrosanct - that word was actually used during a subsequent phone call. I was to find somebody specific to a favoured location, as if this unidentified photographer might present themselves on my doormat like an old-fashioned postcard.

'Visit the Curzon.'

'Why there?' I asked.

'It's well known in the area.'

'And it has to be a woman, a young woman who is local?' I couldn't repeat the details in the email, I had reached the point of exasperation. 'Why?'

There was a lengthy pause and a rasping sigh. 'I'll tell you why the next time you visit. I have a good reason.'

The stubbornness was also familiar and insurmountable.

And then there was the final issue. Who would work for somebody they were never going to meet, or, for that matter, know by their real name? Direct contact was by necessity limited to emails, which had led me to an interesting question, one that I still believe was the key to the deliberate mystery surrounding the project.

'What name will you use in your correspondence?' I asked, and jokingly suggested a familiar one that again brought back fond memories of older conversations.

'Why not? Good idea.'

I offered my reservations, but eventually caved in. I knew full well the name had been appropriated long before it was needed and had been chosen for its credibility.

As for whom I found to take the photographs, well, that is a remarkable story. Over the years, and to the best of my ability, I've made numerous attempts at writing this particular chapter and failed. I owe it to those involved to present it without judgement.

PART ONE

*'What I have dreamed in an hour is worth more
than what you have done in four.'*
Lorenzo de' Medici

ONE

Ashby-de-la-Zouch

*T*HE BREEZE SCATTERS *the wisps of pine needles bringing with it was the smell of horse breath and churned turf. At last, the impatient crowd of the berfrois grandstand, which lines each side of the list, fall silent with wide-eyed anticipation of the spectacle to come. Riding forward, the gleaming, armoured stallion is held in check, and snorts loudly. Steam shoots out of his nostrils and colours the air a misty grey; the frosty night has lingered into the early morning. The horse stamps his hooves on the chalky tilt yard and demands its release. However, no signal has been given; the lance handler has just retreated. People grow restless, rowdy in their chants.*

The tension grates on the rider, who tries hard to keep his steed under control. Through the eye slits, he focuses on the wooden barrier of the list, then into the distance, where his foe similarly struggles with his mount. Oblivious to the cool damp air, he sweats into his undergarments. The weight and oppressive nature of the garb provides no ventilation. Twisting his rigid form, he attempts to spot the scarf, still held up high and blowing in the breeze. Leather creaks as the saddle strains under the extra movement. Discomfort for the rider is inevitable and serves only to make the seconds feel like hours, and it has only been merely ten or so breaths since their lances rose.

The red cloth falls. Floating, for a moment it catches an up current and drifts, unsure. Then it slumps. Briefly, the jittery horses rear with excitement; the command is given. Unfettered by their grooms, both charge in unison towards each other. The joust has begun.

'Are you all right, luv? You look… dizzy.'

I jerked, my eyelashes fluttering. A curtain of sunlight breeched my lids with a golden flash. Above me was the silhouette of the stranger whose chafing voice had interrupted me at a crucial moment. I huffed and grabbed the strap of my handbag. Between the teeth of the zipper, I slipped the camera out of sight.

'Yes, fine.' I rose and hurried off the small ridge.

By the time I reached the edge of the sunken earthworks I regretted the curtness. Glancing back, I searched for the old lady. She had vanished, speedily for one with so many wrinkles and grey hairs. With a shrug, I slowed and meandered over to the Great Tower.

It didn't matter, not really. I'd relived the same daydream every time I visited Ashby-de-la-Zouch Castle. Lost in a slipstream of fantasy, I always, without fail it seemed, inhaled horse sweat and heated metal through my charmed nostrils, and, through my soles, I felt the rumble of the roaring crowd. What was my stimulus for escaping the humdrum of the real world? A solitary, covert yearning; I sought out ruins, chivalry and romantic tales; I was a sucker for them. If only, I mused again and again, photographs could capture my imagination in perpetuity; perhaps then I wouldn't need to keep coming back here and spending fruitless hours pretending I had some magical ability to travel back in time.

Time wasn't on my side and the brisk walk to the car park was accompanied by a flurry of late autumn leaves. Halfway there, I overtook the silver-haired lady ambling along with her shepherd's crook walking stick. I halted, aware of the gnawing discomfort in my belly. Turning on my heel, I approached the woman and bent slightly, hoping not to offend.

'I must apologise,' I said. 'I didn't mean to sound rude.'

The wrinkles multiplied as the lady's face broken into a smile. 'I interrupted you. I shouldn't have spoken. You seemed almost… catatonic.'

I flinched. 'Did I?' A worrying development. Nobody had commented before now on my appearance.

'In an occupied sort of way.' She clutched the walking stick with a hand that was all knuckles and veins.

'I was thinking about jousting.' I glanced past the woman to the severely pruned walls and towers.

'*Ivanhoe* by Walter Scott.' The old dear's voice brightened. 'He wrote the scene here.'

I exhaled and met her gaze; she possessed sharply focused eyes as blue as a summer sky.

'Yes, I know.'

'You've read it?'

'No,' I said. 'I should really, I suppose. I'm more of a visual kind of person. Or maybe it's because I prefer my senses telling a story.' I stopped, realising that what I was saying to a perfect stranger was ludicrous. However, the woman held me in her gaze, nodding sagely in the way an older person does when told something they have mastered years ago.

'You shouldn't be afraid to be what you feel,' she said.

For a second, I thought my hair had stood on end. What she said wasn't weird or unrelated to my own experiences of visiting places like Ashby. To me, at least, she made perfect sense.

'I can't help daydreaming, imagining things.' I was attempting to tell this unknown woman something deeply personal. 'I feel so…' The translation fell apart.

'Here?' She nodded, slowly. 'For me it's food. Great feasts. Roasted swan, smoked eels. Rich aromas. Earthy flavours, right there in my mouth.' She stopped. 'I'm not scaring you, am I?'

My pulse had quickened. 'No. Absolutely not. You've reassured me, in fact. I thought I was… am crazy. It doesn't just happen here.'

'Of course not. Why would it?' Her lips tinged purple, she shivered. 'I have to keep moving or I stiffen up.'

We walked side by side to a turnstile.

'I live in the village,' she said. 'I've seen you here before.'

I laughed softly at my weakness for the castle. 'You probably have. Sorry, I haven't noticed you.'

'It's comforting, isn't it, knowing you're not alone?' The growing smile dissembled her face into a mosaic of blotches.

We hadn't exactly defined what we were truly discussing, and I wasn't sure if I wanted it to be defined with a word, like a medical term from a textbook. Somewhere, somebody probably had a whole vocabulary for what I felt and none of it would be flattering. Mum already had her suspicions of something malign based on certain unexplained events in my childhood.

'Yes, it is. Does it get easier with… age?' I grimaced at the indiscretion.

The multitudinous lines on the old lady's brow deepened thoughtfully. 'I don't remember it ever being difficult. Think of it as a gift. Scott wrote books. I cook. What will you do?'

I clutched the bundle of keys in my coat pocket and stumbled slightly on the roots of a tree. I had never arrived at that conclusion before – harmonising the two things into one. But it made sense. It meant there was a good, or better, reason to keep trying, to not give up.

'One day, I'm going to visit…' I hadn't the words to express my wish and my feelings weren't readily packaged into neat verbal statements. Perhaps I had more in common with missionaries who ventured out with only spiritual needs to fulfil. 'I like photography,' I said instead. 'It's my hobby. I'd like it to be more than that.'

'Then it shall be, shan't it? Us dreamers must never stop hoping.' She held out her hand.

I held it gingerly; the bones under the translucent skin were strong, though.

'Good luck,' the stranger said.

'Thank you,' I said, with genuine gratitude.

I wished I had the chance to share our experiences over a cup of tea and a piece of cake. I would have liked to have known what she meant by a gift, because I'd never considered frequent daydreaming a talent or skilled activity, more of a childish and inconsequential distraction which sometimes caught and dropped me unawares into a scene that was equally as vivid, if not more so, as a book or a film. I had created this longing within me to be somewhere else in time and I was somewhat disconcerted by its growing insidiousness. However, the unexpected conversation had boosted my mood and for once I didn't scowl when I checked my watch.

❖

During the drive from castle to hotel, I concentrated on firing up my work persona. Never an easy task, as I'd yet to establish a resilient one.

Most days I manifested a pleasing facade, a shell that masked my inner voices. The brief excursions to the castle at Ashby-de-la-Zouch helped exercise my body, and wandering mind, and I often ventured out before the start of a late shift on the understanding my idiosyncratic daydreaming had to stay within the confines of that castle after I left it.

The hotel car park was half-empty, and I squared up the cranky Fiesta I shared with Mum next to an executive saloon. Turning off the engine, I stared up at the modern building, which was sadly devoid of any form of architectural beauty – I'd once snapped a few shots, hoping the camera might find something elusive that my eyes had failed to see. The failure supported the argumentative point that a photographer wasn't always the best interpreter of a subject. What the architect envisaged in the concrete moulding and geometric fenestrations was not what I reflected upon when I paused to contemplate the hotel's exterior. The building had a purpose, something useful, unlike ruined castles.

I applied a layer of gloss to my chapped lips. Appearances were everything. I was the first person to greet guests when they entered the foyer.

Every day was the same, or so it felt. For some idiotic reason, I'd chosen the job thinking I would meet people, which I did, and had assumed that through the varied human interactions and small talk I would be immersed in the world outside of the small town. The reality was different. I met plenty of people, but only fleetingly. How was it possible to widen horizons when accosted by crumpled suits, tired eyes, irritated mannerisms and polite indifference to my equally fake charms? I said hello and goodbye to countless bodies walking past the reception desk, dished out the same pat replies to complaints, and only, it seemed, occasionally dealt with the kind of crisis that made a day exciting. Seriously, had room twenty-six ever had a flushing loo?

I tried hard, if only because my work was appraised and judged, and failure was not an option. Today, however, was one of those days when I drifted off, didn't smile enough, and was too slow dealing with a massive queue of receipt lovers. From the outset of the job, I hadn't anticipated the volume of business clients; I preferred honeymooners and quaint old couples. Daily, I adopted the polished fake smile, and worked the queue of suits grasping credit cards, expensive mobile phones and leather briefcases.

At midnight I drove home, yawning, and parked outside the pleasant semi-detached house my parents had bought when I was a toddler. I tiptoed into the draughty hallway. Occasionally Dad was the designated welcomer waiting up for my arrival; usually it was Mum munching on biscuits, wrapped in one of the hotel's towelling robes, watching a late night romcom.

'Hot chocolate, Robyn?' Mum asked, without stirring from the settee. 'Kettle's not long boiled.'

Greeting my mother with a tired smile of gratitude, I stood propped against the doorframe, resting my head on the flaked woodwork. 'No, thanks. I'm beat.'

Mum rubbed her eyes. 'Dad was too. Crawled up there after tea. Long day for him.'

Dad and I often went days barely seeing each other. Then, he would have a spell off work, and he would be the one to greet me, or make lunch when I came off an early shift. The arrangement had its ups and downs, occasions when our body clocks worked against them, and we aimed grouchy barbs at each other. Given the way she was stretched out on the dimpled cushion, Mum must have fallen asleep there. She worked a couple of days a week in a corner shop, carefully rearranging the tin and jar labels on the shelves to face forward. Mum's lips were puckered. Something was about to be said, and it was probably best to wait for the recollection to emerge.

'Yvette rang. Pub tomorrow night. She can pick you up.'

I lowered my eyes.

She straightened up. 'Darling, don't do that. It's got to stop, this moping around. If he's there, ignore him.'

And her. Sally. 'Easier said than done.' I puffed out my weary cheeks. 'He's all over her.'

Craig, the ex, the amicable splitter, who had suggested we went our separate ways, then appeared within days at the pub with Sally. Our mutual friends, mostly from school days, had wisely not taken sides. Yvette was the exception. She understood how hurt I had been by the underhand method of "moving on", and continued to support me through the weeks that followed.

'Don't give up your friends just because you share the same ones,' Yvette had said, handing out tissues in fat bundles.

My mum had agreed. 'Make him see what he's missed out on,' she had said. 'I've heard Sally works her way through men like a bowling ball.'

However, three months on, the relationship was steadfast, glued by the commitment Craig and I had failed to create over our two years of dating. And it was simply dating; nothing had come of any plans to live together, nor had we changed the habits of our lives.

Craig never shared my fascination with castles, their stories, nor the idea of the past living on through heaps of stone, grassy mounds and windswept cobbles. I could hardly blame him; it was why I wasn't surprised by going our separate ways. However, I hadn't expected the rebound to happen so quickly on his part.

I probably wasn't cut out for sharing my life with anyone. What would a fun-loving guy make of a feckless daydreamer who carried a camera wherever she went, glued to her like an unnatural appendage?

TWO

HE WIPED THE DUST off the varnished cedar, emptied the contents of the box, and checked the tips of the brushes. He discarded the frayed ones. One by one, he sorted the small tubes of paints into colours, and noted the gaps. He wrote down what he needed to order from his supplier. Satisfied with the list, he repacked the box and closed the lid.

The lightweight easel wasn't in good shape. He leaned on it, and it creaked painfully. Folded, however, it was perfect for carrying.

There were other preparations to make, and he would stretch them out from one day to the next until it was time to go. The stack of paper required careful handling. He trimmed each sheet to size and sandwiched them between two boards. A roll of adhesive tape was dropped into a khaki rucksack, along with a staple gun, and a few wooden wedges for stretching canvases. From a shelf he selected the inks, and out of a drawer, a range of pencils. And the knife for sharpening them – an easy choice.

The telephone trilled sharply. He located it under a dust sheet. The phone call lasted longer than he would have liked. He pressed hard for more information and none of it was forthcoming. The plan was in motion, he was told, but beyond that he was required to wait. Constantly frustrated by his contact, the artist had kept himself busy with his usual routine, and circumvented questions from his curious colleagues. Most had Easter holidays in mind. He didn't envy them. He was content to follow a different path.

On the spur of the moment he climbed the ladder into the attic and rummaged through the discarded heaps until he found what he was looking for behind the water tank. It would need a decent airing. For the first time he felt excited, almost relieved by the anticipation of leaving home for an extended period.

The arrival of the contract heralded the start of the next phase of his project.

THREE

Coalville

I COULDN'T CRITICISE my parents for the lack of opportunities. They had carried me through childhood with carefully managed finances and muted optimism. They had given me everything a child needed in a kind, nurturing environment. Everything except adventure and holidays abroad. The reason I had failed to escape home wasn't their fault. I was the one who had to break out of the comfort zone of living with amenable parents. My brother, Richard, had managed it; why couldn't I?

The answer had to lie with proper motivation and not magical fantasies initiated by what exactly? The lady at Ashby had called it a gift. I should have forgotten what she'd said, but I couldn't. If I hoped to establish a career, I needed to concentrate on the tangible, believable things in life, like my self-taught photography skills. For technology was fast moving and I'd had little opportunity to experiment with the latest digital cameras that had just come on the market. It was bad enough having to safely store the rolls of exposed films, negatives and photo albums. My bedroom was an archive filled with shoeboxes and cartons stacked on shelves. When I showed my parents my pictures, my kindly mother and father admired them and smiled sweetly. Occasionally Dad asked about the camera settings, nodding gravely at the explanation. Not a token gesture, he listened attentively, but the art wasn't one that he shared with me. He preferred fishing rods.

Who decided that ambition was a necessity for life, and who decided if you were successful or not? I had constructed a career plan at school: earn enough to rent a place that had potential for a studio and dark room; turn a hobby into an industry, and from there, I'd make a name for myself as a photographer. Those ideas fell apart quickly. I hadn't the money, nor had my family, and when I touted my skills, amateur admittedly, to local studios, they only wanted the baby pictures and assistants for weddings. Photographing reluctant babes with chubby cheeks and drool was not even a halfway house to where I wanted to go. Hence, hotels with their shifting sea of people who should have told me where to go, what to see, and who to meet.

The silver lining remained the trips out, the odd adventure to a crumbling historical site, an abbey or picturesque somewhere village. I had my favourites, ones I returned to over and over, to relive the smells and sounds. Yvette, perhaps, out of all of my friends understood the lure.

Yvette was an oddity. The declaration was my own perspective and nobody else's. I clung to the perception for one simple reason: Yvette, armed with a first-class honours and plenty of job offers, had found one locally, as in the middle of England and far from the epicentres of art appreciation. I had been dumbfounded. Instead of delving into past secrets of great artworks, Yvette designed marketing brochures for a fashion house, admittedly haute couture, and niche, but still, it wasn't what her friends or family had anticipated. What about London? I had asked her three years ago, when she returned after her graduation ceremony.

'It's not necessarily where all the talent is,' she had replied with a slightly indignant tone. 'You should know that. Anyway, I realised I was being dragged into academia, which just isn't me.' The nail polish and lip gloss had shone as brightly as the clothes she wore, fresh off some catwalk. 'I could never do what's expected of me. You understand, surely?'

I thought I did, and yet my idea, on the surface, was hardly unoriginal. After all, people travelled; alone too, if that was necessary. But they most probably didn't base their travels on a romantic idea of seeing the past come to life in ruined structures. I needed to connect, to meet people with similar interests; Coalville wasn't helping me find them.

Yvette had a grander view of what I might achieve and had thrust an idea upon me that I should try again to exhibit my work at a local art institute. The last time we had spoken about it at the pub, we'd both been exasperated and tired, and perhaps I had been too defeatist. According to her, I was missing a golden opportunity. It was hardly my fault; I really wasn't qualified to enter a prestigious art exhibition.

'What's the point?' I had said. 'Two years I've tried to get in, a third year is bound to fail.'

'Not this time,' she'd said.

I hadn't shared her optimism. 'There's no point, honestly, it's like I'm so far off the mark for the entry level, I might as well send my pictures to Blue Peter.'

She had sighed and before replying, and with abundant ease, had quaffed a mouthful of Burgundy wine. 'Utter rubbish, Robyn. And you know it. Trust me, darling, things happen when you take risks.'

The darling didn't grate. It was Yvette in her work mode. All lovey-dovey mannerisms coupled with a hard-nosed business mind. No wonder she had shunned an academic life.

The deadline for applicants was four days away, just before Christmas. Yvette insisted three times was the lucky charm. And, yes, I agreed, my portfolio had improved, and I had more chance with the recent batch of pictures.

'It's about putting out feelers,' she said sagely. 'Finding others with similar projects. Artists, historians, authors. Better still, a sponsor, a kind of patron of the arts. You're going to have to be passionate about what you do. Consider your photography an art, not something you do with a camera. It's about expressing yourself. Tell a story. The transition of time, that's your thing. Time and place.' Her enthusiasm effervesced in her voice.

The word passionate haunted me after that conversation. Was I passionate? Was photography a distraction or something I couldn't live without? Without a camera, would the castles I yearned to visit, and the stories attached to them, retain the same level of interest? Did I really view my photographs as a means to bring those castles back to life, like my daydreams? The truth was, beyond storing them, I'd done nothing creative or truly tangible with the photographs – Yvette considered my negligence a big waste.

I lay on my bed in my overcrowded bedroom, reached over to the bedside stand, and picked up an envelope. Inside were the blank spaces of a printed form. I'd failed again to complete the entry application. Yvette would not be pleased. She was convinced this was the best way to secure a patron. But what exactly would I do with one anyway?

She would ring again soon to ask if I'd posted the form, and I knew what she would say. She'd said it at the pub.

'Just fill the damn thing in. The world of creative arts is full of rejection letters. It's what gives you backbone.'

Okay, I thought, I'll do it, but what I really needed to achieve my ambition, the one masquerading behind the photography, was good fortune.

Fat chance of that coming my way.

❖

The invitation dropped on the doormat a week after Christmas, one of the busiest times of year for the hotel. Mum had congratulated me with a cup of Earl Grey. Dad gave me one of his brief hugs and returned to examining the *Angling Times*. For them it was part of a long line of events that I had initiated in the hope of turning a hobby into a career and as for my unspoken passion for visiting castles, they both ignored the obsession, believing it would eventually pass, as had many of my other childhood fancies.

I'd had my first vivid daydream at Ashby Castle just before my tenth birthday. It had left me excited, unafraid and beguiled, as only a child can be when imagination takes hold. I badgered my parents to take me to North Wales during a school holiday just so I could visit Harlech and Caernarvon Castles, and as I hoped, discover my imaginary experiences were portable and unique to each place. What I sensed at Harlech was visceral even among the commotion of other visitors. Short stocky men, clad in helmets and leather tunics, milled around me, calling out in alarm. I distinctly felt the whistle of arrows flying past at great speed. While I had been distracted, Richard had teased me, pretending to wave a sword in my face. It came as no shock when he enlisted in the army, married the caterer serving the barracks, and was now stationed somewhere in Iraq. His wife, Miranda, dutifully sent her in-laws updates. He was safe, she believed. The Americans were close to capturing Saddam Hussein.

Those early imaginary encounters were rather like a blurred canvas lacking in detail, but they still managed to inspire strong emotions in me, and their effect couldn't always be hidden. Mum once found me pinned against the stone wall of the battlements, white as a sheet, eyes tightly shut. She thought I was afraid of heights, or something, and refused to take me to any more castles until I begged her that it was nothing but a dizzy spell brought on by hunger. An easy excuse – what child isn't always hungry?

The morning of the exhibition, I could barely eat a thing she put on my breakfast plate. It was a relief to hear the doorbell.

Yvette's car was slightly bigger than mine, the one on loan from Mum. The generous boot space swallowed the stiff boards between which were sandwiched the precious prints. Weeks of deliberation, and I'd finally chosen the images for the exhibition, and spent a small fortune on enlargements.

'I still can't believe it. What if they take one look at my portfolio and banish me from the premises?' I nibbled on glossed lips.

The weather wasn't helping my negativity. March had brought rain not sunshine. The damp start to the day was an unfortunate harbinger of anxiety.

'Will you put a sock in it?' Yvette said; her lips twitched, and she shifted her grip on the steering wheel. 'Didn't I say three's a charm? You spent ages making the selection. I think what you've chosen is spot on. Classic photography, good compositions. Some unusual, off kilter for the subject. Going black and white—'

'It's daring, I know.' I wasn't in the mood to critique my choices.

Yvette smiled. 'I'll help you set up. Then I'll leave you to it.'

The Curzon Institute for Art was a private college for those with deep pockets and excellent connections. However, once a year, it opened its doors to non-residential talent and put on an exhibition worthy of its reputation. Most, nearly all, exhibitors paid for their stands in the hope their profile would be lifted to new levels. Critics came from as far as London and Edinburgh, even Paris.

The only possibility of me making it into the exhibition was by the route offered to a handful of locals, and those lucky artists were exhibited for free. Although fine art was the norm for the Curzon, for this particular show they permitted a broad spectrum, including photography.

Yvette and I arrived at the institute mid-morning, approaching the grand old house along a shady avenue dotted with daffodils and crocuses. It was touching, watching Yvette fuss over the transportation of the prints from car to hall. My attention was slightly distracted by the polished brass doorknobs and Baroque ceiling, a permanent exhibition of zealous wealth.

The lighting wasn't especially good.

In an hour or so the place would be buzzing. The caterers had already popped open the corked bottles and served dainty petit fours on platters. There would be dealers with fancy galleries or private clients, the kind of people who prized provenance and attended auctions in Sotheby's.

One man had arrived early. He fingered the stem of his champagne glass and picked up a brochure. The expression on his face was difficult to read. Scanning the contents of the programme, sipping occasionally, he lingered by the entrance, several long paces from my stand, which was beyond the last window and where the lesser artists were carolled, nervously adjusting tilted picture frames.

Yvette squeezed my hand and left me, as agreed. It was the right thing to do; I had to manage on my own. What great artist hadn't begun their career with a lowly status and little money, she espoused. I pointedly remarked that many had died just as impoverished.

Yvette walked toward the door, and as she passed behind the man with the champagne flute, she nudged his shoulder. He jerked, nearly dropping both brochure and drink. Yvette said something; probably an apology, smiled, and pointed in my direction. Their conversation was brief, and reminded me that Yvette was comfortable in this environment having studied art and visited countless galleries. She continued on her way without looking back.

Pacing in front of my portfolio, I fidgeted with my watchstrap. The nervous habit was hard to break. I shouldn't have worn short sleeves. As for the skirt, it was ridiculously long. It hung limp and colourless like worn out drapes. The smile I attached to my face was acquired from my repertoire: charming and well-practised. Underneath it, I was a shivering bundle of nerves.

The man moved purposely toward me. The streaks of grey hairs behind his ears sharpened into focus. What brought him in a direct line to me? Perhaps the ancient aspect of my compositions had caught his eye. I liked to think I'd trapped the fascinating vividness of detail and made it appear timeless. Scale was always a problem with buildings, whether old or new, and instead of vast landscapes with rolling hills for surroundings, I focused in, tighter, closer, and made the building material my subject.

In one image, at the bottom of the tower, the stone walls, roughly hewn, held together with crumbling mortar, were crisp, textured and honeycombed. The distorting tilt was obvious, and unfortunate. I remembered the day. I had stood at the base of the tower and aimed upward to a solitary unglazed window. The light spun out through it in a glorious halo. Even in black and white, the warmth emanated and drew the eye to a distant, invisible horizon, a hint of blue sky, without the blue.

A castle, obviously. Where, he wouldn't know. It didn't matter. The point wasn't to recognise a specific place.

I stepped to one side and sensibly said nothing. He worked systematically through the portfolio. The prints, varying in size, were unframed, but mounted on plain boards. Courageously, I had done something different. The subject – the flintstone tower wall, the isolated window with weathered carvings – was the central feature of each photograph. What changed was the light, the angle or distance, the focal pointed shifted. In one, I had levelled myself with the window.

'How?' he asked.

Intuition told me which photo he was looking at. 'A mound opposite.'

Another picture was snowbound, icy and bleak. The next wet and rain soaked. I wasn't afraid to venture out. The spring image – daffodils in one corner – was awash with greyscale, highlighting the missing colours. The contrast in shade and light was razor sharp. I liked to think I couldn't have done a better job than an artist with a paintbrush.

'Daring,' he admitted. 'One subject. Where?'

'Ashby-de-la-Zouch. A portrait of seasons. The tower is the time traveller.'

Given his pouting lips, the premise was too basic. I would have to come up with more reasons for the sequence of pictures. He waited, his gaze flitting from my face to the photographs. His narrow face was handsome, and he was married, according to the ring. Middle-aged, he possibly had children that were my generation. Elegant in a dapper kind way, he was dressed smartly but casually, no tie, tweed trousers, pointy shoes. I was struggling to place him in a profession that matched his jumbled appearance.

The need to fiddle with something mounted so I hooked my forefinger around my watchstrap. If I wanted to engage with these people, a touch of exuberant arrogance was required on my part; an emotion that didn't come naturally for a customer service type. I cleared my throat.

'I hoped to demonstrate how time… the day, the year, all can bring a difference. Some days, walls trap you; other times, they protect. Light in a window offers hope of escape.' I blushed. 'I'm rambling.'

'You *hoped* to demonstrate? Have you?'

Balanced on my tiptoes, I was bursting to speak about the details. Shyness, though, wasn't my natural state. Yvette had suggested holding back until I was sure. Was I though?

I finally unleashed my hands and gestured. 'I have I think… here…'

What followed was detailed. His eyes glazed over a few times when I mentioned lenses or shutter speeds. So not a photographer. Using a tone that reminded me of an inquisitorial teacher, his questions focused on composition.

'It's about atmosphere,' I said, remembering what Yvette had suggested when we explored my collection for options. 'These pictures give the castle character, a sense of longevity and purpose. I'm hoping the viewer will see what I… feel.' My mouth had gone horribly parched.

'You must have gone there—'

'Many times.' I laughed; a ticklish, dry giggle. 'A few years of them.' I washed the smile away. 'I refuse to be embarrassed by my obsession.' The word escaped before I had a chance to think.

'Obsession?'

'My need to revisit.'

'Never satisfied?' Of course, he would know that photographers had the advantage over painters. A quick snapshot, again and again; no waiting for the paint to dry on the canvas before touching up.

'I'm not a perfectionist,' I said, firmly.

He nodded as if in agreement. 'Finishing projects is important, though. But you're seeking something?'

I shuffled back onto my heels. 'Is it that obvious?'

'It's the way with most artists. And you're right. Revisiting a subject isn't a sign of failure. I'm sure da Vinci didn't think so with his sketches.'

'Then these are my sketches.' I added a sweep of my hand, which felt overly melodramatic, so I dropped my arm. The intense heat of my flushed cheeks spread to my neck.

It was a tipping point for the conversation. He retreated a few steps, and catching a spotlight, the dusting of silver hairs around his temples sparkled. He discarded the empty champagne glass on a nearby table. I opened my mouth to thank him – my interested viewer – and his question collided with my gratitude.

'Why castles?' he asked.

My lips trembled. Yvette had suggested I shouldn't mention the motivation that kept me returning to Ashby, and other places. When we had set up the stand, she had reminded me the purpose of the exhibit was to demonstrate I was an artist and not a castle enthusiast – the subject, she had said, would tell its own story. It was my story, too. Should I bend to it and not the critics?

Who was this somewhat pensive guy, who stared at me with an inscrutable expression, and why did his appearance hover ambiguously between businessman and something more down to earth? He had to be an academic, probably on the institute's staff. What he might have initiated, letting me feel welcomed, now following his awkward questions, was something different.

My coarse throat ached to speak and frankly, what had I to lose if I simply stated the truth?

'I want to visit every castle in the country.' I didn't know where to look. Not at his face, which was bound to show that amused expression of incredulity.

However, when I glanced up, he remained expressionless, as he had done since he arrived at the stand. If I spotted anything reactive, it was a slight widening of his granite eyes.

'And photograph them?'

'That part isn't essential. It helps, when explaining to people, to give a reason. So yes, if you like, I will photograph them.' Now I had blown my credentials – I was an utter idiot.

He stepped forward. 'My name is David Carmichael. I'm professor of Art History at Charnwood University.'

Charnwood University was where Yvette had studied art history, and the nugget of information explained why she had exchanged words – she must have known him and suggested he visited my corner.

'You're not surprised by my ridiculous ambition?' I mocked myself without hubris.

'To the contrary, I'm delighted by it. Although, I can't offer you help with the "all" aspect. There must be hundreds—'

'You can start with one-hundred and fifty, unless you count those that are gone without trace.' My collection of books on castles was squeezed next to the photo albums.

'Why?'

I shrugged. 'Why not?'

He shot me down with the kind of disappointed expression he might give a student awarded a poor grade.

I let down my defences begrudgingly. 'Because they talk to me. And I'm curious about what they tell me.'

'Talk?'

'In my head. Not words, per se, images of the past that come to life. I smell… hear… I know, just ignore that side of me. I'm here in a different capacity—'

'Which interests me. But so do the castles.' He focused in on my name badge. 'Robyn Yates – you want to time travel as well as take photographs?'

I nearly scowled at his mocking tone and thought better of it. 'I doesn't matter what I want to do, I can't recreate the past with photographs.'

David Carmichael tucked his hands behind his back and straightened. 'I disagree. In fact, I have a proposal for you. I need a photographer for a special project. The trouble is I can't provide a wage, only very generous expenses and whatever equipment you need. Neither will the job last more than a couple of months. You need to be available over the summer. And… be prepared to travel, although nothing arduous. I have a client, if you like, somebody who lives abroad and can't do the task due to poor health.'

My jaw dropped, leaving me gaping with surprise. An avalanche of adrenaline-soaked thoughts followed. 'To take pictures of what?'

'Castles. In Northumberland and Yorkshire primarily. So sorry, not all of them. About fifteen or so.' It was his turn to blush. 'It's remarkable, isn't it, that you want to do something similar to my friend?'

The pause dragged on. It seemed it wasn't a topic either of us wanted to explore. Fate had brought us together, why was best left unknown.

'This person,' I said. 'Who are they?'

The pink tinge deepened, the pause lengthy. 'I can't say,' he said quietly. 'There are good reasons for anonymity, I'm sure. It's an unfortunate limitation, among others.' The embarrassment was poorly hidden.

I blinked. 'Oh.'

'I know,' David shrugged. 'Eccentric is perhaps an understatement. My wife and I owe this friend…' He left the sentence hanging for a second and his eyes seemed to lose focus before sharpening again. 'I can tell you that you both share a love of history, and especially castles, and their architecture and purpose. An academic, like me. But, beyond that, the purpose of the request is to remain secret. I'm to give you a list… a specific itinerary.' He stuffed his hands in his jacket pockets to hide the trembling and cleared his throat. 'Are you interested?'

The answer came immediately without hesitation or wavering. 'Absolutely.'

We exchanged business cards. His was laminated, mine thin cardboard.

'I'll email you,' he said. 'Give you more details. But I do need to know soon. The project needs completing by the end of August.'

'Sure,' I said. *August*! I had a job and a life that wouldn't accommodate a summer of travelling.

More people were edging their way to my part of the exhibition, possibly drawn by David's presence. He waved at one. The man had connections, which meant whoever he was working for, probably did too.

A strange setup was in the making. I would have to approach the hotel about a sabbatical. Then there were my parents, who wouldn't want me to take up any job that wasn't paid.

He slid a foot back and opened up the space between us again. His dark eyes reflected a beam of light, and they glinted, brighter than last time, burning a fire inside of him, it seemed. I'd call it enthusiasm. His whole posture suddenly lacked the stiffness I had seen when he spoke to Yvette. An invisible burden that had troubled him was gone. If I had to pick a moment to take a snapshot of him, one that captured him fully, then this would be that second. Perhaps he wasn't a bad choice for a go-between.

FOUR

THE EMAIL ARRIVED THE NEXT DAY, my day off, so I had time to think about the proposal. With my parents out of the house, I had the family laptop to myself. The "slab" at it was known - metallic grey and not really portable – lived on the dining room table surrounded by a mountain of clutter and ironing. I read the message through several times. My clammy palms were super itchy, and I scratched the skin almost feverishly. As for the pace of my heartbeats, there was a manic edge to the rhythm. What I was reading was an unbelievable opportunity.

The list of castles included ones I'd always wanted to visit, and the good news continued. Somebody, a nameless person, was going to pay for food and board, a rental car and fuel, and all the photography equipment I needed, which I could keep afterwards. If that was the deal, then there was no need for a commission fee. What else was I going to spend my money on? What I had to do was deliver on specific requests. The mysterious client of David's had to have a good awareness of each location because the details were strikingly complex: this angle, this direction. What he hadn't suggested was the technique of photographing the views; only the subject was decided in advance. However, as David pointed out at the end of the long email, I was free to take whatever other photos I wished as long as I prioritised the agenda.

The oddest request was right at the end.

Please don't deviate from the schedule. The castles must be photographed in the order given between July and the end of August.

I wasn't keen on that constraint. It smacked of micromanagement, and what if the weather was appalling? Surely flexibility was key to the success of the project? But after I shopped around for an expensive digital camera, I changed my mind. Thinking about it calmly, the route was logical, from north to south, and there was more than enough time to visit other places along the way, which as far as I was concerned, was a must. I was a free agent and without more commissions, I had to consider other ways I might bring extra earnings. If I focused on the famous ones, then I might be able to sell the images online or to an agent. If the season was important, then it was advantageous for light and warmth - no grim black and white shots. Mr "whoever" wanted summer scenery with full foliage and white clouds, not rain and dewy grass. As he lived abroad, he probably had little understanding of how unreliable English weather was during the summer.

I spent a few more hours researching, checking accessibility of each castle, the days they were open to the public, and the local amenities. I would have to book hotels… No, not hotels. Bed and breakfast, or lodgings. Travelling was likely to be a lonely affair, and this was the chance to meet people. The thought of banishing myself inside a hotel room was abhorrent, and too much like a busman's holiday.

With my brain ignited, I couldn't stop, and I fired off a stream of questions to David. How would I receive the expenses? I needed money up front for fuel and board. What if I had to query any aspect of the project – was I always going to get an appropriate answer from David? Why couldn't I communicate directly with his friend? If I used libraries or internet cafes on route, couldn't I email him, or telephone him?

Direct communication would be an awkward issue. David anticipated it would be limited. His friend wasn't to be bothered too much due to some unspecified health problem. David understood my concerns and I received nothing other than weak sympathy in reply. Then, I touched on the biggest bug of all. What did I call the client? Because surely, there would a contract, an agreement of some kind? What proof had I that he even existed?

The agreement would be with David, as the representative and UK resident, and he would take possession of the prints, manage the paperwork, including any fees demanded for the taking of commercial photographs, something I'd overlooked. It would mean signing over the copyright of the photographs to him; I could keep copies, but never publish them anywhere. Okay, that made sense. As for the money, he would arrange for a weekly allowance. Any discrepancies we could argue over later, but he didn't anticipate any major issues.

Easter approached, the deadline for my final decision. David had sent a draft of the agreement and I kept it by my bed, in the drawer. A routine check of my inbox revealed an email from an unrecognised account. I hovered over the delete button, and assumed it was spam. Something alerted me, a sharp taste in my mouth, almost bittersweet. I paid closer attention to the email address:

LDM1449

What was the significance of the handle?

The subject of the email was simply *Castles*. Could this be the elusive friend of David Carmichael? I fumbled with the mouse buttons and opened the message.

> David passed on your email address. I hope you do not mind me contacting you. I am pleased you have decided to help me with this project.
> I know this must be daunting. I don't make too many demands of you, I hope. There is something of a connection between us – our love of the past, the beauty of structures that embody it, whether intact or ruined. From what David told me, I understand you seek the same things as me.

I did? Somewhat presumptuous of him. What had David told him? I doubted he understood my true motivation for agreeing to the arrangement and I wasn't going to discuss the reason via the medium of email. Worryingly, there was an implication he had seen something of my photographs, but how? David hadn't taken any of them with him, not even copies of the ones I used in the exhibition. I read on:

> Once you send me your first batch of images – I'm glad you have chosen a digital camera, it is convenient for us all – then we can discuss things further.

What things? The castles or the images?

> The reasons for my anonymity must be strange to you, but please put your trust in me and allow me this privilege. I look forward to receiving your photographs of Bamburgh Castle.

Bamburgh was the first on the itinerary. It was a must see.

As for his signature at the end – he referred to himself simply as "Medici". I looked up the name and found an entry that fitted with his email address. Lorenzo de' Medici, nobleman of Florence and patron of the arts, was born in 1449. My mystery man was keen on staying in the shadows. We might as well be playing a game of cat and mouse. This email had left me far from excited at the thought of visiting this distant castle, and slowly, like a creeping sensation of coldness, I was beginning to understand why I had lost my enthusiasm.

I backed off handing in my notice for the same reason I couldn't tell my parents: I was no longer convinced I was the right person.

FIVE

THE WIND BUFFETED the easel, causing it to rock slightly on its spindly legs. Stretched across the board and held in place with strips of tape, the white paper was marked with faint pencil lines. He tapped the paintbrush on the edge of the small bucket dangling below and waited for the squall to die down. A week after Easter and the weather remained unsettled.

The wind dropped. He looked up and focused on the central point of the landscape. Carelessly placed, as if dropped with little thought onto the far end of the triangular ramparts, was the stone windmill. The rounded structure rested on a square plinth and there were features to note: tiny glazed windows; cone-shaped roof; smoothed stones with no visible mortar. The windmill, sadly, held no other facets of interest having lost its sails. The artist had little time to dwell on history of the building; the guidebook was buried in his rucksack. With the weather and time set against him, he would create a rough draft and finish the rest later.

The view beyond the windmill distracted him from time to time. On the horizon, the billowing greyness of the sky blended into the turbulent seas. It remained an impressive landscape even with the lack of bright sunshine.

People pried, who wouldn't? Strolling past they stopped to look. Some commented in an appreciative manner, and he smiled with his lips only. Eventually, the audience drifted away and left him to flick the brush across the canvas in relative solitude. The paint coverage was good; the wind effective in drying the canvas. At his feet was the paint box, and he crouched to retrieve an unopened tube. The outside of the lidded box was the worse for wear; it had been on many journeys, right across Europe, but the inside was in better shape. He traced the initials faintly etched into the wood – LDM – with the tip of his finger before rising again.

He maintained a firm stance, standing with his legs apart, his broad shoulders slightly hunched. The palette rested somewhat precariously on one arm, the brushes in a pot by his feet. He worked reasonably fast. Pausing between strokes, he sniffed the salty air, and turned to glance up at the darkening sky. The wind had shifted direction. The shelter provided by the walls was no longer sufficient. As if aware, the easel shivered and wobbled on its thin legs. He swiftly mixed the last batch of colours, applied the wet, silky fibres to the paper and covered the faint sketch marks of the windmill with a dapple complexion.

The warden came and stood next to him, nodding appreciatively. 'Sorry. We're closing soon.'

'Just about done.' The artist cocked his head to one side, and rapped the brush handle on the palette.

'Impressive. But why the windmill?' The warden gestured behind them to the vast structure looming high above their heads. 'Isn't this what you've come to paint?'

'It isn't what you expect, though, is it? A windmill on a battlement.' The artist wiped his brush on a rag.

'Will you be back tomorrow?' the warden asked.

'No. Tomorrow I'm off to Alnwick.'

'Ah. Not the same as this, is it?'

The artist zipped up his fleece jacket. 'No. Bamburgh is different to Alnwick. I have to go there next.'

SIX

Kenilworth

'**I CAN'T DO IT.**' I flopped onto the sofa. With Mum and Dad both out, I took the opportunity to call Yvette.

'Why?' Yvette asked.

I switched the phone from one ear to the other, curled into a ball, and propped my head against a cushion. 'I'm not qualified. It's that simple.'

'You haven't handed in your notice?'

'No.'

'Or told your mum and dad?'

The idea of it twisted my stomach into knots. 'No,' I said, painfully.

Yvette effortlessly directed me down the fraught path of indecision.

'You're running out of time, Robyn.'

I sighed. 'I know.'

'And you've not warned David that you're having second thoughts?' Yvette, of course, knew David. She had studied under him, one of many students.

'He wants me to sign by Monday. He's not harassing me. I think he knows that it's a big ask: giving up a job for something this short-lived.'

The emails from David were business-like. The contract was in his name. He hadn't declined any of my requests, and I couldn't fault him for supporting me with the logistics. But he wasn't a photographer and didn't appreciate why I needed the extra equipment until I explained why.

'It's Saturday tomorrow, and you're off. Take me somewhere that inspires you. Not Ashby. What's that one near Warwick?'

I straightened up. 'Kenilworth.'

'Take me there. I'll drive and bring sandwiches. The weather looks reasonable.'

I suspected this trip was the intention from the outset of the call: Yvette cajoling me into a state of motivation. The weeks had ticked by since the exhibition, and the half-hearted enquiries that I'd received about the exhibition photographs had dried up. I'd sold three prints.

'Okay,' I said slowly. 'If you can't convince me, I'll tell David I've changed my mind.'

'And if I do, you'll tell your parents.'

I pictured Yvette's confident, yet friendly smirk.

❖

Yvette didn't waste time. As soon as her foot landed on the accelerator, she launched her first question.

'Why this… I was going to say obsession, but that sounds unfair.' Yvette hesitated. I waited for her to adjust her language. 'Why are you so interested in castles and seeing them in person?'

'Why not?' I fingered the outline of the glove compartment. 'If I was a sports fan, nobody would question my desire to follow my team to every stadium. I like to see what's left of history.' I shrugged.

'I do get that. I like looking at history through the lens of contemporaneous pictures. What I mean is, why castles in particular? What do you see in them?' She was referring to something I didn't like to discuss.

I understood the nature of the emotions that stirred me to travel, but not the extent of them, especially my need to embroider stories into the fabric of those derelict buildings. I superimposed events over the missing walls, and then breathed life into them until I felt I was there. Yvette preferred to let pictures tell their own tales, as she was trained to do, and not cast fantasies. If I couldn't go back in time in person, my mind seemed capable of it instead. Pure escapism and probably symptomatic of deeper needs.

'Oh, you know, history played out,' I said feebly, and stared at the tarmac ahead. My cheeks flamed, hinting at my embarrassment.

'Don't be ashamed. I know you, Robyn. You're a born romantic. I'm more pragmatic. History is what has been and gone. It's fascinating to study and interpret, but I'm not hankering to go back in time.' Yvette reached over and patted my thigh, then swiftly recoiled to her side of the car.

I smiled softly. Yvette described her family as cold fish who had never embraced displays of affection. I veered the direction of the conversation toward my comfort zone.

'Sir Walter Scott wrote a novel set in Kenilworth. Tourists have visited for centuries. The first guidebook was published in 1777.'

'I bet you've read it.'

'Not that one. I have this little guidebook by this guy called Braithwaite. It's rather quaint.' I retrieved the tattered book from my bag, opened it at the page on Kenilworth, and began to read. '*The Duke of Lancaster's original stronghold was turned into a palace with its ornate gardens, hunting lodges, pavilions, and marble fireplaces. When Elizabeth the First stayed with her entourage for nineteen days, she almost bankrupted the Earl of Leicester, Robert Dudley, her favourite.*' I closed the book. 'He hoped she would marry him, but she didn't.'

'Ah, that failed romance. What do you see in it?'

She was persistent. What did I see? 'Castles are complicated pictures of history, don't you think?' I said. 'Built over centuries, altered according to the wishes of their owners. We're left with a ruin, and yet for hundreds of years it would have been a vibrant place, buzzing with people.'

❖

We walked toward the gatehouse, buffeted by a gentle, cool breeze, then wandered through an open court, passed Gaunt's Tower and under the outer Water Gate. Climbing a steep incline, we entered the Great Hall via a porch.

The unpleasant dizziness arrived suddenly. I dropped back, allowing Yvette to move on, then when the brief attack of vertigo waned, I joined her. My legs weakened at the knees and my heartbeats thundered in my ears. All familiar symptoms.

The dimensions of the Great Hall were suitably imposing. Two walls remained, as did the perpendicular window tracings and the foundation stones of vast pillars. The intervening wooden floors and roof had rotted away, and below, the stone vaulted ceilings of the undercroft had been demolished. What we stood upon was the cellar floor while above people's heads, the grand fireplaces were interspersed along the walls. Heating the space had required several hearths. Only two remained, bizarrely perched half-way up the walls.

Yvette dashed off to the toilet, promising to be quick. I lingered in the Great Hall.

Rivulets of dampness had encouraged moss and lichen to impregnate the stonework and I perched on one pillar root, absent-mindedly poking at the fuzzy growth. The tingling started afresh. My scalp prickled, electrified by something that wasn't visible. If there was energy loose in the air, I alone had access to its magical powers. Heavy lids shuttered my eyes. I ignored the other visitors and released my imagination, succumbing to this gift that had no purpose or explanation. I breathed, and waited for the inevitable transference. It always happened here in the Great Hall.

A flash of colour. Greens, some blue and the hint of red. I assimilated the weave of threads, and saw, hanging on a stone wall, an extravagant tapestry of a deer hunt.

The air tasted sooty. Fierce crackling erupted.

A roar of shooting flames licked the vast hollow of the blackened chimney opening.

I panned out, pushing myself away from the pillar where my body remained transfixed and immovable, to a wall, and from that vantagepoint, I explored the panorama.

The numerous occupants of the hall were cosy, perhaps too hot. Corralled at the lower end of the hall, wiping sweat from their brows, belching loudly…

The youths are squashed on the cramped benches. They gesture at each other over the hullabaloo as they tear apart hunks of bread. Away at the other of the hall, on the dais, is the lord of the castle, regal and colourful, deep in conversation. Between him and the lower tables is a chasm of status. Up on the minstrel's gallery, the musicians pluck strings and toot on whistles. The smoke fails to mask the stew of flavours rising from the tables. Dish upon dish is carried out of the kitchens by an army of liveried servants, creating a display of culinary opulence. A collective gasp of hungry mouths greets the youths. The guests eat with gusto and no manners. The hounds bask in the rushes by the fire until baited by scraps tossed from the tables. They growl and snatch with claws and fangs.

Beer spills down the wiry beards of the knights and juices splatter onto the wooden boards. Knives slice effortlessly through cheese and meat, their blades clattering on the pewter plates. Raucous laughter drowns out the music. The lowlier men accost the fairer sex and sink their smeared lips on sweeter mouths. Rank odours settle on tongues. Flies swarm. Somebody wretches. The stench of an endless feast...

I gagged and pressed my clammy hand over my mouth.

'I'm back.' Yvette jumped off a low wall.

I swallowed the bile, and conjured up a smile of welcome. 'Come on then.' I hurried ahead of Yvette, inhaling gulps of air. The nausea swiftly abated. Had she noticed? Probably, but she was kind enough not to ask me. Many might not be so sensitive.

We climbed to the top of the Strong Tower. While Yvette snapped the distant views with her compact camera, I turned my back on the scenery and focused on the castle ruins with a reliable lens.

'You mentioned a book,' she said to my back.

I hooked the camera strap over my shoulder. 'In Sir Walter Scott's book about Kenilworth, he implied Robert Dudley's first wife stayed in this tower. She didn't, it was fiction.'

'I wonder why he altered the facts.' She carefully peered over to look at the sheer drop.

Heights rarely bothered me. 'Made for a better story, I suppose.'

Back at ground level, I led Yvette into the Great Tower, the keep, which formed the oldest part of the castle. A Norman structure, the kind I preferred. Yvette wandered aimlessly and kicked a pebble along with the toe of her shoe.

I pressed the camera shutter, the icy metal. Without the tripod, the camera was exposed to the slightest shiver of the hand. I retreated to shelter by an interior wall and, with my blue-tinged finger, traced the unusual wall of sandstone blocks; each one eroded into a unique pattern by a constant barrage of wind and rain, forming pits like miniature caverns. Time had ensured the erosion had been kind, creating a beautiful array of patterns and smooth indentations; a unique façade of tiny pockets, rather like the grooves of fingerprints, and impossible to reproduce artificially.

Between shutter presses, I returned to stroke the contours. There was no warmth, no transmission through the stones; it wasn't how it worked, or so I believed.

An expressionless Yvette studied the ruined walls. 'Shame it didn't survive. I've seen paintings of Elizabeth I, portraits extolling her beauty and elaborate clothing. The virgin queen with her pure white face. Underneath…. Do you think it was all a game to her? Courting, being wooed, when in truth she was quite content to remain single?'

'Possibly.'

'But all those royal progresses entertained her. She loved being the centre of attention. I think she played it right. Rule in isolation; a life without men.'

'Do you think I want to emulate her? That by travelling, I escape my responsibilities? My grand plan to avoid commitment, is that it?' I tried, and failed, to sound sarcastic.

'Robyn, please,' Yvette said with a slightly impatient tone. 'If you're inferring parallels, they're of your own making. I'm talking about Elizabeth.'

My fragility had been laid too bare.

Yvette had painted a different portrait of Kenilworth. I preferred to see it as embodying romantic court life with indulgent feasts; a castle "modernised" in the hope of creating love between friends and not the dark scheming of a power greedy earl. If exploring history uncovered variants of the truth, then at least I could rely on the camera always capturing solid and informative facts. Was that the reason I hankered for Medici and his strange project?

Yvette's canvas lace-ups were soaked.

I pointed at Yvette's shoes. 'Sorry. I should have suggested you wore boots or something,'

Yvette answered with a little shrug of indifference. 'Did he marry again? Dudley?'

The abrupt question echoed within the walls of the gatehouse. 'Yes. Lettice Knolls.'

Yvette chuckled. 'From Elizabeth, the Great Queen Bess, to somebody named Lettice. I bet she was a bit limp after the grandeur of a queen.'

Dudley had found happiness, of sorts. My shoulders slumped and I sighed, miserably.

'Penny for them,' Yvette said, fishing out the car keys from her exquisite handbag.

'Just, you know, thinking,' I said vaguely.

I wanted the camera to be my tool and enable me to record a historical landscape that might one day be lost to time. Cautious about who I spoke to and how I shared my thoughts, I had bottled aspirations and avoided expressing them to others, including Yvette. Until David's offer had partially resuscitated me, I had been paying the price for that introversion. And now the perceptive Yvette, sensing my reticence, had brought me to Kenilworth. Examining the camera, I noticed I'd used a forty-eight exposure of film. It couldn't go on, this lunacy; reel after reel with no purpose other than to sit in a box waiting for an occasional viewing.

I opened the car door. 'Thanks for bringing me here.'

'My pleasure. Thanks for the tour. I think I understand a little better what it is that inspires you.' Yvette disappeared below the car roof, hiding her windswept features from scrutiny.

I doubted Yvette understood; she'd not asked the right questions. A spot of rain landed on my nose, and I ducked into the car.

The engine started.

'I'll tell Mum and Dad tomorrow. Sign the contract. Hand in my notice.'

Back at home, Yvette followed me into the house to greet my parents and engage in friendly chit-chat. Mum, though, rose from her seat before Yvette could speak, and with knotted eyebrows, addressed my friend.

'Everything okay?'

I exhaled heavily and stepped between them. 'It's alright, Mum.'

'No funny turns this time, or dizziness?'

'No.'

'Good.' She expressed her pleasure with a nod at my father. 'See.'

I didn't know what was meant by that little remark, nor did I want to know. Yvette, sensing there was a much tougher conversation coming my way, declined a cup of tea, and after pecking the air between my cheek and her lips, she said goodbye and left me to deliver the news alone.

A wave of butterflies stormed my delicate belly. I couldn't remember the last time I had been both excited and terrified. Probably when on board the corkscrew rollercoaster at Alton Towers, hovering at the top before the whooshing descent. However, a rollercoaster ride lasted only a few minutes; this crazy adventure would last over two months.

SEVEN

LEARNING FROM PAST EXPERIENCE, the artist wedged the easel's legs between the rocks, leaving it precariously balanced, and hastened to complete his sketch before everything blew away.

He mixed various colours and kept a record of them on a scrap of paper, noting which smudges realistically reflected the ambient shades. He crossed out a couple with a pencil and wrote "sea" next to one.

Satisfied, he sketched out an outline on the paper, then swept the brush across the white canvas. The uneven line of Dunstanburgh Castle's walls, with their jagged edges, gradually materialised.

Several times he paused, dropped his arm and tapped the brush handle on the side of his legs, ignoring the careless splattering of paint, and re-assessed the emerging illustration. He struggled with patience. A weakness of a restless body. When a gust of wind buffeted the easel, he steadied the tripod and muttered a curse. He repeatedly glanced from his wristwatch to the gloomy sky with its bustling clouds, then the white crest breakers of the sea, finally back to the painting.

A passer-by walking the path to the castle entrance stopped to admire his brushwork. The slightly wizened man, whose pewter-coloured hair flapped up and down in the wind, leant on his shooting stick and hummed. He muttered a few incomprehensible words, which were sufficient to distract the artist. He frowned and kept his back to the interloper.

'Looking good,' the pewter man murmured. 'Watch your blue. Not enough azure, perhaps?'

The artist's eyebrows rose into points. He ignored the suggestion.

'Have you come with a group?' Pewter man searched the empty hillside.

The artist hesitated; brush poised for another sweep. 'No.'

'It's not a bad time to visit. You've had a good spell of weather these last few days. I sometimes come during May half-term and spend a little time on the coast.'

The artist turned. 'Half-term. Are you a—'

'Teacher? An art teacher, as a matter of fact.' He crept forward and closed the gap. Peering at the detail in the picture, he nodded. 'Such a popular castle to paint, Dunstanburgh. Very few get it right, in my humble opinion.' He unfolded his shooting stick and perched on the seat.

The two men admired the view and talked, comparing techniques. They had a polite discussion about the best landscape artists. The connection forged, the artist returned to his work, unperturbed by his audience of one.

After half an hour, the man folded his portable chair and offered the artist a handshake in farewell. 'You'll be back in the summer, then?'

The artist wiped his hand on a cloth before clasping the firm hand. 'That's the plan. I've a schedule to keep, and limited time.'

'Good luck with everything.'

Alone again, the side-tracked painter raced to complete his task. The clouds parted and a bright spotlight struck the distant stone walls and the sky beyond.

He stepped back, examined his scene, and the one above, and sighed heavily. In a blink of the eye, the sunbeams had altered the landscape. What was once grey and murky had transformed into sharply-focused stones, and saturated vivid colours, especially the turbulent sea, which now reflected the changing skies.

'Azure.' He picked up his palette. 'Gonna need more of that for the sea.'

Later, in the evening, he called his contact and was greeted with a rude response.

'What are you doing? You should have waited.'

PART TWO

'*It is advisable to play and spend good times.*'
Lorenzo de' Medici

EIGHT

Bamburgh

Bamburgh manages to host an imposing castle and remain merely a village. A large village admittedly, but certainly not a provincial town. Built on an outcrop of seemly indestructible rock that forms a pier jutting into the North Sea, the castle's location is ideal for demonstrable fortifications. Starting out as a six-century timber fort, each conquest brought new dimensions to the promontory, until the Normans arrived and claimed the castle as theirs.

Travellers, when approaching the village, will be taken by the sight of the castle rising high above the houses, perched on the rocky base, and though impressive, it still seems to emulate a semi-collapsed wedding cake with differing levels and elevations. Somewhat confined by the rocky platform or sill, it is host to a number of wall enclosures, bringing the visitor up to the inner square keep and some unusual features.

Bamburgh Castle is without doubt a spectacularly beautiful sandcastle of red rock, almost romantic in its landscaping with its tiers bursting out of the coastal beach.

~ Alistair Braithwaite's Touring Guide of Northern Castles

ARRIVING IN THE VILLAGE of Bamburgh, head throbbing, sore eyed and exhausted by the journey, I resisted the lure of the spectacular silhouette of the castle perched above the town's outline, and went in search of my accommodation. I needed a well-earned rest after the longest drive of my life.

The Vauxhall Corsa, bright red, and in immaculate condition for its age, had appeared a week ago outside our house, right on cue, as David had arranged. Dad had insisted on giving the car a "good look over", which amused and annoyed me at the same item. He never gave Mum's rust bucket the same treatment. Unsurprisingly, Dad's mechanical skills were limited to topping up the oil and a tyre pressure check. For ten minutes he had unproductively fiddled with things under the bonnet.

'It will do,' he had said, slamming the bonnet shut.

The boot space disappointed him. 'A tad on the small size for your gubbins. You've got luggage, camera stuff, tripods, Wellington boots.'

I had shooed him away with a wave of my arms. 'Dad, it's summertime.'

'Welly boots.' He had snorted. 'It's the *north*.' He said the word as if he was describing a foreign country with an extreme climate. The furthest north we had ever been was a trip to the Viking Jorvik Centre in York.

My first Northumbrian bed and breakfast was a typical family home. The pebble-dashed semi-detached house was on the outskirts of Bamburgh and part of a small row of similar housing. The couple on the doorstep greeted me in unison and helped unload the car. It wasn't long before I realised the elderly couple operated like conjoined twins to the extent they completed each other's sentences. Beverly and Bert – they insisted I called them by their first names – were retired and relied on the busy summer period to bring in extra income.

The two bedrooms they let to boarders had been their sons'. Divested of childhood trappings and replaced with ubiquitous Laura Ashley, everything matched in perfect harmony. I offered them a weary smile of gratitude. Beverly chatted amiably about her grandchildren, or grandbairns, as she pronounced in her Northumbrian dialect, while re-arranging the tea set on the dresser. My weary limbs yearned for a long soak in the bath.

'Dinner?' Beverly asked. Bert held the bedroom door open for her. 'For an extra fiver; it's not a problem.'

I grabbed the offer without hesitation. Any plans I might have had for eating out on the first night disintegrated at the sight of that bed. The food turned out to be delicious and homely. I made appreciative noises as I ate.

'Why are you up here?' Their voices blurred into one unit.

I wiped my mouth with a napkin and for a few seconds an awkward silence descended while I composed an answer. Foolishly I hadn't prepared myself for the curiosity of B&B owners with their empty nests. A minor flaw in my plans. The exact nature of the project was something that I had glossed over when I had told my parents my news. Mum had fretted over the fact that I didn't know Medici's real name, nor the purpose of the photographs.

'All I have to do is take photos of these castles,' I'd said, 'send him the digital files and I get a very expensive camera to keep. Think of it as a commission. I've got a job and I'm being paid.'

'Expenses,' Dad had muttered from behind the barricade of his newspaper.

'A very generous living allowance. Okay, what about this. I'm a student studying castles and improving my photographic skills to boot.'

'Pity there's no qualification at the end of it,' Dad had said, dryly.

In the end, after I'd persistently repeated the benefits, Dad had proved more sanguine; he simply shrugged his shoulders. 'If he's paying you, giving you the money, then you should go with your gut feeling.'

I needed a less revealing answer for my hosts and an explanation popped into my head. 'I'm a freelance photojournalist.' Not quite truthful, but it summoned up my activities without having to explain the mysterious arrangement with Medici. 'I'm photographing castles for a commission. Nobody famous…' I ended limply. I asked if they had internet access. 'I have to check my emails.'

Bert cleared his throat. 'We have a computer. Our son Graeme set it up for us. We use it to check bookings.'

'Do you mind if I quickly used it?'

'No problem.'

The boxy computer rattled and huffed during its lengthy boot-up and then took several attempts to load my webmail account. I sent a mail to David, asking if there were any last minute requests from Medici. With my parents and Yvette, I opted for a quick text message. The mobile reception was reasonable.

Beverly provided me with a pile of towels and a hair dryer.

'You're welcome to join us in the lounge.'

'Thank you, but I'm very tired. It's been a long day. Tomorrow, perhaps.' I backed away.

Beverly's dimples deepened. 'Of course. Photographer. Castles.' She nodded, slowly.

Post-bath, I arranged the photography equipment on the bed: three lenses, spare battery, pocket tripod and the newly acquired Canon EOS digital camera, which had arrived three weeks earlier, giving me sufficient time to practise at Ashby-de-la-Zouch. There was some adjusting to its weight and feel in my hands. Each piece of apparatus served a purpose. A fixed length wide angle lens for the scenic shots, a zoom lens for detailed close ups and the luxury object: the tilt and shift lens, which enabled me to take shots of buildings without distortion. The latter happened to be key to the types of photographs I needed to satisfy Medici's requirements. In his detailed breakdown of views and locations, he had been particular about angles, whether upward or downward. There was also my trusty film camera, looking slightly scratched and neglected next to its juvenile digital cousin.

Black, polished and fiddly, the new camera had a beauty to it, something that I would not find in other modern devices, like laptops and mobile phones. The mechanism was unchanged from the early days of photography: look, hold steady, click. The fundamentals would be as familiar to a nineteenth-century photographer as they were to me. And yet, this digital camera was also magical, and beyond my comprehension. Bytes and pixels, the language of a computer, now applied to what I held in my hand.

Did it matter, my woeful ignorance? Probably not. I'd never be the geek at the photography shows spewing out technical jargon to fellow enthusiasts. I only had to know what I was capable of doing with it.

I checked, re-checked everything, then packed the lot in a shoulder bag. The bag bulged and stretched the stitched seams. Weight remained an issue.

The next morning, hoping to escape the house without been accosted by my kindly but chatty hosts, I crept out, gently closing the door behind me. Out of the corner of my eye, I was certain I saw lace curtain twitch.

When I'd driven to Bamburgh the previous day, catching sight of the castle, a wash of contentment had lifted my spirits. The evening sun had illuminated the stonework and it glowed crimson, almost as if to remind the visitor of bloody battles. Arriving at the gates, the intact keep signalled something different: Bamburgh Castle was occupied, a home. There were state rooms, an armoury and museums; stuff that informed but left me uninspired. My love affair was with deconstructed buildings; I preferred to recreate them with blocks of imagination and whispers of forgotten people.

The list of requirements was equally uninspiring: shots of this tower, that gatehouse, and several looking up at the battlements from below, especially out by the windmill. I adjusted the mechanism on the tilt and shift lens until the lines of walls were straight, and released the shutter. By now, I'd a stiff neck and aching wrists.

The windmill lacked sails and much else. It was a perplexing addition to the battlements. Presumably, the bleak construct had been dumped on the edge of the escarpment outside the main walls so the wind could harangue it. I ignored the building and looked out to the sea. Brushing a strand of hair out of my eyes, I snapped pictures of the distant isles using my film camera. I had my own requirements: no people, as they added a modern slant to an otherwise purely historic perspective, and certainly no aerials, aeroplanes or vehicles of any kind in the background. I shared those kind of stipulations with Medici. However, whereas my benefactor wanted rigidly architectural images, I extended my shots to include ambiance. I preferred silhouettes without detail, letting the cracks and breaches in the walls vanish into the gloom. Then there was the sea, a perfect backdrop.

The world before me shimmered, blurring a fraction, and I lowered my camera to check the settings. It was then I smelt salt, not the sea kind, but the human kind that came with sweat. I wrinkled my nose and wiped it with the back of my sleeve. Something rippled in the air, and it wasn't the wind. Air didn't have substance to it. This was what I had come north, given up my job, to explore and capture, not with lens and film, but with my imagination. I knew what I felt wasn't real, only my ingenuity created a realism to it, and as I prepared myself, I didn't care to call it a gift or a talent. What did it matter what it was? For a few minutes I would feel so alive, and nobody need know how I achieved this buzz, this explosion of senses.

I closed my eyes, held my breath and listened to the distant hubbub. I swayed, slightly, buffeted by the warm wind, and imagined what it was I might be hearing. The faint tooting of a piper – was that the real thing, being piped into battle? Drumbeats, which I felt through the soles of my feet, were accompanied by ferocious cries. There was, in my head, an army marching towards the castle. Were these the shouts and caterwauls of the barbarian clans approaching from the Scotland? The lords of Northumberland trapped behind the castle walls had had to face Celtic marauders time and time again for centuries. I smelt hot oil, the kind thrown over the side of the ramparts to smother the enemy. Would I see anything, like I did with the joust? Flying arrows whistled right by my ear. I was moving closer, building a more complete picture. Any moment now, I might see something. I braced, my heart beating faster than the drums, and readied myself... Another arrow shot past me.

I ducked and opened my eyes. I wasn't alone.

'You like this spot?' The man stared at my baggage and tripod, his hands tucked behind his back; a glazed bald patch reflected the sunlight.

I blinked, and like the shutter of a lens, that simple action ended what I'd heard but had not seen with my own eyes. Crouching lower, I pretended to fiddle with the rucksack's zip before standing up. It would take longer for my heartbeats to steady.

An official, probably, since he wore a uniform of sorts. Was he checking I had permission, which I had in the form of a letter in my pocket? David had helped with permits.

'I can explain why I'm here.' I held the letter out.

'You're a photographer, I can see that. It's popular.' He ignored my outstretched hand with a bemused expression. 'With artists too. Painters with their easels.'

I stuffed the crumpled envelope into my camera bag. 'A bit blowy standing here.'

'Aye.' He smiled. 'Doesn't put them all off. This one man, he came at Easter, painted that windmill for a few hours. No interest in the castle. I asked him why, and he said he had to. Odd fellow.'

I felt a twang of sympathy for the guy. 'Well, I'm after the castle shots.'

'Postcards?'

'Excuse me?'

'There'll be for postcards. They update them from time to time in the souvenir shop.' He scratched his peeling nose. 'Hope the weather stays fine. They say this summer is going to be a scorcher.' He ambled away.

What a great idea! From now on, I would tell people I was taking photographs for postcards as it was a better excuse than being a photojournalist.

An hour later I was finished. I checked through Braithwaite's guide one more time for anything that might have missed my attention. The final page mentioned the windmill.

It took three hundred years for Bamburgh to be rescued from ruins and returned to its former glory. Bankrupting one owner, it was once the home of a bishop in the 18th century. He had grand plans, including the bizarre addition of a windmill for civic purposes, producing grain for the locals. In the end, a family of armament makers acquired the castle in 1890, and ironically the castle was rebuilt using the money made from selling the kind of weapons that had destroyed it the first place.

With such a novel feature, I changed my mind and followed the path out to the escarpment and, using my personal camera, took a few close-ups of the windmill with no sails. Would Medici care for the oddity? In my opinion, it added humanity to the fortifications.

I checked my watch. Since I was ahead of schedule, I had the opportunity to carry out one particular wish before hunger drove me back to the B&B.

❖

The thin covering of clouds had largely evaporated to allow the sun to stage a late appearance. The tepid sand, pristine and pale gold, tickled my toes. Sat on the beach, I soaked up the heat rays. The tide was out, and the white tipped waves sloshed back and forth. By nightfall, the tide would race to meet the line of drying seaweed and cover the rippled plateau and pocket rock pools. Voices fought the whooshing wind and waves as children, screeching, built sandcastles. A few had the ability to structure complex designs with moats, while others stuck pebbles and seashells to disintegrating humps of sand. Above the heads of the young architects a real castle beat them hands down.

Ever since I'd first read about the Bamburgh many years ago, this was the view I had craved to see. The idyllic castle was perfect for postcard material with its location adjacent to a long stretch of sand and the backdrop of an azure sky. Armed with my faithful old camera, I made the most of the scenery, but not to the extent I'd anticipated. The view was unchanging; the castle had been locked into that landscape for eternity. A few shutter clicks and I was done.

Or so I thought.

A familiar tingle in my scalp rooted me to the spot. Here? This wasn't a castle; I was some distance from the outer walls. Perhaps the marauding Scots had fought on the beaches and I was about to revisit the battle. I dared to close my eyes for a moment or two, to calm myself and wait, then I opened them to stare at the empty swathe of sand. What was I expecting to see in this vast openness?

Nothing audible teased me like it usually did, nor did I smell anything other than salt and seaweed. Instead, a curtain of pink rays descended, like a filter on my camera lens, and it tinted the air as if the sun was setting. There was no hint of a blood red sun on the horizon; the sand below this shimmer was a glorious saffron, the sea a continuous hue of aquamarine. And yet, something floated past me; a veil, or so it seemed, and staring from behind it, eyes shadowed and lips pale, was a young woman's face. I inhaled sharply and a terrible sense of sadness engulfed me. There was no joy in this vision; it wasn't what I expected. I shivered, ice cold and feverish, and as I attempted to dismiss the unwanted illusion with a rough shake of my head, I heard a sob of despair.

I looked around but none of the children were crying. Turning back, the pink haze had vanished.

The forlorn feeling of loss abruptly lifted and the warm breeze cocooned me once again. The moment, the slippage of time, was over. I had not enjoyed it. Until recently only a few of the visions had left me bereft or uncomfortable; most were uplifting, even exciting. But after Kenilworth, when I had come close to vomiting, I wondered if they were symptomatic of a disease, a malfunction of the brain. I wasn't prepared to contemplate the idea, so I decided that this one, like Kenilworth's vision, was best forgotten.

My stomach rumbled on cue. Back at the B&B, I anticipated many questions from a curious couple.

I picked up a knife and fork and braced myself for more questions from Beverly. She quickly obliged and I answered.

'I'm more interested in the mystique that surround castles than the significant dates. So much history, and yet we only record the facts. The beach is lovely too.'

'Oh, there's plenty of things to see around here. And as for the castle, you should be careful what you wish for,' Beverly said.

'Here we go,' Bert said.

'What?' I asked.

Beverley lay down her fork and ignored her husband. 'It's said that there's a princess who fell in love, but her da wouldn't let her marry the boy. They were separated, the lad sent away. The poor thing was naturally sad. The king feeling sorry for her, had men go look for him. When they came back, they said he'd married somebody else. So the king had a pink dress made for her—'

'Pink?'

'Aye, to cheer her up, her being a girl, of course.' Beverly clucked her tongue disapprovingly. 'She put it on and flung herself off the castle tower onto the rocks below. Turns out, the lad hadn't married anyone, and he came back for her.'

I swallowed a hardened lump of unchewed food. It wasn't possible. I didn't see ghosts; I imagined things and made them feel real. If this tale was new to me, how had I managed to conjure up a vision of a pink woman, and heard her crying? Staring at my half-eaten dinner, my appetite was obliterated.

'You're awful pale, lass. Was that not a good tale?'

'Very interesting,' I stuttered. 'Too good, almost.' I imagined my photographs of the beach. Would there be a hint of pink, a veiled face hovering above the sand? A real blurring of fiction into fact? I'd been in that worrying place many times, knowing it was meaningless to go there: nothing ever showed up in the photographs. An overactive imagination wasn't the same as seeing ghosts, and the evidence was clear in the images I snapped. Nothing was ever there.

'Every seven years she appears, wandering the battlements,' Beverly continued, excitedly stabbing at her food. 'Glides, they say, down to the beach, gazing across the sand and sea, looking for her lover. Yes, you're right, a good story.' She paused, fork half-way to her mouth. 'Somebody should make a film of it.'

I recalled little else of what Beverley said during the remainder of the meal. Forcing down the last mouthful, I said my thanks, and asked to use the computer again.

David hadn't replied to my email, but Medici, unprompted by me, had sent one. The message was just two lines of text.

Congratulations on your safe arrival in Bamburgh. Looking forward to seeing your photographs. I'm sure they will be perfect. Did you see the windmill? Fascinating addition, most unusual, worth a picture for yourself.
Hope you enjoyed your time on the beach.
Medici

How had he known about the beach? I couldn't bring myself to reply to him to ask. Not yet, not until I was sure how best to ask him. In any case, the castle was next to the sand dunes, and it would be logical to take pictures from the northern aspect; it was a famous landmark.

I logged out of the account and dashed upstairs to the privacy of my room. I would tell him, though, that I liked the windmill.

NINE

Alnwick

The Norman invasion of England, which crushed the native Anglo-Saxons and remaining Viking settlers of the Dark Ages, heralded the arrival of those early wooden buildings with their ditches and ramparts. Across the English landscape, the advent of the motte and bailey style signalled the growing power of the barons who built and occupied them.

Alnwick was one such location.

Malcolm the Third of Scotland became the first failed besieger of Alnwick in 1093, and from there on, the castle expanded, from wood to stone, until it passed into the hands of the Percy family, who built the famed octagonal towers, and the subsequent Dukes of Northumberland have remained its inhabitants into modern times. A continuous occupation for centuries. Quite an achievement.

~ Alistair Braithwaite's Touring Guide of Northern Castles

I WASN'T EXPECTING THE GROUNDS of Alnwick Castle to be so crowded and hostile to taking photographs. A Monday, and not yet the school holidays, I had assumed unhindered views for my visit. Listening to the lilt of the Scots dialect, I remembered, belatedly, that the Scottish schools broke up earlier than their English counterparts. It looked like a coach load of holiday clubs had deposited their energetic cargo in the heart of the castle.

Thwarted, I went for an early lunch in the café and squashed myself in a cramped corner, next to a harassed mother and her brood. I devoured a sandwich and scalded my mouth on hot coffee. Ignoring the hubbub, I read a few passages from Braithwaite's guide on the arrival of the Normans.

> **The idea of a castle, a defence structure inhabited by a lord or knight, was an invention of the Normans. Prior to their invasion, such private fortifications had been banned. It was the duty of the king to defend his nation. Building your own castle was forbidden by Alfred the Great. In the land of the Gaul, the invasion of the Viking Norseman led to the creation of a new Duchy – Normandy. The French king's power disintegrated when he failed to repel the Norsemen. Other men filled the power vacuum, built their strong fortifications and the king, unable to stop them, had been left with a small country surrounded by fiefdoms. The era of the domineering feudal lord had arrived.**

For Alnwick, that feudal power lay with the formidable Percy family.

Offering up my table to another boisterous family, I decided to visit the Constable Tower where there was an exhibition on Henry Percy, better known as Harry Hotspur, a warrior knight since childhood. Wandering around the exhibits, I deciphered letters written by him, the pictures of the castle as it appeared in his lifetime, and read of his gruesome death in battle. There were plenty of quotes from Shakespeare. I didn't recognise them; my English syllabus had chosen *Macbeth*.

What was it about men and war? Had the castles those great medieval knights built fostered a love of destruction and chaos, or were they constructed to avoid conflict by threatening their opponents with long sieges and unnecessary hardships? It was probably a mixture of both. As usual, I tried to look past the killing aspect of the architecture to the indestructible elements and sheer scale of them.

The Percy family lineage dated back to the same Viking invaders who conquered Normandy and settled there. Could such an ancient lineage be proved beyond doubt? The Percy women had between them produced a long line of nobles. My parents knew little of their own ancestors. Mum in particular was cagey and uncomfortable talking about it. The excuse given was reliability. Granny Izzy, my late maternal grandmother, had a form of dementia, and had a tendency to make things up. She liked to tell entertaining stories that kept the younger members of the family spellbound. As for my dad, he bounced any questions about his family back to me by saying, 'What's the point?' A staple answer for anything he didn't know; he would rather deflect the question than admit ignorance.

I stepped outside and rummaged in the pocket of my rucksack. Opening my notebook, I reminded myself of the structures to be photographed. Most of Medici's requirements were odd features of the octagonal towers of the barbican, which included stone figures standing guard on the parapets. The life-like guardians were a pretence to fool attackers into thinking there was a significant garrison. I picked a spot away from the crowded areas and fiddled with the tilt until I had the angle right, then I zoomed in on the caricatures. They looked miserable and weather-worn, although today, the sunshine was roasting them. I peeled off a layer of clothing.

Something about Alnwick failed to capture my imagination – I hadn't experienced a single episode, not a hint of sensory overload nor even a tingle. My nostrils flared unproductively, picking up only neutral smells. As for the atmosphere, there was nothing to stimulate me. Was that due my inability to wholly relax or the history of the place? It felt a pity that the castle, given its fantastic history, wasn't in ruins. A selfish thought, cold-hearted, perhaps.

Job done, I lugged my equipment with a weariness of spirit, and headed towards the gatehouse and exit. It was time to find my resting place for the night.

'Robyn?' The door opened a crack to reveal a shockingly pale face.

My hand recoiled from the doorbell. 'Yes. Mrs Farley?'

'Ms Farley.' The wary expression deepened just short of a frown. The welcoming technique was the opposite end of the spectrum to Beverly and Bert. I felt like an uninvited intruder and not a paying guest.

She yanked on the door handle. 'Call me Meg.'

The proprietor of Petals Bed and Breakfast was considerably younger than I'd anticipated. Probably because an antique couple managed the last establishment, I had assumed retired folk were the norm. I tilted my head back, then a bit more. Meg was a bean pole with cellophane leggings stuck to her skinny legs and a limp t-shirt with visible ping-pong ball breasts underneath the thin fabric. She flicked a strand of jet-black hair behind her ear. Obviously dyed – her eyes were blue.

'Breakfast at seven-thirty,' she said. Her spider legs bounded up the stairs, while I heaved the suitcase up each step. 'I have to work tomorrow.' Her booming voice echoed down the stairwell.

I staggered and nearly toppled backwards.

The room featured an iron frame bed and a pinewood chest of drawers. From that minimalist starting point, upon closer inspection, the details went downhill. Grey-cream walls, flaking paint around the windowsill and crooked Venetian blinds. The room smelt of pine scented furniture polish applied in a frenzy. This was my introduction to the cheap end of the B&B market. My skin immediately started to itch, as if unwashed and grubby.

Meg unsuccessfully attempted to realign a broken blind. 'Bathroom's opposite. Please remember to lock the door.'

I dropped the heavy holdall on the floor and gently lowered the camera bag on to the bed.

'Thanks,' I said.

'Sorry, no telly. You're welcome to watch with me, downstairs.'

Meg wrung her hands together, as if begging me to decline, which I did politely. I waited expectantly for mention of dinner.

She held out a solitary key on a piece of string. 'Front door. I put the chain across at ten. Best be back by then.'

I was under the strong impression she wanted me out of the house.

'Sure. Ten.' I noted the hand holding the key, especially the pale band of skin on the ring finger. Recently divorced? Desperate for cash? Meg was noticeably uncomfortable in her role as landlady.

She backed out of the room, smiling awkwardly, moving with adolescent gawkiness. She fumbled with the door handle. 'Anything. Just ask.' She pulled the door shut behind her.

I kicked off my shoes and lay on the bed, which had a hard mattress and a lumpy feather pillow, and stared at the cracks in the ceiling. The brief respite ended. I had things to do. Hunting around, pulling furniture away from the walls, I discovered the room had one plug socket. I sorted through the day's pictures, deleted the failures off the nearly full memory stick and noted the good ones. It all took time.

Done with the camera, I fished out the Nokia mobile from my handbag and sent a text to Mum. I couldn't face ringing her and admitting I was lonely. What I texted was a bit like a night watchman's report at the end of a shift:

Everything fine. In Alnwick. Speak tomorrow.

My text to Yvette summed up my mood more precisely.

Shitty B&B. Got to eat out. Lumpy pillow.

Yvette, unlike Mum, who hadn't replied, came back instantly.

You should write a review of B&Bs.

My friend was trying, without success, to make me smile. Before I could reply, the phone went ping again. Yvette, somehow, across the distance, had sensed my subdued misery.

It's going to be lonely. Enjoy the scenery. The weather, OMG, it's boiling here.

I hugged the phone to my chest, then wrote a short reply, my thumbs skidding around the numeric keypad.

Thanks. Tomorrow will be better. Dunstanburgh.

My stomach grumbled and I swung my legs off the granite hard bed, grabbing my coat at the same time.

The front door, apparently spring loaded, slammed shut behind me and almost caught the heels of my shoes. The key dangled from the string. I dropped it into my handbag. Rain pitter-pattered on my face. Barely visible, it floated down, a misty grey visage that smothered the air with tiny droplets. It was the kind of rain that penetrated everything it touched, straight down, no breeze to shoo it away. According to the weather forecast, this was an interlude; the heat was set to return.

I hoisted up my hood, squeezed past the immovable rusted gate, and headed towards the town centre, hoping to stumble across a restaurant or cafe. The first one I encountered was shut. It was Monday, not the best day of the week for eating out. Moving along the main street of the town, I peered at the menus and walked past a bistro twice before accepting it was the best option.

Sipping on a glass of water, waiting for the spaghetti Bolognese, I mulled over my current situation, starting with the man holding the purse strings. I recalled the emails between David and me, the thread of communication that had begun my northern adventure. David handled me; he was in control. Since our one and only face-to-face encounter, he had continued to instruct me remotely, and I'd not taken the time during the preparations to clarify the relationship I had with him. By Easter, not only had I ceased questioning his role in the arrangement, but I had failed to establish exactly who Medici was. David was deliberately concealing his identity. He referred to everything in the first person. *I* will provide you with a rental car and expenses.

The forkful of spaghetti hovered by my lips, my mouth frozen half-open; the strings of spaghetti slipped off the fork. David had accepted the nickname, Medici, and used it in all of our correspondence. Medici this, Medici that, the pair of us knocking the name back and forth. Medici himself seemed to appreciate the moniker.

The fork clattered on the plate. Were David and Medici one in the same person? Had I overlooked the obvious explanation?

The idea of being manipulated into believing I had been communicating with two different people, when they could well be the same person, irritated me. No, more than irritated, infuriated me. Was the mystery man a trickster taking advantage of my naivety?

It didn't make sense. Why pursue the charade of pretending to be somebody different? I'd only spoken to David a couple of times on the phone and he came across as trustworthy and honest, but also forthright and unswerving in his decisions. David's writing style was unlike Medici's, although I had few examples to compare. Medici remained resolutely focused on addressing what he needed from me: the photographs. Only once had he touched on other territory and it had been to discuss my views on history, specifically my quest to visit as many castles as possible. The wording of the email had caught my attention and still did.

David tells me of your ambition. An intriguing goal. Is it to immerse yourself fully into the past, the history of each location, or to photograph every possible architectural feature of the period? I know which I would prefer.

I had given the same answer that I gave to David, who after the exhibition had never discussed my love affair with castles or photography. Medici's response indicated his preference. Lacking any kind of emotive language, he described architectural concepts using exact terms, some of which were new to me, and I had to look them up. Only at the end of the email had he referenced my goal.

You should see and experience as much as you can. Envelope yourself in history as if you were there. I envy your opportunity.

Again, I tried not to read too much into the insightful remark, but all the same, it unnerved me how close he was to the truth. In contrast, practically-minded David had proposed the annual membership to English Heritage, rather than buying tickets at each castle, and other things relating to travel that I'd not considered.

David was proving more useful, if less enthusiastic.

I retrieved the fork. David and Medici were not the same person. Medici delegated and David, for whatever undiscovered reason, carried out the instructions, and I in turn did the same. I recalled a conversation with Yvette when she described the benefits of patronage, the role of a benefactor, and the definitions certainly applied to the context of my situation. Why would Medici be bothered with the details? Should these issues matter to me anyway? The money was there in my account, proof of both men's legitimacy.

❖

The rain was spewing out of the guttering and striking the front doorstep. I turned the key and for a moment the door refuse to budge. A firm wriggle of the key and it still held fast. Nausea bounced into the back of my throat at the thought of all my camera equipment being flogged on eBay. I shoved harder against the wood, the door yielded, and I stumbled over the threshold. Behind me, the door shut with a recoiling bang. Rainwater dripped off my nose. I flared angry nostrils. Apparently my host cared little about hospitality. Having shaken my head free from the damp hood, I listened with a cocked ear. Raucous laughter broke the uncomfortable silence. Meg had company. The front room, which I hadn't troubled to enter, was the source of the man's brassy baritone and Meg's high-pitched giggles.

'Oh, you bad boy,' she squealed. 'Do that again.'

I froze. There was no mistaking the panting or Meg's over-egged moans.

'Don't stop!'

I bolted up the stairs and straight to my bedroom. Breathing heavily, I leant against the door and drew across the bolt. The unwanted and embarrassing noises of Meg's rowdy play acting were still audible through the floorboards.

'Oh, yes!' Another burst of clichéd dialogue followed. I lay on the bed and covered my ears with the pillow. Meg didn't have a self-conscious bone in her body. My arrival, crashing through the front door, obviously added to the excitement. Perhaps she'd deliberately kept the door stiff, a cue to put on a performance for her guests. The shrill tones continued for a few more minutes. I cringed at each exaggerated moan and groan.

The quietness was abrupt. An eerie nothingness enveloped the narrow house. Easing myself upright, I tiptoed towards the door and pressed an ear to it. Softer voices, normal in volume and tone. A door creaked.

'Same time,' the gruff male said.

The heavy front door clanged shut. That was it? No post-sex chatter or a nice cup of tea? A simple hump over the settee and done? Sliding back the bolt, I opened the door and stuck my head through the gap. Meg was trotting upstairs, her face rosy cheeked, her ruffled hair angled upwards. The spaghetti strapped top barely covered her breasts and as she moved along the landing, the black PVC mini-skirt squeaked, her long, elastic legs bowing outwards.

I shrivelled at the sight of the caricature of what I knew her to be. The lack of comforts in the bedroom was evidence of her abandoning her lodgers for a more lucrative business. But it was too late to avoid her. Meg had spotted me.

Her colouration deepened, and she pursed her lips. 'Lodgers don't pay as much as I'd thought,' she said, with a brisk shoulder shrug. 'And that bastard of an ex-husband doesn't cough up a penny. Needs must.' She ran her fingers through her tangled, sweaty hair. 'Goodnight.' The satisfied smile, which spread across her face and creased into her flushed cheeks, had a glorious edge to it. That will-o'-the-wisp charm had to be appealing to a night visitor.

Alnwick, the home of the troublesome Percys and centuries of warfare, was no different to my hometown. What had I been thinking?

I washed my hands thoroughly in the bathroom. I was mortified by my mistake. By my ignorance. I had greeted solitary businessmen staying the night in my hotel workplace with courtesy. What a dolt I'd been, assuming their crumpled suits and tired eyes were due to hard work while their companions, smartly dressed and heavily laden with make-up, were supposedly their work colleagues. It wasn't often, but occasions had arisen when the cleaners rolled their eyes when questioned by the duty manager, who turned a blind eye to the practice. It wasn't worth damaging the hotel's reputation to draw attention to them. "Escorts" was the manager's preferred term.

Before I went to bed, I reviewed the list of B&B bookings and crossed out another cheap one. I would replace it with a three, no, four-star one as soon as possible. David didn't need to know why and even if he did ask, I had my personal safety to consider. As for my planned second night at Meg's, it wasn't happening. I would find somewhere else to stay.

I checked the door was locked before turning off the light.

TEN

Dunstanburgh

A massive fort, battered by weather, destroyed by war, it sits proudly on the headland, refusing to be cowed still. Other than the natural rock known as the Great Whin Sill, there appears to be no apparent strategic purpose for the location of the vast castle. Upon the same rock, many a fearsome structure had been built - Hadrian's Wall, Bamburgh Castle and Dunstanburgh. The Normans were not the first to pick the site - at one time, an Iron Age fort stood upon the outcrop.

Thomas, Earl of Lancaster, who built the current castle in 1313, associated himself with Arthurian legends, and created his Avalon Island with the use of water features. None obviously survive, but the golf course benefits from the lower plateau. Isolated from nearby settlements, even to this day, Dunstanburgh requires sturdy legs and a brisk walk to reach the gatehouse, avoiding the golf balls along the way. Ideally, don't pick a rainy or blustery day, you'll be hugging the walls for shelter.

What brings visitors to this bleak outpost is the aesthetics of landscape and the castle's rugged determination not to crumble and expire into the sea. The once mighty, rather aloof castle, perched on a spillage of magna rock, has all the elements of an abandoned fortification robbed of its stone - forgotten, bleak, inaccessible and haunted by its past. Turner painted here, and Gothic writers penned antiquated myths as splendid as Lancaster's own ambitions.

Bird watching is also recommended.

~ Alistair Braithwaite's Touring Guide of Northern Castles

I RE-PACKED THE CAMERA BAG for a second time and, regardless of my efforts, its weight remained uncompromisingly heavy even after I'd sacrificed the tripod and a zoom lens. I heaved the strap over my shoulders and attached a flask of water to my trouser belt. The weak sunshine was welcome, the energetic breeze less so.

The walk from the car park in the village of Caster to the castle was approximately one blustery wind-swept mile along a coastal footpath. Unlike many fortifications, no habitation had blossomed at the base of the castle, unless you counted the golf course. A few hundred yards down the track, I paused to take a swig out of the water flask and cursed the feudal lord whose idea it was to build a castle on the rise of a bleak promenade of cliffs and rocky coves.

The earl, whose name I'd forgotten, should have taken sound advice. Walking briskly, I conjured up the equivalent of a feng shui consultant standing with the earl, evaluating the outcrop's potential. The nervous advisor muttered a word or two about bad vibes and the wrong energy, and dispatched a perplexed look of disbelief at the choice of location. He suggested, as politely as possible, that the sea air was too harsh. He wrung his hands, imploring the earl to think of the masons and carpenters who'd have to labour in such remoteness. Then, there was the obligatory, 'The cost, my lord!'; the lord's reply, 'You're dismissed.'

Yet, Dunstanburgh had been built, and later its gatehouse was enlarged. Its fate was decided by a series of civil wars and, unlike Alnwick and Bamburgh, no one cared to rescue the crumbling fortress and transform it into a palatial home like Kenilworth. Lifeless and alone, Dunstanburgh suffered the ignominy of neglect. For lovers of ruins, it was a blessing, and worthy of my daydreams.

From a distance, the giant gatehouse and crippled keep seemed to be all that had survived, and Braithwaite was keen to point out its size.

The gatehouse is on such a grand scale it diminishes the rest of the walls. So big, it is impractical and unsophisticated; Dunstanburgh remains the largest castle ever built in Northumberland. The space inside the walls was mostly unoccupied, a testament to its use as a garrison fort rather than a home. With much of the original structure missing, one is required to be imaginative about what else might have stood within its bailey.

I smiled. Imaginative? This was why I liked the little guidebook. I liked the idea of Alistair lost in his own daydreams, just like me.

As I approached the gatehouse, other features emerged and brought shape: elongated walls, steep inclines and half-formed towers. Humbled by the fragments of a once enormous fortress, and wretchedly aching from my exertions, I paused to sympathise with the weathered shell, robbed of its stone and fractured into remote parts. My own life had often felt equally fragmented. Walls implied strength, but without care and maintenance, they amounted to nothing, and so it had been with me. Friends and colleagues thought I quietly persevered through life's mishaps and hurdles, but the reality was that I lived a directionless life, compartmentalised and unfulfilled. This summer, I'd broken out of that routine and done something different, surprising friends and family in equal measure.

Arriving at the bottom of the hill, I grappled with the straps and zipper of the bag, and fished out my film camera to take a few wide angled views to add to my landscape collection. Medici wanted, unsurprisingly, something different to my choices.

Dunstanburgh was little more than a line of uneven grey stone sandwiched between patchy clouds and a sheet of swaying grasses and yet it had so much to offer me.

'You're truly dramatic. Tell you what,' I said, aiming the viewfinder at a window, 'we can be friends for the day, can't we?' Each shot seemed to present the castle as lonelier than the last and I commiserated with its melancholy isolation.

My brother, Richard, the soldier accustomed to camaraderie, had been quick to point out my fears in a rare call home, not long before I'd left Coalville.

'The loneliness will drive your bonkers,' he said, his voice breaking up with the weak connection.

I had huffed with annoyance. Mum had said the same thing. 'It's not for the rest of my life,' I had said.

'All the same, sis, you'll pine for home cooked food and company. It isn't even a proper job.'

'There's a contract. I'm being paid expenses. In any case, I never said it was a job; it's not a holiday either. When are you coming home on leave?' The conversation limped on after that into safer territory.

Regretting how easily Richard had kicked my confidence, I strode up to the ticket kiosk and flashed the English Heritage membership card.

My preferred company came in the form of sturdy bedrock, colourful stone, swaying grass, open azure skies, the cresting waves and squawking seagulls - and what I conjured to accompany it. What would it be this time? An archery competition, a mock sword fight, the beating of weapons into shape or the smell of hot metal from the blacksmith's forge? A burst of energy propelled me onwards, as did the wind, which harried me from all directions.

I wasn't the only creature in need of shelter. Perched on the cliffs below the castle was a flock of pigeons. I focused the zoom lens on one and spotted the leg ring. Racing pigeons. Poor things. Where were they bound? Was this a regular stopover point? Somewhere, somebody was waiting for them to come home. I tried not think of my parents, my bedroom, the comfort of familiarity.

A gust grabbed my camera strap and whipped it across my face. I decided it was an appropriate time to have lunch and ducked behind a wall. I hunkered down on my bottom, my knees tucked up to my chin. A shadow crossed the grassy expanse and reached my toes. The sun was fighting a losing battle.

The half-eaten sandwich was returned to its wrapper, my appetite gone in an instant. I slowly unwound a tangle of messy thoughts, allowing them to coalesce into a single stream of conscious self-awareness. I stilled every inch of my body, ignored the calls of the seagulls and the rustling of long grass. With nobody nearby, I was in an ideal situation to drift into a dreamscape and let it develop. I closed my eyes.

There was no "sight" of anything. Not even a smell. I heard a blast, a noisy wail that wasn't human, or animal.

A horn. Then it came, an instant dull ache behind the eyes. A buzz of tingles shot across my scalp from nape to temples, while another flurry of electricity spiralled around my ankles. Something bright startled me. A bolt of lightning flashed and yet the sky was clear of thunder clouds. The static prickled more harshly and I nearly opened my eyes. What came to me wasn't a crowd of people, the familiar scene of castle life lifted from an illustration. Instead, the grass parted, shifting open like a gaping mouth, and from out it, something emerged.

He rose above me, out of the ground, and seemed to be part of the silvery sky. The figure of a man, vast and ancient in his armour. I went with him.

He sees something amongst the flashes of lightning, and thunderous rainfall. A high cliff. But he isn't up at the top where the gatehouse is barred to him, but below, by a pitch-black cave entrance. The wind howls painfully in his ear, yet, inside the cavern it is quiet, and brighter. A swirl of light on the tip of a staff draws him in, along slippery staircases and dank corridors, until he rises up into the castle itself. There in the murky darkness, a wizened faced man, his guide, points beyond the sleeping army of knights and horses to the centre of the scene.

On a crystal plinth of carved snakes and skeletons lies a beautiful woman, and a horn. He must awaken her. But with a steely sword or the horn? He chooses the horn, lifting it to his lips, he blows.

The knights wake, roaring and angry, charging toward him with brandished weapons and…

A seagull squawked right by my ear. The dream crashed out of my mind leaving a vacant hole. The last image I saw was the man's gauntlet clutching the curved horn.

I groaned with disappointment. It had the makings of a good tale, one that I thought would lead me to this very spot where I sat. An armoured knight seeking shelter in a storm, a secret cave, some kind of Merlin-like creature, a dazzling woman, and that horn blasting. Adding to my frustration, the gull had stolen my sandwich.

There was no mention of this particular legend in Braithwaite's archaic guide, and if anyone liked an eccentric tale, it was him. I had no clue as to what I had witnessed in my mind, and why the imagery was filled with fantastical symbols and devices when usually I stuck fast to historical depictions. Apparently the ghostly Pink Lady at Bamburgh wasn't a unique experience; myths were occupying my subconscious. However, for now, the spellbinding moment of escapism had ended and pondering over its meaning wasn't productive.

With my pulse calmed, I gathered up my things and continued to circle the outer walls. The wind, which had seemed unbearably harsh, had dropped, and the sun hopped out from behind the clouds to warm my brow. I fished out a hat and covered my head.

Medici had wanted shots of the gatehouse from both sides, within and outside. From inside the walls, the arched doorway was in a gully and only just visible, and the grounds of the castle rose higher than the door. I set up the tripod, aligned the viewfinder with the apex of the archway, and widened the shot to include the sea in the background. Medici had described the gatehouse in an earlier email; his exact wording was, "seek out the underbelly of the gatehouse's D shape". What a strange guy he was.

Job done, I folded the tripod legs and packed the camera away. Whatever Medici was searching for in these photographs, it wasn't anything related to the waking dream I'd experienced. He maintained a forthright interest in architecture, and nothing else. While I yearned to understand the meaning behind my slippages into the past, he was happily critiquing the builders' designs. Perhaps that was why I had never studied history formally. Factual analysis wasn't my thing. Given today's experience, paranormal would have been a better choice.

Avoiding a repeat of my overnight stay with Meg, I took a room at a hastily booked roadside hotel, which was on route to Warkworth Castle. I slept fine, except for the blasted phantom horn, which woke me up a few times, and, although I couldn't recall the night-time dreams, I felt sure I was reliving that vision in the cave.

In the morning, I sent a text to Yvette and asked her to research Dunstanburgh's legends.

ELEVEN

THE ARTIST WAS RELIEVED to be almost back on schedule. He had returned having avoided the rainy days. As before he had packed light, not bothering with the unnecessary things like razors and shower gel, just a bar of soap and a tin opener. He missed his studio. He wasn't missing juvenile students with their limited attention spans.

He easily persuaded the lady in the ticket office to let him back into Warkworth Castle without paying; he adopted a well-practised charm when needed. She was a different person to the previous day, but fortunately, he still had the ticket receipt in his jacket, and having produced it, he explained why he needed access to the grounds.

He walked straight to a spot a little distance from the angular keep, circled the area, kicking up the tufts of grass with the point of his shoe. It had probably slipped out of his pocket when he had bent to dip his brush in the water pot. He hadn't expected to care that much; it wasn't as if somebody important had given it to him. But it mattered; he had kept it in his possession for a long time.

The sun glinted on something. Crouching, he hunted with his fingers. The object was wet with early morning dew. He wiped it on his jeans, ran his fingernail along the ridge and teased the blade out. He flashed it briefly, admiring the shimmer of cold metal. Snapping the blade back into the handle, he stuffed the penknife deep in his pocket.

Carrying a knife was purely habit, a hangover of his youth. His father had probably suspected he carried, but had said nothing. Better knives than drugs, he would have thought; one might protect you, the other never could. Fortunately, the penknife had only ever been a status symbol, occasionally revealed to warn off a bully.

Now, years later, it was a multi-purpose object. The knife was useful for sharping pencils and the tiny screwdriver came in handy for adjusting the easel when the hinges played up. He patted his back pocket, reassured the penknife was snug, and strode through the long grass toward the gatehouse and the exit.

He waved goodbye to the woman in the ticket office; proof he was telling the truth, that his visit was cursory. He done all he needed to do the previous day.

In the car park, a young man was unloading a buggy from the boot of his hatchback. His companion, a yawning woman, hugged a sleepy baby to her hip. The man appeared keen; the woman exhausted. There was another car reversing into a space, a red Corsa, the features of its sole occupant were indeterminate under the shadow of the trees. He decided it was a woman, which was more than he needed to know; he shouldn't be nosey as it wasn't polite to intrude; he knew what unwanted attention felt like.

And that was it for Warkworth Castle; little to report, not that Camilla wanted details. He grimaced, dwelling on things that had not been said. He had misconstrued his agent's motivations. She hadn't the wherewithal to understand what it meant to paint under such difficult circumstances. He and Camilla had speculated about the reasons for the commission during phone calls and a rare meeting in the pub. When he grew weary of her vague answers and threatened to withdraw his services, she had sworn him to secrecy, as if he was painting the crown jewels for the queen. 'It's for a gift,' she had said during their last tense encounter.

'If that's what you say it is.' He wasn't convinced Camilla was telling the truth; her rosy cheeks weren't entirely due to alcohol, and she had fiddled with her earrings. A gambler would describe it as a tell.

Standing by his car, the artist turned and inspected the towers one last time. He wouldn't be back here again. Tomorrow, his destination was further afield and in the direction of Newcastle. He wasn't planning on stopping there for long either.

TWELVE

Warkworth

As if all their other residences were not sufficiently grand, the Percys finally had a prestigious castle, their chief residence, and Warkworth kept that status even after it fell into decline. The symbolism of the Percys' success was carved on to the entrance of the hall, the location of the earl's bedchamber, the exclusive room of the castle. The heraldic sculpture of the Percy Lion, their dynastic badge, includes the three fishes of the Lucy family, an important provider of inherited land, and the incorporation of the Herbert's portcullis, another related family. Weathered by time, the bold statement of ownership has stuck fast to the tower, helping create an interesting focal point for photographers.
Moving on through the castle, don't forget to visit the Little Stair Tower with its spire.

~ Alistair Braithwaite's Touring Guide of Northern Castles

TOTTERING PRECARIOUSLY on a low stone wall, which were the remains of a structure that once reached for the skies, I slipped and twisted my ankle.

'Ah, ow!' I hopped on one foot, comically clinging on to my camera, and, failing to keep my balance, I dropped onto the slippery stones, and screwed my eyes shut.

'Please, please,' I muttered. 'This can't be happening.'

With my lips pressed tighter, I tried hard to ignore the throb, but when I placed any weight on my leg, the pain worsened.

'Are you alright?'

I shaded my eyes and looked up to find a man looming, his face cast into the shadows.

'Hurt it?' he asked.

'Not sure. I fell off this wall.'

'Stones are treacherous after rain,' he said with a strong Yorkshire accent. 'With somebody?'

As if summoned to my side by some invisible emergency siren, he hovered expectantly, his broad shoulders hunched, and his hands shoved into the depths of a black bomber jacket. I couldn't help noticing his jeans were streamline and low around his hips. I paused before answering. The issue of lone working had concerned Dad and he had made suggestions. 'Make something up. You know, boyfriend popped to the bog or something. Don't let anyone, especially a man, know you're alone.'

Mum had expressed an interest on my behalf in self-defence classes. I hadn't seen the point; I wasn't capable of flinging anyone over my shoulder. I could appreciate why she would have been panicked by the situation I was in; there was nobody else in the vicinity and one strange man had me at a disadvantage.

I opted to deflect the stranger's question. 'You?'

He straightened, revealing a young face in the sunlight, unremarkable in character except for what seemed like an excessively short nose.

'Wife is in the car with the sleeping bairn.' He grinned. 'She's probably gone to sleep too.' The smile extended into dimples. 'It's only, I'm a nurse. So if you want, I can take a look at your ankle?'

'A nurse,' I said tentatively. Was the whole "wife in the car" speech just an excuse to wriggle into my pants. Did perverts hang out in castles? I smirked - *unlikely, Robyn, get a grip*. But there again, what was wrong with a little flirtatious indulgence? After my doomed relationship with Craig, I needed to regain some trust in men.

'Aye.' The nurse crouched in front of me. 'Leeds General Hospital. The wife comes from these parts, so we're visiting.'

Before I could protest, he had the heel of my shoe in the palm of his hand.

'Do you work in Accident and Emergency?'

'No,' he said, gingerly loosening the Velcro strap. 'Orthopaedics. So I see a fair share of sprains and breaks.'

'I hope this isn't broken.' I winced.

'You'd be howling more if it were,' he said, cheerfully. 'Does this hurt?'

He tugged on the heel and lifted my foot out. A twinge of pain, but nothing else. I felt like a fraud. 'Not really.'

'Good. Promising so far. Wriggle your toes.'

I did, and he massaged the ankle joint at the same time. When he touched the knobbly bone, I exclaimed. 'Yes, there, a bit.'

'Aye.' He rotated the ankle gently, then slipped the shoe back on. 'Nothing broke or sprained for that matter. A little twist. Might swell a little. Keep your weight off it a bit and keep it up when you sit down. Bag of frozen peas is helpful too.'

'Sit down?' I frowned. 'I've not finished.'

'Finished what?' He rose. 'That's some equipment.'

'I'm taking photographs. I'm on a schedule.' I carefully tightened the Velcro shoe strap.

'A hobby?'

I lifted the bag onto my knees. 'No. I mean, yes it is, but I'm actually taking photos for somebody else. A commission.' I liked the fancy word.

'Really?' he said, without sarcasm. 'You're not local, though.'

'No. I'm touring the area, taking photographs.'

'Nice area, but I'm biased. I used to come up here to volunteer on archaeological projects. But I'm not really cut out of the outdoor life.' He grinned with renewed charm. My chivalrous, floppy-haired knight held out his hand. 'Let me help you up. See if you can take your weight. Not that you have much, kind of fly-weight, aren't you?'

I squirmed at the observation; it wasn't my fault my metabolism burnt its way through food. I felt no shooting pain, merely a harsh throb. He let go of my arm and I balanced equally on two feet.

'Sore?'

'Just a little.'

'You really should keep your weight off it.'

Standing next to him, I wasn't as intimidated by his height. He came across as a genuinely nice guy. I hobbled forward and although the pain wasn't bad, it certainly wasn't improving. 'Oh, f—,' I muted the curse and fretted instead. 'I've still got stuff to do. How am I going to hold a camera steady when my leg is shaking?'

He pursed his lips. 'I'm quite a good photographer myself. Why don't you tell me what you want to photograph and I'll work the camera. It's digital, isn't it? So you can delete the crap ones.'

No way was a stranger holding that precious camera. I was about to say a polite no when I stumbled on the uneven ground. The pain wasn't nice.

'What about your wife?'

'She's been up all night with the kid. I needed to stretch my legs before driving home. I like Warkworth. She brought me here not long after we got married. It felt romantic, taking snapshots of her against the walls. They had some kind of mock tournament on too.'

My ears pricked up. 'I would have liked to have seen that.'

'Ah, it weren't that good,' he said, sheepishly. 'My wife will be fine. She can see us from the car park.'

'Okay. If you could take the pictures exactly as I ask.'

'Sure thing.' He eased the camera bag over his shoulder. 'I'm Mitch. This is some weight.'

'Robyn. I'm getting use to humping it around.'

'So, your photographing specific things?'

We were next to the Lion Tower, one of the items on the list. I had memorised today's agenda.

Moments ago, I'd been sceptical and doubted his credentials, but a few minutes later, I happily told him the essentials of my project, although I omitted the role of the mysterious Medici. Mitch attached the camera to the tripod and familiarised himself with the menu options.

'This is some camera.' He poked about in the bag. 'This lens?'

There was a low wall, and I rested against it and pointed upwards. 'Use the zoom for the lion.'

Less of a lion, more a sheep with a woolly neck. Closer up, it looked even less dramatic. Perched on a stone shelf, the lion's body was half missing, the back legs resembled skeletal bones, and it seemed to have saucepan on its head. A helmet, I supposed. Medici had requested shots of the different colouration of the stone, the lack of symmetry, and the Percy coat of arms, the archway beneath, too, which meant switching to a different lens and moving further back.

'Take your time,' Mitch said, helping with the tripod.

He turned out to be a reasonable photographer, and happy to take directions, and we progressed like an actor and director in partnership. A satisfying hour later, Mitch packed the camera back in the bag.

'Ah, the lad must be awake.' Mitch waved across the open space at a woman; the small figure gestured frantically.

'Thank you, so much,' I said, awkwardly. 'For helping.'

'My pleasure.'

There was that moment, the uneasy hesitation of strangers who knew too much about each other and probably would never meet again.

'Can you manage from here?' he asked.

Something of a guilty expression swept across his face. He had a wife and kid, and wasn't supposed to be spending his time with me. I, too, felt a little ashamed I had stolen him.

'Sure. Ankle hardly hurts at all now. I can walk to the car park.'

'Good.' His hands were back in the pockets. 'All the best with everything. And keep off that foot tonight, tomorrow too if you can.' He headed off to the car park at a brisk pace, one that I couldn't possibly keep up.

Rather than walk, I elected to sit in the middle of the castle's inner ward, and waited.

I thought no amount of patience was going to trigger an awakening. There were other distractions. More people posed in front of the lion or climbed the little spired tower and waved from on high. In my solitude, I was never quite alone to think.

The grass glinted in the sunlight. At first I thought what I saw were dewdrops, the leftovers of an early dawn. As I stared, things took shape, and I found myself imagining I was an archaeologist discovering an artefact buried in the soil, less in the past, more in the now. Hands digging, a trowel poking in the dirt, and the revealing of something metallic, silvery. An arrowhead, a dagger's point, the edge of an axe?

I knew little about archaeology, but I did know objects buried for centuries didn't emerge bright and shiny from the ground. I pursed my lips, undisturbed and intrigued by the illusion created by my mind. The dream seamlessly shifted. I could no longer see any grass. The hands, now gloved in faded coarse leather, scrambled in the dirt, frantic in their search. A souvenir hunter? What was I imagining? I was slipping back in time, tumbling from here to then. I saw something else down there in the shadows. A dark crimson stain on the edge of the metal. Drawn up and out of the ground, the weapon was bloodied. The sturdy, faceless figure rose with it, arm outstretched, blade raised, and with a purpose it began to move toward me.

I leapt to my feet and let out a cry of pain. 'Dammit.'

The figure evaporated. The ground around me returned to lush greenery. The weapons of the past no longer visible. Subliminally, I was probably warning myself not to be tempted into joining archaeological digs. God knows where that would lead me.

I was ready to leave. I took one last look at the Percy Lion, and for a second, I perceived a wink from under his saucepan helmet. He must have seen history unfold from up there. Probably many mock tournaments, too.

I predicted my next landlady, Mrs Dyllis Bartholomew, to be a stooped pensioner, knitting scarves and reading *Women's Own*.

'I'm Dyllis. Welcome.' The curvaceous carrot-topped woman stepped to one side.

I dragged in the suitcase. Within five minutes Dyllis had informed me that she was thirty-six and a widow.

She nudged the bedroom door open with her elbow. 'My husband died two years ago, during the night, in bed.'

'Oh, I am sorry,' I said, alert to a strong whiff of lavender.

'Testicular cancer.' Dyllis' eyelashes thickened with tears. 'Yep.' A lock of red hair tumbled over her face, and she left it there.

Too much information was heading my way. 'How sad.'

The room was perfectly acceptable, if a little on the small side. Plain walls and carpet, matching curtains and duvet. The king-size bed with its purple cushions propped against the faux leather headboard dominated the space.

'Do you have a boyfriend?' she asked, her attention focused on the bed.

'No.' I heaved the suitcase onto a stand. Did clothes become heavier with use?

'Well, my advice, pet, is when you do have one, grope his balls from time to time. I wish I had.' There wasn't a hint of embarrassment in her manner.

I clawed back a witty remark. The woman was deathly serious. 'I'll keep it in mind.'

Her abstract expression paled. 'Yep, wish I had.' She handed me a key. Mrs Dyllis Bartholomew wasn't a sleazy Meg. The frankness might have similarities, but the reason for it was very different.

'I will, you know, check.'

'Comfortable bed.' She gestured without touching it. 'His and mine, but after he went, I couldn't bring myself to sleep in it. He died in it. I got a new one.'

A dead man's bed. I wished Dyllis was better at filtering out the personal stuff. What could I possibly say to that snippet of grief?

'I'll leave you to it,' she said. 'Bathroom's down the hall. There's always hot water.' She hovered by the door with her back to me. 'Um. You're welcome to join me in the lounge. I usually watch Emmerdale, then I can cook us a bit to eat. Would that be all right with you? I'm partial to sausages and mash. I do onion gravy too, if you like.'

I usually preferred staying in the room, but something about Dyllis lured me into needing an inconsequential chitchat.

'Sure, that would be lovely,' I said, and smiled.

Later, having unpacked and plugged the batteries into recharge – ample sockets – I joined Dyllis in the lounge. She was curled up like an armadillo at one end of a black leather sofa, the television in her direct line of sight. I perched, uncertain as to the formalities of being a guest in the host's private space.

I wasn't a fan of soaps. As soon as I arrived in the lounge, Dyllis started a lengthy run-down of the storyline, which had been going on for years. Or so it felt. Each thread was dissected until my head buzzed with over-the-top plot twists and a cast of forgettable characters. Throughout, Dyllis paid no more than the slightest interest in the current episode.

I unhooked my gaze from Dyllis long enough to glance around the room. I saw ordinariness, except, from my perspective the absence of pictures, especially photographs. Where were the portraits of her late husband? Banished out of sight? If Dyllis was my friend, I might have asked, but instead, I nodded and smiled at her monologue, aware of the aching rumble of my stomach, the droop of my eyelids. Finally, the programme ended and Dyllis switched the TV off.

'Just enough time to cook something.' Dyllis uncoiled, forming limbs out of nowhere, and rose. 'Then, it's *New Tricks* on. I do like a good bit of detecting, don't you?'

The bangers tasted delicious. I made sure to compliment the onion gravy. Conversation during the meal was stilted and awkward. We sat across a tiny kitchen table and our toes constantly bumped into each other.

'Busy this summer?' I asked.

She nodded. 'Better than the winter. What brings you to these parts, a woman travelling alone? Are you in sales?'

I rolled out the postcard excuse and kept it simple.

'Bamburgh is lovely. The beach... We had many a picnic on that beach.' Dyllis' trembling finger traced the outline of the plate. She sighed, heavily, and ducked her eyes down.

All the crockery was plain white. Plain was a major feature of the interior of the house. I rotated the mug.

'If they crack, I chuck 'em,' she said, examining her mug.

I removed my hand. 'I'm sorry?'

'We had a different set. Royal Doulton; fancy bone china. His sister gave it to us as a wedding present. He fussed over them and always insisted on washing them by hand and not in the dishwasher. Bloody palaver. I sold them on eBay. His tastes weren't always mine. I'm a purist when it comes to decorating; he liked a splash of this and that on things. All the same.' She looked out of the window, avoiding my searching gaze.

I offered to help wash the dishes.

'Ah, don't trouble yourself. Dishwasher.'

Faced with an evening of watching more television, I made excuses.

Crestfallen, a meek expression slipped across Dyllis' face. 'I can open a box of chocolates. Dairy Milk.'

It wasn't that her company was unwanted or unpleasant, I hadn't the energy to stay awake. I hesitated on the threshold of the lounge. Dyllis, however, had happily curled up on a nest of cushions and was already focused on the television.

'No, no. I'm fine.' I yawned, stretching my mouth as wide as possible. 'I'm beat. Goodnight.'

I stood at the bottom of the bed. Which side had he slept on? I lifted the covers. Was there a man-sized dimple somewhere? Why it bothered me probably had something to do with the hotel. Two weeks before I finished work, a guest had died of a heart attack during the night. The undertakers quietly came and left through a rear fire door. Two days later the room was back in use. Nobody, not even the cleaners, said a word about it.

A bed was a bed. All the same, I was shivering just thinking about Mr Bartholomew. There wasn't a single photograph to remind Dyllis of her absent husband, and yet the woman spent a lot of time remembering him. If her grief was fresh, perhaps she was in denial, refusing to move on. Wouldn't it have been sensible to remove the bed altogether? Then I understood what she wanted. When she was ready, Dyllis would use it again. I was optimistic for her. Dyllis was pretty, and deserved having company at the kitchen table. Then, she could give up the B&B. Strangers were no substitute for a husband.

It was nearly ten o'clock. Back at home, one of my parents would be up and we usually would drink soothing hot chocolate together before going to bed. I missed Mum and Dad. Far away from them, I had underestimated the importance of those little daily rituals. Regardless of how boring and reliable their routines were, stability was important for their happiness. The problem was that I had relied on my parents' habits and they were woven into mine, glued in place by time. By ignoring my ambitions, I had used their choices as a crutch, another reason to avoid striking out on my own.

Remembering a promise, I sent Mum my usual one line report and, for the first time, received an immediate response. Mum had been up waiting for it.

Have you met nice people?

She used to ask those kinds of questions when I started at the hotel. They dried up eventually when the replies were the same. This time, I considered my answer to be genuine.

Yes. Somebody helped me today carrying things.

I stopped there. I didn't want to mention the ankle, which continued to ache.

I was still waiting for information on Dunstanburgh. Yvette had promised to get back to me with any ideas as to the origins of the horn and the cave, which she said seemed Arthurian and something somebody might have painted – so perhaps I had seen a picture of it somewhere. I racked my memories, but nothing came back to me.

I outlined the dead bed dilemma to Yvette.

Is there a ghost in the house?

Yvette's humour fell short of laughs. It wasn't what I needed. If I was tumbling into a rabbit hole, the last thing I wanted was jokes about hauntings. I flung back the cream duvet and opted for the best solution. I slept in the middle of the bed.

THIRTEEN

Prudhoe

Prudhoe means "proud hill" and has been the site of a castle since the Norman Conquest. The steep embankment overlooks the River Tyne, and presented besiegers with a disadvantage. It is the one castle in Northumberland that the Scots failed to capture. While the castle itself fell to pieces, the owners, descendants of the Percy family...

...the Georgian mansion sits inside the walls and its interior is fittingly in the Regency period. Quite at odds with the medieval...

Strange happenings are recorded at Prudhoe in the form of bouncing balls, grey women flinging themselves from ramparts and shifting white horses vanishing into thin air. There are reports of underground tunnels...

I TOSSED ALISTAIR BRAITHWAITE'S GUIDE onto the passenger seat. Having reacquainted myself with the castle's one page outline, I was probably better off not reading too much into his ramblings. He hadn't helped me at Dunstanburgh.

Already sweating slightly, I lugged the camera bag over my shoulder and followed the signs. The energetic sun baked everything, and nearing the end of July, the heat had turned the grass yellow, wilted the daisies and dandelions, and cracked the dry mud.

Familiar natural features were incorporated into the scenery: a winding river, as opposed to coastline, and grassy embankments upon which were added man-made defences. Dominating castles were traditionally built on a promontory in a bid to escape siege engines and flying arrows. Even with those commonalities, each castle was unique; a happenstance that continued to feed my appetite. No two were the same; there was no blueprint for the perfect castle.

I used my film camera, frequently stopping to adjust the settings or change a lens or filter. The tilt and shift attachment proved invaluable. Gone was the distortion of converging vertical lines that plagued my earlier photographs. I preferred playing at using the worm's eye – viewpoints from the ground; I also wished sometimes that I was a bird. Aerial shots were impossible without a helicopter.

The tree-lined and steeply inclined path led up to the gatehouse. The climb triggered another wave of drenching perspiration. I glugged on the water bottle. Inside the inner bailey, and on my left, was the manor house glued to the remains of the keep. The glazed panes and drainpipes were a sacrilege in my opinion; it was like fitting PVC windows on a four-hundred-year-old cottage. Mansions needed deer parks, duck ponds and follies, and shouldn't be enclosed in medieval walls.

There was one item on my list for Prudhoe: an oriel window in the chapel. I rounded a corner to find what I was supposed to be photographing.

'Oh.' The disappointment was a grave addition to my existing one.

I had expected tall perpendicular window frames jutting out in a prominent position. Instead, the chapel's oriel window was a boxed bay situated halfway up the exterior of the gatehouse, supported underneath by a shelf of stone that itself rested on a wall. Oriels were often used to show off stained glass, especially the family coat of arms. This one had narrow windows and no glass. According to Medici's notes, it was the earliest oriel window in the north of England.

I performed my duty diligently and without enthusiasm, snapping both exterior and interior shots, trying to magnify the small appendage by augmenting the narrow windows with my zoom lens. And that was it. Done and dusted. One minor window with little merit; it told no tales nor excited my imagination.

Tears welled under my eyelids. Suddenly, without any kind of emotional build-up or logic, I lost my sense of purpose. The whole "photographing castles" adventure was rapidly declining into an anti-climactic self-indulgence. Whoever Medici was, he wasn't interested in the romantic undertones, the stories buried beneath the surface of stone and grass. He couldn't help me conjure up the things I felt. He was fascinated with eccentric details and architectural oddities. Why the heck had somebody like David, an eminent professor, attached himself to this lame project?

Fulfilling Medici's requirements had left me jobless, alone and with nothing that might set me up as a pro. The camera equipment was a big incentive, but there was no prestige to be gained in a portfolio of somebody else's eclectic photographs. I had not given any thought to what I might do with all the rolls of film I had used.

Conscious of other visitors, I hurried across the bailey and escaped attention in the farthest point: inside the east tower. In the shadows I hid, eyes downcast, and sniffled my way to a pathetic conclusion. I crouched on the floor and repacked the camera bag, slamming things into the foam casing with an uncharacteristic lack of care. Anger had replaced despair and embarrassment; I brushed away the wetness on my cheeks.

Enough, Robyn. I was wallowing in self-pity, and it was loathsome. I was obliged to finish the project whether I wanted to or not. What I needed was a couple of days in Newcastle in a proper hotel to fix my crazy hormones. I settled on my haunches, there in the dark corner of the tower, and slowed my breaths. The temperature dropped, plummeted to icy, and the hairs on the nape of my neck bristled. I went to move, then hesitated.

Ping-pong. Ping-pong.

A ball bounced down the stairs opposite me. Metallic and loud, it echoed sharply. I walked over to pick it up. A child probably dropped it. There was a floor above me, and I might not be alone in the tower. I reached out with my hand, fingers hunting across the stone floor, and found only dirt. I grasped at nothing.

There was no ball. The coldness I felt in my bones wasn't from today, but from a different time. My mind had been travelling yet again. This damn gift wasn't under my control at all. I stumbled backwards, aware of the eerie silence, the utter lack of reasoning that could account for the deception. It had never happened like this: eyes open and mind distracted by other things. I had to be meditative and calm, self-aware and open to the past. I raced to think of an obvious trigger, something hopefully innocuous. For the first time, I was afraid I was encountering actual ghosts. Standing up straight, with the sunlight streaming through the doorway, crossing my path and illuminating the ground, I remembered then what I had read. On this occasion Mr Braithwaite's anecdotes were definitely to blame. Prudhoe was full of wild tales, and highly suited to my active imagination.

Hearing things had to be a sign of fatigue or something insidious. First the horn, now this bouncing ball. I seriously needed a proper break. I would email Medici an apology; I wouldn't be able to keep up with his tight schedule. I grabbed my things and hurried out of the tower.

Outside, I nearly collided with an easel. I dodged around it, muttering an apology, before turning to see who I'd disturbed. It was a man. An artist.

I wasn't intending to be nosey. I couldn't help it. I might have stared too much at first, mesmerised in part by his stillness, which only served to amplify my opposing state of mind. With a few metres between us now, I allowed myself that privilege of curiosity, something that was probably inconsiderate, but I couldn't resist peeping.

The long fingers of his left hand thrummed on his coarse denim jeans. His face was obscured. I imagined pursed lips or eyebrows furrowed in concentration. There wasn't a hint of grey in his hair or any thinning around the crown, but that didn't mean anything. Men's ages were hard to determine. Very tall, or so it seemed – he might be the same height as my brother but, unlike meticulous Richard, this guy was scruffy, and perspiring. I sympathised: the heat was relentless. In his right hand, he twirled a pencil, moving it independently of the drumming hand. I was slightly jealous; I wasn't ambidextrous.

On the flat top easel was a sheet of paper attached with strips of tape. What kind of artist was he? A hobby type, or a keen amateur with grand ambitions, or the professional with well-received exhibits on display in an art gallery; maybe famous in some part of the art world? Intrigued, I inched along the wall until the drawing came into view. He wasn't working on anything grand; he had outlined a plinth, carefully recreating the arrangement of supporting stones. Definitely an eye for detail, like me in some respects. I deduced the subject of the picture: the oriel window.

As I moved a fraction closer, he turned, and spotted me. To my surprise, he was young with darkly clouded eyes that matched his short umber hair. Unshaven stubble, too. When he returned to tinkering with his sketch, I nearly said something, but words failed. The interruption was registered by him in a fleeting expression of distaste, the kind that I might wear when disturbed. He returned to his painting, and the frown lines dropped from his face.

I swung the bag, for once oblivious to its weight, and retreated along the wall of the gatehouse with toe to heel steps and, just in case he was looking, I pretended to be fascinated with some distant feature, then hurried away. The encounter lasted seconds, no more than half a minute. It was sufficient; I knew when I had overstayed my welcome.

❖

The drive into Newcastle was fraught. The road atlas lacked the details of one-way streets and lane changes. I circled the centre twice before spotting the hotel's sign. I had no time to think through the day's events. I checked in, unpacked, and laid the camera equipment on a table for a dusting down. Sandy particles impregnated everything, including my skin. Only when I sank into a bath of aromatic bubbles and tipped back my head was I able to process things, starting with my night with Dyllis, then the ominous bouncing ball. The latter I decided to dismiss as a frivolous adventure. The interior of the tower was dark, and I had been stupidly emotional and hot, so that was a good enough excuse.

As for the oriel window, it seemed a messy construct, which was probably why Medici had included it. Odd that the window had caught the attention of the painter, too. Surely the Gothic mansion in the middle of the ruins was a more romantic vista for watercolours. I wished I had plucked up the courage to ask him what he saw in the oriel.

After the obligatory text message to my mother had been sent, I finally allowed myself the pleasure of closing my eyes.

FOURTEEN

THE EFFICIENT CITY HOTEL had two computers in the foyer with internet access. Smelling slightly of roses, I reconnected with the outside world to catch up on news – I wasn't a newspaper reader – and checked my emails.

I tapped my fingers impatiently on the keyboard. The webmail was slow, the volume of emails far greater than I anticipated. There were three from David, one notifying me the next week of expenses was due to arrive in my account, another that he was going on holiday soon, and would be hard to contact, which seemed somewhat inconsiderate. The third was to remind me to send the first week's memory stick to him as soon as possible. Officious in nature, his emails troubled my already worried state of mind. He wouldn't take kindly to my request for an extension; I was supposed to be competent, a semi-professional. I closed the messages; I wasn't sure how to reply without revealing my weaknesses.

My phone chirped. My text allocation was nearly depleted; I would have to top up somewhere. The reply from Yvette suggested looking up the story of Sir Guy the Seeker. I suspected a joke again; however I had asked for some ideas and Yvette had taken the time to do the research for me. I sent a brisk thank you.

The internet crawled through pages of junk, words that had no context to castles or myths. I was being asked to view plenty of dating websites: Guy and Seeker weren't useful terms. I added Dunstanburgh, and one potential link popped up. Unfortunately, it led to a dead end. On the verge of giving up, I tried one final click on a website listing poetry, and there it was, the missing connection, and as I expected it was steeped in Arthurian mimicry.

The legend of Sir Guy the Seeker had grown out of a poem written two hundred years ago. The lengthy poem wasn't provided, only a synopsis of the story. I read it through, twice. A cold wave of tingles travelled along my spine, circling my neck, and ending its journey in a flurry across my scalp. Each sentence sent out another set of shivers. I was sure the tale was new to me, yet I had witnessed in my mind each layer of it while at Dunstanburgh. What I had missed was the ending.

Sir Guy had chosen to blow a horn, bringing a horde of knights down upon him. He survived their slashing swords but woke up back in the cave under the castle by the shoreline. The wizened creature who had guided him was a wizard, according to the narrator, and he accused Sir Guy of cowardice for not drawing his sword and choosing the horn instead. Cursed forever, Sir Guy hunted for the alluring, beautiful woman he had seen, but never found her, nor could he leave Dunstanburgh. Like the lady in pink at Bamburgh, Guy was the resident ghost but this time in the form of poetry.

The story itself wasn't insipid, if anything it was a glorious epic waiting to be filmed by a Hollywood producer, but it had been forgotten and faded into obscurity. Which led me to the heart of my worries: I had always assumed that my imagination, the vivid daydreams and visions, were facsimiles of things I already knew about and carried with me to a location. Sir Guy wasn't part of that mental repository of myths and anecdotes, and thinking back, neither was the lady in pink at Bamburgh. Re-evaluating my daydreaming, which wasn't the slightest bit prosaic, it didn't feel like a gift of any sorts. The knot in my stomach tightened.

I logged out, closed the browser and switched on my phone. What could I say to Yvette? What would she do anyway? She would pragmatically remind me to focus on the photographs. But I wasn't in Northumberland purely to work on a commission. If there were reasons for my strange affliction, the answers weren't going to be at the end of a lens. Medici, my patron, had put his faith in me, and in return I was committed to the contract.

The next day, after sleeping fitfully, dreaming of bouncing balls and horns in equal measure, I posted the first memory stick. The small thing – something of a miracle in my understanding of technology – was packed in a jiffy bag, which I addressed to David Carmichael at Charnwood University. I paid extra for recorded delivery, as he'd requested. With the stick I had added a sheet of paper with numbered lines and details of each photograph. That had taken me quite a chunk of the morning to do, as I had to review each and every one, and check them against Medici's list.

The rest of the day was mine.

I relied on the wide-angle lens and my faithful older camera, nothing else, and walked the streets and quayside, snapping the Millennium Bridge and other heritage sites. The bustle of people and the fog of cars added to the heat. A sheen of pollution loomed above the city; the dusty sky was neither blue nor grey. I drank coffee, ate a veggie burger somewhere, elbow to elbow with shoppers, and bought a few necessities.

Back in the hotel, I regretted not asking Dyllis for use of her washing machine. The grime had filtered through the fabric of my clothes onto my skin. I wasn't accustomed to cities; at home, I rarely visited the nearest city, and relied on out of town shopping centres. I managed to resurrect a few items of clothing by washing them in the bath with shower gel; Mum would be both proud and embarrassed by my initiative.

One of the computers in the lobby was free. I logged back onto the webmail, and before I could type a message to David, informing him of the incoming jiffy bag, I spotted the unopened email in the inbox.

David informs me I should expect your first batch of photographs soon. Very excited. I know they will be perfect.

I gulped. His optimism buoyed me. I needed it. The email had been sent ten minutes ago. I risked a reply.

Thank you, I hope you find them useful.

I paused, tempted to ask the question that kept my palms clammy – why do you want them? But David had been specific from the outset; it was none of my business.

I thought of Guy and the phantom dream at Dunstanburgh. Would Medici have a theory? I was sure he had used the term "seeking" when he had first contacted me.

Do you mind me asking? Do you think myths and legends have any basis in history? Yours, Robyn the photographer.

Given the nature of our arrangement, I wasn't anticipating a speedy answer. Touching the mouse, I hovered over the close window icon, and was just on the verge of clicking, when a reply bounced back.

Dear Robyn, immortal castles are witnesses, and without them, memories of the past are lost. Who would care to keep those myths alive if it wasn't for them? Objects and places are storytellers as much as poems and books, the stuff of legends. Do you not think so?
Your kindly Medici

He described a castle as if it was a living thing.

Yes, I do think so. I saw Guy the Seeker at Dunstanburgh.

I hesitated, then clicked send before I changed my mind. But something told me that he would understand. What led me to think that was as inexplicable as my visions of myths. Through all my reticence about Medici's motives, I had no doubt that something of a connection had formed between us that went beyond the castles we both admired. I waited, feeling foolish at revealing such a silly thing as a reference to an obscure poem. Why the heck had I used the word "saw" when I had read about it? What would he think of me now?

The reply took longer this time and arrived without a subject header. No preamble, only four lines.

I pushed the chair back, creating space between me and the monitor and keyboard. The shock hit my stomach, churning up the veggie burger. I hadn't expected him to know the poem. Why had he picked that particular verse? I remained awkwardly frozen by his knowledge of something I assumed was so obscure.

The inbox synched again. Another message with no subject heading.

> I haven't scared you? I have taken you by surprise, I think. I ask for photographs, but I suspect you have other means to see things without a lens. Would it not be exciting if we all could have this ability or something like it? We could reach out and be together, but unfortunately we are not all the same. Don't let it dissuade you from persevering. There is still time, I hope. Prudhoe would be disappointing. Such a mean oriel window is hardly stimulating. Maybe the next ones will offer you more inspiration. Sorry, Robyn. I cannot always answer your questions. I will be absent soon. Keep using a camera, if it helps you. If I could, I would too. You'll find out what David doesn't know about me soon, from somebody you've met but know little about.

Know what and from whom? He was implying that he knew about my visions, too. His enigmatic writing style was really starting to piss me off, even freak me out a bit. I hammered the keys, demanding an explanation for his weird choice of words. In the midst of it, David sent a text.

> Just to let you know. Medici will be offline for a while. Please refrain from making contact until I speak to you.

My head spun. I was online, emailing him. Had I upset him? Was David with him, reading my emails? Was that how they worked together? Nothing made sense. Medici, who always seemed one step ahead of me, was now telling me he couldn't answer my questions right before David texted the same thing. Whatever was communicated behind the scenes, the message was clear, I was not to engage with Medici.

The secrecy riled me, driving out unwanted anxiety, and I replaced it with a fresh burst of outraged confidence. I should pull the plug on the project and reclaim my old job while I had the chance. But lying upstairs was a very expense camera and it wasn't an unconditional gift. I had fallen in love with its versatility and the opportunities it offered me. I wasn't prepared to part company with it yet. I had places I wanted to go, things to see.

I chewed my lower lip and made a decision. Tomorrow, I would visit Durham, photograph the cathedral because I wanted to, then on Monday, I would begin week two of my peculiar assignment and stick to the list and complete my obligations.

As for my so-called gift, this increasingly childish ability to fantasise, it was best I kept my thoughts to myself from now on; not even the inquisitive Medici was entitled to know about it. As for my family, they could never appreciate any of this strangeness, except one person, and she was gone forever. If I was truly able to go back in time, I would have asked Granny Izzy what she thought of it all.

FIFTEEN

BOWES CASTLE WAS A HUGE STONE BOX with no lid.

The artist walked around the keep three times, his eyes shaded from the bleaching sun by a raised hand. Sunglasses were for gangsters and posh people in flashy convertibles. But today he regretted not owning a pair.

In places the walls had cracked apart, revealing a honeycomb of stone and mortar. A painting needed a balance of texture and shade, which meant plenty of light to cast the right pattern of shadows. He hoped to create a composition that delivered grand dimensions and not flat, featureless stonework. The latrines, of all things, were satisfactorily ambiguous, and easily mistaken for windows, of which Bowes Castles had few. The wall beneath the dark holes had collapsed, revealing the chutes. The recipient of the painting probably wouldn't know the purpose of the holes, they could imagine what they wished. If they did know, well, perhaps they had a sense of humour. God, he hoped they did. He'd been given no instructions as to what to paint, other than the pictures must contain some feature of the castle. At Prudhoe, he'd decided on the little window because it was technically challenging to paint, and back at Bamburgh, he'd considered painting in the style of Turner – washes of intense colours – but after a brief rethink, he'd laughed it off; it wasn't his style. Romantic visions weren't him at all, and these paintings were becoming weirdly influenced (afflicted?) by his personality, with their clear lines, well-defined natural colours, and the important feather-light brushstrokes that captured the invisible spaces, the air he enjoyed breathing in.

He would paint the latrines because he had that freedom to do so. Another artist might pick defensive barbicans or curtain walls, the typical structures of a castle, but he was adamant not to end up with a portfolio of unremarkable, beautifully executed, yet similar features.

He settled the easel into the ochre grass that covered the rock-hard ground. It took time to prepare everything he needed – the paint, brushes, the pre-stretched paper. The sun was awkwardly high; he had arrived later than planned. He hadn't slept well. The combination of heat and flies had been unbearable.

As he swept his pencil over the paper, marking the key points, he noticed her, the same girl who had nearly crashed into his easel – the one with melon hair, slightly skinny arms and a thumb-sized nose. She carried her camera bag with stooped shoulders and clutched a water bottle, which was understandable - the air was turgid and closing in. Later it would be too humid to paint; he needed to work fast.

Whenever he glanced up, she was there, taking long shots of vertices, the highest apex where two walls met. The sun was behind her. She fiddled with the tilt of the camera; angles were problematic with photography, less so with painting. A painter, one accomplished with the tricks of his trade, could adjust distortions and create parallel vertical lines just as the eye saw them. She wasn't ignoring him either. Now and again, when he allowed his attention to wander away from the canvas, he caught her staring at him. It was natural, they were both creative types, and since she had also been at Prudhoe, she had to be working on something specific, like him. An odd coincidence, but his life was full of them, mostly the good kind, except for that one ruinous time that he would never forget.

Immediately, he felt the familiar stabbing pains of a headache and the weight of the invisible burden pressed from above onto his back, driving him closer to the ground, as if he was falling. However, the flashback was brief, and he shot it to pieces before it took hold. He'd become adept at managing them. Years of practice and an empty heart helped.

Something else was wrong, though, and the agitated taps of his brush against the easel sped up. He wasn't prone to theorising, nor was he likely to judge anyone without talking to them, but from the expression on her face, the girl with the camera was disturbed by his presence, and in turn, he was perplexed. The sharp gaze of mistrust that she dispatched in his direction intensified when it became apparent he was in the wrong place. She aimed her lens at the latrines, and he stood in the middle of her view. With an angry thrust of her chin in his direction, she collected her bag and marched away out of sight.

Having completed a rough sketch, he munched on a cold bacon sandwich. The flies harried him, and he swatted them away with his paintbrush. He glanced up and frowned. The weather was changing quickly. A bank of translucent clouds was forming, and the haze was like a pale lavender field suspended in the sky. The sun was barely visible. He might need an umbrella. But he didn't own one of those either.

SIXTEEN

Bowes

BRAITHWAITE HADN'T BOTHERED with an entry for Bowes Castle. I wasn't surprised. It was a simple keep with nothing to explore, no winding staircases or towers, nor dungeons beneath. The only issue had been the presence of the painter. He had stood right in front of the turret containing the latrines, the very thing Medici had wanted photographing. Why Medici had picked the banal feature was a mystery. Another one of his quirky requests, but if that was all he required, then at least Bowes should have been quick. Except it wasn't. I had to wait for the guy waving his paintbrush around his head to budge from the crucial viewpoint.

Giving up, I left the site, bought a sandwich, and sweltered in the car.

I moaned to Yvette via text.

I'm melting!

The reply arrived ten minutes later.

We all are. It's due to thunder tonight.

Thank God. I emptied a water bottle down my parched throat and started another. The hour hand moved on my watch. He had to have finished by now.

Ring me, tonight. Where are you staying?

B&B in Darlington. Couple who bicker constantly. Quite entertaining.

The issues were trivial and piled up in rapid succession, as if not arguing was a scary state of affairs. The tension in the house drifted up and down the stairs in tune with their quiet undulating voices. At night, they had fallen silent, although I was convinced I'd heard a rhythmic creaking.

After Meg, I had, for the purpose of staying on top of my emotions, procured a thicker skin. The people I encountered on my journey were snapshots, like photographs. If I had chosen to keep a journal, I could have filled the pages with insubstantial character sketches and fleeting descriptions of life. I certainly wouldn't forget them, and they had the potential to colour the life I might choose to live.

The relatively short time on the road had widened my perspective. The big city life wasn't for me; the realisation wasn't a surprise. I hadn't felt a spark of anything in Newcastle. As for Durham Cathedral, while the Norman architecture was grandiose, the churn of people through the great doorway had given me no opportunity to absorb and reflect. Ruined abbeys were likely to be better suited to my "gift".

While I waited, I returned to Medici's last message. It's odd wording haunted me still. What had he meant by my need for inspiration and persevering? Was he hinting, possibly implying, that I should seek out my visions? There was that word again – seek. Bowes was a shell, and my mind was empty too. I wasn't fascinated in the slightest by the stonework. The heat further lowered my expectations. I wiped my brow with a damp handkerchief and rummaged in my rucksack. What else could be coming my way? Next up was Barnard Castle, which according to Braithwaite…

High above the River Tees, cut into the rocky cliffs, Barnard Castle is named after its builder Bernard de Balliol. The castle passed into the hands of the Duke of Gloucester, later Richard III, during the War of Roses. His plans to enlarge and expand the castle came to nothing when he was killed in the Battle of Bosworth. The boar, Richard's armorial emblem, is carved into the oriel window…

Another bloody oriel window!

I put aside the guidebook. Preparation for tomorrow's trip wasn't stimulating either. A glance at my watch resulted in a sigh of frustration. I had one hour before Bowes closed its gates to visitors. I slammed the car door shut and re-entered the castle's grounds.

Fortunately, the spot under the wall was empty and I planted the tripod on the trampled grass where the painter had stood and used exactly the same vantage; the upward angle was perfect for a vanishing point somewhere in the hazy sky.

Perspiration glued my t-shirt to my back. On the horizon, the strangely ominous clouds, purple and heavy-looking, barrelled into one another, blocking out the sun. Not a leaf moved, and the birds stopped singing. Alone at last, my mind was open and absorbent like a dry sponge. I didn't know why, given my doubts and lack of faith, but I needed it to happen. I needed an entertaining vision, triggered by some kind of spell that bound me to the past. It would surely be a respite from the frustrations of the present.

I swayed, feeling it enter me like an ethereal mist. Where would I end up? I had no idea. I allowed myself to float away, surrender to the paths of history. No horn this time. What I heard was like a deep rumbling. The earth below my feet vibrated up into my knees. I touched the arid ground with my palm and felt the movement. Flat on my back, the shaking spread along my spine. Above my head, the sky went dark, illuminated only by explosions of light. The booms smashed against the castle wall, stones flew in all directions, but none of the shrapnel struck me. I wasn't really there. I never was.

The air tasted of blood. My nostrils singed and burned with the smell of gunpowder, sulphur and smoke. All around me were the cries of men in panic and fear, although I saw no figures. I had conjured up battle scenes before and heard the whistle of arrows in flight, but none of those daydreams captured the raw terror, the pandemonium of a tower under siege. I was among the hectoring assailants and not within the walls defending. Nowhere was safe from missiles flying through the air and there was no escape from the stench of boiling oil and tar pits. The flashes of light were fleeting and blinding, and if there was anything to "see", it was the silhouette of the castle's crenelations and the crossbow bolts on route to their targets.

The spell ended abruptly, possibly it had lasted mere seconds. The rough vibrations ceased, and I felt instead the shards of prickly grass through the fabric of my t-shirt. Cannon fire faded into nothingness, only to be replaced by the rumble of thunder.

I had been wrong about boring Bowes. Something had happened here and left its presence, an echo of a battle, and my imagination had seen it, bringing the carnage back to life. War wasn't the past I craved to see. Jousts and feasts, the laughter of folk making music or dancing, the kiss of courting couples or the tales of the travelling Chaucers; these were my flights of fancy, the indulgence of my daydreams, not this horror that left me rigid on the ground.

Why were my visions increasingly gruesome and filled with foreboding? I'd become afflicted by something, or maybe somebody. Was it possible other people's emotions were influencing my moods? Rising to my feet, I stared at the flattened grass, the tiny specks of dry paint on the wilted blades. I knew exactly who had stood on this spot an hour earlier. There was no denying it: this new conduit was open and active, no matter how much I tried to pretend I wasn't receptive to it and whether a gift or plain madness, I seemed to have less and less control over my daydreaming.

The pit of my stomach ached not with hunger but the familiar sensation of nausea that came with worry. Insanity, the medical version of madness, had I inherited it? Would I end up institutionalised, like my grandmother? I raked my trembling hands through my damp hair, feeling the heat of my scalp, and yet I had a strange urge to shiver, as if a fever had taken hold of me.

Now I was imagining the worst kinds of things.

Enough, Robyn.

The simplest solution was the best: castles had much more to do with war and death than my charming folk tales of medieval life.

I packed up the camera equipment and left to spend another night with the warring couple in Darlington.

SEVENTEEN

Barnard

THE THIRD TIME I SAW HIM was in the shelter of a tower. The thunderstorm had lasted into the middle of the night, and intermittent downpours had spilled over into the next day, adding an extra layer of saturation to the already sticky humidity. There were hardly any visitors venturing out in the rain.

I located the oriel window in the Great Chamber of Barnard Castle and cushioned my disappointment by telling myself that this was the nature of the business – what I wanted to photograph wasn't important. If Medici valued a barely discernible stone carving of a boar then that was his choice. I zoomed in, opened the shutter, and released. One image of a crippled boar, supposedly once white and now eroded, captured for my patron.

According to Braithwaite's guidebook, there was evidence of Richard III's boar emblem in many places in the region. It was stamped on seals, etched onto glass and carved into stone: a reminder that he had once been powerful and popular in the north of England. I supposed the purpose was no different to the garish logos of big brands. Money was power, whether it came from land or commerce, and it granted those who had it the licence to do as they pleased. I wondered if Medici was that wealthy he could afford the same honours. In the end, it didn't work out for King Richard, and his grand plans for upgrading Barnard failed. He was killed at the Battle of Bosworth.

The boar wasn't the only item on the list. There was the Round Tower, a cylindrical pepper pot cut-off midway, as if sliced horizontally by an executioner's axe. I tried to picture what it might have looked like with a roof. Circling it a few times, I chose spots to take a range of photographs, some with my own camera.

The downpour arrived without warning. I grabbed the bag and equipment, and raced inside the tower. High above, the haloed sky was laden with charcoal clouds. The shelter was minimal and reeked of distant seaweed and mildew. The temperature drop was palpable, and the dampness potent, and the shade darkened the verdant moss and lichen that inhabited the stonework. Rivulets of rainwater ran along grooves of the weather-worn mortar and collected into puddles. The strap of my camera bag dug into my shoulder, and I leaned against the driest wall to ease the burden.

Opposite, there was a high niche, an embrasure as thick as the walls, and below it, another one with the window barred. At first, in the darkness, I was oblivious to his presence. Then my eyes adjusted, and his form took shape.

He had taken refuge in the window nook and was peering through the criss-cross of metal grating. There was no easel, only a rucksack resting nearby. His back was towards me, but I recognised the short-cropped hair and the loose-hipped jeans. Scrunched into a ball, he was balanced on his haunches and hugging his legs in a self-embrace, while his fuzzy chin rested on a flat-topped kneecap. He was a silhouette of human greyness bundled into a monkey-shaped package. He remained there, absorbed and isolated, coiled as if ready to spring into action, rocking back and forth on his heels, and gazing out.

Why was he here? What had brought him to the same places at the same time, again and again, timetabled like me to perform a duty. I recalled a man at Bamburgh mentioning an artist painting there before I had arrived, and how he had chosen the windmill as his subject. The coincidence was beyond supernatural; it had to be engineered. There was no explanation other than the obvious. I had been fooled into thinking Medici was old and foreign. Yet, here he was, fit and young, moving from place to place, painting, spying on me, then lying to me in emails. Medici was doing what I was supposed to do on his behalf – capturing his castles.

Ridiculous. David said Medici lived abroad. But the exact wording escaped my mind. Abroad back then, but not now maybe?

Was this why he was incommunicado – he was actually on the road like me?

The temptation to open my mouth and provoke him was overwhelming. Something stopped me; a little voice nagging inside my head. I couldn't bring myself to disturb him. What if this man had nothing to do with Medici? He could be a kindred spirit, a secret admirer of the ruined structures, or a romantic artist inspired by landscapes. Or maybe he was like Yvette, an art-loving historian or a student, mature in years, and completing an assignment.

The rain shifted from drenching to a trickle. The cessation brought to an end the need for shelter. Still in a defensive frame of mind, I walked out of the tower determined to ignore the man, but, glancing over my shoulder, I saw him turn his head in my direction and stiffen again. It seemed he had recognised me.

Outside, the humid air was a wall in itself, and I waded through it, annoyed with my cowardice. I had every right to ask him why he was at Barnard. He might be a castle enthusiast, or he could be following me for nefarious reasons. I had to know which for my parents' sake, and my own; I had promised them I would act sensibly. I also felt indignant: why hadn't he chased after me to ask the same questions?

EIGHTEEN

'**NO EASEL TODAY?**' the young woman asked.

Her shrill voice bounced around in the tower. Above their heads, doves took off, spraying a fan of water onto their heads.

She had remembered him and returned, which wasn't a surprise given their previous encounters. On this occasion, she wasn't going to ignore him, which he welcomed as progress and necessary.

She fidgeted with a silver hoop bracelet. Her honey-dew hair, cropped short, was shaped under her chin, the sleeves of her t-shirt puckered around her shoulders. The shorts were long to the knees and didn't suit her; the linen fabric hung limp and colourless against her bronzed legs. The scuffed shoes meant she didn't mind the rough terrain. She was though, woefully slight in frame, and young. And there was plenty for an artist to admire, too: the high cheekbones of her oval face were classical; her eyes were set wide. Once again, he was examining a new face in the same manner he might an oil painting hung in a gallery. Her thin lips broke into a frown, which still managed to be both perversely charming and awkward. She was probably better at smiling. Underneath the put-upon stiffness, she was shivering slightly – a bundle of nerves, or cold?

He stretched his legs out, and picked up the rucksack. The look she gave him was hostile – once upon a time, he might have thought such an expression worth painting. Why the anger? She had followed him here and there, arriving when he was ready to depart, leaving while he was in the middle of a brush stroke, and at Bowes Castle, to his bemusement, she had dispatched dagger-like stares while humping the camera equipment and tripod in circuits around the grounds. The constant movement was far removed from his preferred static style of artistry. How could she concentrate?

The way she spoke, the slight snarky tone, was a clue to her apprehension. He could understand it; he felt the same unnerving flutter in his stomach too.

'No,' he said, answering her curt question on the absence of the easel.

She blocked the exit. He stepped sideways, hinting, but she refused to budge.

'Then why are you here?'

'I'm waiting for the rain to stop. Then I'll get my easel and paints.'

'So you are painting today.'

A rhetorical statement. She already knew the answer and he left it hanging while the thin frame of her shoulders slumped. She backed into the shadows, hiding her face. A moment ago, he had thought she was angry. Now he wasn't so sure.

He gestured to the sky above. 'Or tomorrow, if it doesn't clear up. And you, are you taking photos?' He was barricaded in place by two filthy puddles and a strange woman who maintained the advantage. He stood his ground while the interrogation continued.

She hitched the bag strap up. There was a substantial rucksack on her back, too. She had to be a professional photographer working for somebody. Did she think they were in competition? He nearly laughed. It wasn't possible. They weren't moving in the same sphere. His project might have weird stipulations, but he didn't consider them unique to him or sinister – commissions sometimes came with foibles and peculiar requirements.

Her fierce expression magnified. 'You know I am. You've been at Prudhoe, Bowes, and now here.'

'They're close to each other, relatively, so…' He thought back further. 'Warkworth. You were in the car park. A red Corsa.'

Her whole demeanour gravitated downwards, as if on the brink of a collapse. He reached to catch her elbow, and missed.

She'd leapt back, wide-eyed, and landed in a puddle. 'You went to Bamburgh, too.'

How had she known he was there at Easter? What had seemed like remarkable coincidences, now rebounded into something sinister. His heartbeats weren't normal. Neither was the tremble of his hands.

'Who are you?' she asked quietly. Her cheeks were colourless porcelain.

He wanted to know the same thing. He cleared his throat, and feeling generous, he stretched out his hand. 'I'm Joseph. I'm a freelance artist.' Naturally, he avoided using his family name, and if pushed, he would use a different one as a precaution.

'What kind of artist?' She kept her arms bolted to her sides.

He might have to explain a few awkward things, which he suspected she wouldn't believe.

The sunbeam hit the wall above her head and illuminated the fine features of her face. A pretty face.

'Tell you what. Let's meet up later for a drink because I really need to take advantage of the sunshine.' He lowered his hand, accepting it was premature. She was cautious for a reason, and he wanted to know why. 'I'll tell you what I'm up to, and you can explain why you're stalking me.'

Her long-lashed eyes widened into moons. The indignation was back. 'Okay, you're on.'

PART THREE

*'How beautiful is youth, that is always slipping
away!*
*Whoever wants to be happy, let him be so: of
tomorrow there's no knowing.'*
Lorenzo de' Medici

NINETEEN

WHEN I WAS A YOUNG BOY becoming an artist never crossed my mind. Those who witnessed my early accomplishments assumed it was my destiny, while I considered myself a fledging who would never take off. The art teacher at school encouraged me to seriously consider becoming one. Bullied me, perhaps, to be truthful. I wasn't a cooperative student, and I made a point of letting her down without remorse.

However, her persistence worked in the end, and I asked Dad to give up some of his precious garage space. Begrudgingly, he did, and I turned the concrete cavern into a poorly-lit studio that was barely fit for purpose. Money was always an issue; supplies were expensive. I worked odd jobs for the neighbours and during the summer holidays I helped out in the local bicycle shop. Cycling was my other hobby.

Fortunately, I instinctively shied away from exotic materials, and chose watercolours, pencils, the odd piece of chalk lying around, and occasionally, I fashioned a figurine in clay. There were no whacky junk sculptures made out of car parts and greasy rags, the things Dad left lying around in the garage. Against all expectations, I followed the path of fine art, and showed no interest in breaking out into other styles. Nor did I hanker to go to art college. I blamed my youth, a lacklustre father, and the complex behaviour of my brothers. Instead I opted to learn to teach. My reasoning I thought was sensible: I would have a steady income while I indulged in necessary isolation during the long holidays.

I never relished teaching, even when the private school provided me with plenty of art supplies to keep me from quitting. It wasn't that I disliked children; I could tolerate them in art classes, and there were the good ones who paid attention and tried hard. Unfortunately, for a significant majority art was the relax and chat class, the muck around and waste time lesson. Much of my precious time was spent tidying the classroom up after each lesson. The mess generated by teenagers in one hour was spectacular and detestable.

The suggestion, by one wiser friend, someone with connections to the local council, was adult education. I cut back the school hours, and branched out into evening classes for retired folks with time on their hands for frivolous hobbies. It suited me perfectly. Between classes and during the holidays, I was able to pursue what I should have stuck to in the first place. In a cluttered studio, finally free from that childhood dung heap called a council house, I took up brush, pencil or palette knife, withdrew into my personal headspace, and cocooned myself there for hours, often without food.

It was a beginning, and it felt like it should go somewhere better. Friends from teaching college where I had trained threw ideas my way once again, and one went as far as setting up a website to showcase stuff I'd painted. I paid scant attention to its maintenance. Clients sent me photographs of loved ones and I turned them into an artistic representation in watercolours or pastels, sometimes a pencil drawing. It supplemented my modest income. However, the idea of drawing countless faces of people and pets wasn't appealing. Illustrating children's books was another suggestion. I backed away from that idea; I struggled to relate to the mind of a child, so how could I possibly illustrate their world if I lacked empathy?

The illustrators I met suggested other specialities. One painted meticulous representations of botanical plants for a horticultural publisher. Beautiful, I agreed without envy, knowing that she fancied me and wanted that level of exactitude in her love life too. I told her, honestly, it wasn't my thing, turning a living thing into object d'art. We parted company amicably, or so I thought. She presented me a framed picture of a beetroot, garishly red, bleeding almost, with a fork stabbed into its side.

Okay, said another one of my colleagues, what about architecture? Initially I had rolled my eyes in a sweeping dismissal until I thought through what I liked doing best. When I saw open spaces, I wanted to capture them. The vast terrains, brash colours, subtle textures. From then on for the summer weeks, I travelled around Europe, carting with me a slim-downed collection of brushes and paints, and tried my hand at different scenes. The Alps generated a reasonable period of feverish activity, though I preferred the warmer climate of the Pyrenees. Then I ventured into forests, but trees brought me back to living things, and there wasn't enough space between the branches to feel that emptiness. Finally, three summers ago, I reached Greece and, in amongst the rugged rocks and arid heat, I discovered the relics of an empire, the toppled columns, epic amphitheatres and cavernous tombs of kings. The oven-baked air was crisp and tangy, filled with the rich aroma of olives, and I breathed it in until I was sated. Nothing beat that feeling that comes with a vast emptiness. Clogged streets and tower blocks would never be my home again. I lived for that distant summer in the perfumed meadows with the cypress trees, eating apricots and feeding my obsession to draw.

The feeling stayed with me on the leisurely journey home, allowing me to fill my notepad with endless sketches. What my father considered odd was the lack of photographs. I tapped my forehead. 'It's all up here.' I grinned, wryly. Nobody quite knew how my brain operated. All I needed was a sketch and an outline of colourful brush strokes to aid my memory.

Those paintings of Ancient Greece produced the first genuine sales via galleries I had approached. I went back to Greece, taking my time in Italy along the way. The connection of space and substance created a specialism of my own. I steered away from urban vistas and concentrated on landscapes with features, human endeavours overlaying natural ones. Stonehenge was the next project, then on to Glastonbury Tor, followed by Hadrian's Wall. Experimenting with various media, I became versatile with works ranging from a quick charcoal sketch to elaborate oil paintings. I still depended on teaching for an income, but now and again I pocketed extra cash with a sale or the occasional commission. For those odd jobs I relied on an agent with fingers in many pies, and unusual ones, too. The only stipulation I gave her was that I used an alias. The habit had evolved to the point where I had abandoned my real name, except when I had to use it for legal reasons.

Still, the castles commission took me by surprise, especially the scale of the project and the money on offer for completing the collection – mega bucks, as Dad would say. All I was told by Camilla was that it wasn't for a book. It was a gift: a collection of paintings for somebody who admired castles. I wasn't fussed because it meant I could escape the city, disconnect myself from all the aggravation that followed me around like a ball and chain. No phone, television or computer. Just brushes, easel, and a tent.

TWENTY

WHILE JOSEPH PAINTED, I had a few hours to kill. I wandered through the small town of Barnard Castle, visited a museum, browsed shop windows, and as the hour of our appointment approached, I returned to the river to snap a few shots of the castle from the distance. Situated on the banks of the River Tees, the castle was prominent and, unlike Dunstanburgh, was part of the community. I took advantage of a bench and waited.

A light breeze had shooed away the last of the rain clouds. The weather forecast was for a heat wave over the coming days. In the blue skies of my thoughts, I pondered the stranger, the man whom I had trailed from Bamburgh to Barnard. But who exactly was following whom? Could this artist really be working on a similar mission to mine? Was David in on it too, and Medici? My patron clearly loved theatrical secrecy.

I fiddled with the barrel of a zoom lens. There were images to sort through and another list to compile. I couldn't figure out why my motivation was close to rock bottom once again, although this time it wasn't anything to do with my lack of professionalism. Something else was wrong. I inhaled deeply. The air was sweet with the scent of green foliage, freshly awoken by rain, and I had no sense of anything else on the wind. I was unaffected by my surroundings, as to be expected; this was entirely the wrong place to free my mind.

The pub had a beer garden, and I chose a table away from the pollen-laden rose bushes and a swarm of tiny flies. I expected him to be late. Perhaps if he had sense, he wouldn't come at all. My questions were likely to make him uncomfortable as I was justifiably inclined to be inquisitorial. However, he arrived promptly at six o'clock, carrying a pint of beer in one steady hand and a packet of crisps in the other. There was none of the trappings of easel or paint box.

'Hello,' he said, and pulled up a metal garden chair to the table.

With the benefit of evening sunshine, I assessed Joseph's face. He obviously wasn't vain about his appearance: hollowed eyes, dusty black stubble and a sheaf of uncombed hair. The collarless plain shirt was daubed with paint flecks, and his hands were speckled too. I liked the grubbiness on him because it wasn't pretentious and spoke of his commitment to his art above anything else. Having wiped the beer froth off his lips, he scratched his chin and gave a small shrug, as if to hand the reins of the conversation over to me.

I launched myself forward onto the front legs of the chair. 'Do you know David Carmichael?'

His perplexed expression was best described as bemused and wary in equal measure. And genuine. 'I had hoped we could have a chat, not an interrogation.'

I adjusted my stance and the back legs of the chair sank into the grass. 'Sorry. I didn't mean to be rude. I'm just very confused by what's being going on recently. I'm photographing castles for a client and David is my contact.'

'Ah.' He took a mouthful of beer and swallowed. 'He's not mine. I have an agent who throws work at me from time to time. Camilla Brooke.'

I stared at a smudge of white paint on his sleeve. 'An agent?'

'I'm also a part-time teacher. I work in a private school in London. Camilla usually handles book illustrations, which I don't do, but now and again, something advantageous crops up. I've been using her for a couple of years. She came highly recommended.' He tore open the crisp packet and held it out.

I shook my head. 'By whom?'

'A friend. Friends like to keep me occupied.'

'You're working on a commission?'

'Yeah. Don't know much about it. Don't really care to be honest. It's a job that gets me out of London—'

'London.' That explained his accent.

'And you? You're not from these parts.'

I cleared my throat. 'The Midlands. I love castles. I want to see as many as possible, but this project is specific to those in the north of England. I've a list of castles to photograph.' I paused while he ate the crisps in a constant stream of munching. There was no point selling him the postcard excuse. 'I don't know why I'm photographing them.' If the heat of sunshine hadn't been on my face, I would have been sure that it was the blush that was warned my cheeks.

He stilled, his hand halfway toward the packet. 'You don't know? Interesting.' He shrugged off the lack of information. 'Camilla has commissioned me to do a portfolio of paintings for a gift. I don't know whose. I've free reign to paint what I like, as long as I stick to—'

'A list of castles?' The knot below my ribs tightened. I was glad I hadn't eaten.

'Yes.' His brow furrowed. 'You too?'

Finally, I caught his attention properly. Now, he might understand why I was questioning him. 'Yes. All in Northumberland and Yorkshire. Starting with Bamburgh—'

'I went there at Easter.'

Joseph's timings didn't fit entirely with mine. He had started way ahead of me, probably before I had even signed a contract. Our schedules were supposed to match perfectly if my assumption was correct.

He continued. 'During the spring break: Alnwick and Dunstanburgh. Weather wasn't great, so I stopped there. May was a washout.'

'You were contacted before Easter?' I thought back to the exhibition at the Curzon. There was no hint from David that anyone else was involved in the project.

'I got the commission earlier in the year, but they're supposed to be summer paintings.' He shrugged. 'Foliage, pretty flowers. I prefer realism, not impressionistic styles.'

I felt bad for calling him a stalker. It was quite the contrary. 'I suppose if you started before me, you're not following me.'

'Well, I was supposed to do it all in the summer break, then I looked at the schedule I'd been given, the time it would take to paint all these castles, and realised I couldn't deliver all the paintings by the end of August.'

'Why not?' From what I knew of watercolour paintings, they were quick to do.

'I like to do a number of drafts and a colour palette for reference. I usually add the finishing touches later. I didn't want to rush. I couldn't exactly come up at weekends – too far – so I did three castles at Easter.' He smiled, mischievously. 'If I'd know how great the weather was going to be, I needn't have worried. I touched them up with warm summer colours. A little bit of fakery gets past the untrained eye.'

'Like a filter on a camera.'

'Yeah. But May was a wash out. I can't paint in the rain.' The grin evaporated.

'What?'

'Camilla wasn't happy with my early delivery. She was annoyed actually. She insisted I had to do them in situ and not rework them later, but that's not what I wanted to do. She backed off a bit after I told her the issues. Things got a bit awkward between us. I don't think she's done a project like this before. Me neither. Anyway, I picked up when term broke up.'

'At Warkworth?'

He lowered his beer glass. 'Yes. Where I saw you in the car park. Who are you working for again?'

'I don't know. He's not telling me his name. He's like,' I cringed, 'my patron.'

'Ah, patronage. Handy to have, even these days. Although sponsorship is a better tool. More money.'

'Yes, so I'm told. But we're way past the Renaissance.'

He leaned on his elbows. For second, his eyes sparkled. 'You know why they became patrons? They made their money through trade, not titles or land, so they had to show off their status by getting the best to work for them, the renowned painters, sculptors, musicians.'

I shrugged. 'Except I'm not an artist.'

He admonished me with quite a stare that belonged to a stern teacher. It sent a wave of unfathomable tingles down my spine.

'Don't cheapen photography. It's modern media. Creating pictures with a camera is art. It might not be like Michelangelo and the Sistine Chapel, but it's still great having somebody supporting you. Michelangelo's patron wasn't royalty. It was the Medici family… What?'

My blush had caught his eye. 'My friend Yvette told me all about patronage. When he emails me, which isn't very often, he uses the name Medici. It's a bit of a joke thing,' I added lamely. It could also be covertness, malicious, or simply about anonymity.

Joseph laughed. 'How appropriate. It might turn out to be very advantageous for you. Doors open, fame beckons.'

'I'm not interested in being famous. I could enter more competitions, but I don't want to.'

'I guess it will become easier to spot artistic talent now that we have the internet and can do things virtually.'

Yvette had said something similar. 'My friend reckons such things will soon be all the rage and flash-in-the-pan celebrities will become cheap commodities promoted by high profile people. She's brilliant at predicting trends, like fashion. She's an art historian. It makes perfect sense, doesn't it? History always repeats itself at some point.'

Any evidence of amusement was replaced by that serious look again, but this one was less critical and more appreciative. 'I'd like to meet your friend. And this Medici.' He paused, then spoke with no hint of humour. 'He's got a list, an agenda, like Camilla.'

I rummaged through the contents of my handbag and pulled out a printout. 'He's very specific with details of what I photograph.'

He leaned over the table to look and squinted at the small lettering. 'Well, mine isn't.'

I pointed at the first item. 'You painted the windmill.'

He drew back, his eyes narrowing into pinpoints. 'How do you know?'

'Somebody saw you, a member of staff, and he told me. I was standing by the windmill photographing the sea, for my personal collection. Medici requests peculiar architectural features.'

'Like latrine chutes? I just thought they were fun to paint. Whoever gets these paintings can work it out for themselves.' He grinned a cheeky smile that broke the stubble into waves of light and umber.

I smiled, partly because it was contagious, but I remained slightly perturbed by the mystery painter. The same fifteen castles were too significant to dismiss. 'So you have a list, but nothing specific to paint.'

'I only need to stick to the same canvas size, and watercolours.' He drank a good measure of beer.

'Which, I have to say, are really suitable for castles. Is that your speciality? Have you exhibited your artwork?' I rattled through questions, thinking about David's approach to finding me.

'I'm diverse. But watercolour landscapes are okay with me. I'm not a portrait artist. I have exhibited, but not in a long time. A few works go out to galleries. Most of my income is teaching. This is quite an undertaking for me. I enjoy travelling and needed the break. What about you? Are you new to it?'

Something about my questions had alerted him to my inexperience. 'I'm an amateur. This is my first commission. My first big project. I work… worked as a hotel receptionist in Coalville.' I lowered my eyes.

Around us the tables filled up, the evening crowd with louder voices and trays of glasses. Food orders were arriving. My stomach rumbled voraciously for food I didn't fancy. I smelt caramelised onions. Dog breath from a nearby Labrador. My headache intensified.

'Are you okay?' he asked.

I looked up, blinking rapidly. 'Yes. It's just the storm. It's left me on edge.'

He nodded. 'And so has my presence. I'm not stalking you, you know that, don't you?'

I twisted my fingers into a ball. 'I thought… it's silly, I know, because I've not met him. I don't even know what he looks—'

'I'm not your Medici person,' he said, firmly.

I squirmed. 'I know that now. But when I saw you in the tower, in the rain… You've been everywhere I've been, and it can't be a coincidence.' The sun dipped behind the slate roof of the pub. A cool shadow struck my scorched forehead.

He fingered the rim of his beer glass. 'No, I agree. I tell you what, I'll contact Camilla and see if she's heard of… what did you say his name was?'

'David Carmichael. He's a professor of art history at Charnwood University.' I collected the papers before they blew off the table. 'I didn't know him until he asked me to do this. He found me exhibiting at an art college in Coalville, near where I work.'

'I see.' He pursed his lips. 'Weird. Where are you going next?'

I examined a crumbled sheet. 'Richmond, then Bolton—'

'Yeah.' His frown deepened. 'That is disturbing. And I guess you're on a predefined schedule too?'

Now the nausea churned up into my throat, which tightened, and I spoke hoarsely, 'The order of castles is an obvious north to south route. I suppose he might just be helpful with the planning. I have to finish by the end of summer.'

'Me too. I don't think Camilla is lying to me. The collection will be a gift for somebody. But yours isn't?'

'I don't know. I post the digital memory sticks to David.' I halted. There were other things to consider. 'Are you being paid?'

He guffawed. 'Yeah, of course. The whole collection, though. Don't get anything for each painting. Has to be complete. I won't embarrass you by asking you how much—'

'But I'm not getting paid. I'm getting this.' I patted the camera case. 'Equipment. A digital camera. I can't afford it on my own. Plus expenses for accommodation and a car for the duration. It's just a rental.'

'Considerable costs covered though. I don't get expenses, except for a modest down payment for the paints. I'm using my savings. So I'm camping—'

'Camping?' I stared at the nearly empty pint glass.

He gestured over his shoulder with a jerk of his thumb. 'Camp site the other side of the castle. I come into town for food.'

'I'm in a bed and breakfast in Darlington. With this crazy couple…'

His eyes glazed over; he didn't paint portraits. Another small similarity. I cropped people out of the photographs.

'I don't know your name,' he said.

'Robyn.' I left off my surname because he had, and it felt like his trust had to earned. Perhaps we hadn't been supposed to meet. What were the chances anyway? We could have got our days out of synch or gone off schedule and re-ordered the route. Maybe that was the crucial part for Medici's plan, being different, and creating original pieces of artwork. What if the opposite was true, though? This very meeting could have been engineered, like a collision course. But why? I needed to find out more about Joseph. I tried the casual approach.

'Joseph. Not Joe or Joey?'

His eyebrows furrowed as if I'd said something distasteful. 'Robyn, not Rob or Robbie?'

I opened my mouth to say, don't be daft why would I pick a boy's name, when I realised his preference was perfectly valid and none of my business. 'No, of course not,' I mumbled, my cheeks flushed with heat.

He rose and shook off the crumbs from his sleeves. 'I'll be at Richmond tomorrow.' He stared over my shoulder to the willow trees by the river. 'I've never worked like this before. It's breathless in its pace. Unnatural. I'm not sure… It's uncanny this… what exactly? Two commissions running in parallel? I guess it's possible we're working for the same person. You're right, there's too many things in common.'

'I know what you mean.' I stood. I was desperate to email Medici. David wouldn't be happy, but he was supposedly on holiday. Another option was Yvette. She might find out why Joseph was mirroring my work.

'Robyn,' he said again, as if to savour it. 'I don't think it matters why to be honest. Maybe your Medici guy is playing a game of sorts, and he wants two different sets of pictures for some reason. A special exhibition? Yeah? I don't know and if we aren't working for him, we can still keep each other company. It can get lonely some days. Let's just go with it.'

I wondered if that nonchalance would stand the test of the next few days. We might come to resent the similarities and see ourselves as competitors. We also deserved an explanation from our go-betweens and distant financiers. But Joseph didn't strike me as the curious type or ambitious either and neither of us were in it for immediate financial gain. Somebody had promised him a fair payment, yet he camped out to save money, and I had only my equipment as final payment. We'd settled for a lot less than perhaps we deserved. Why were we both willing to tolerate bizarre obligations?

The loneliness was true. 'I've got a mobile number—'

'I don't have one. It's the way I like it.' He shoved his hands in his pockets. 'No computer either. So I'm off the grid, so to speak. It's why I like the camping. And if I have to, I'll use a pay phone to ring Camilla, if I can find one that's working.' He smiled. 'World's changing fast, and I'm only… young.' The smile widened.

How young? He was in his twenties like me, or a bit older. I couldn't tell with the stubble.

'Oh. Okay. Then I'll see you when I see you.' I picked up the camera bag.

He didn't offer to carry it to the car, which was still in the town's main car park. Instead, he walked with me, ambling around the drying puddles. His long shadow stretched across the road, dwarfing mine.

'So you like castles,' he said abruptly.

'Especially their history, the stories they tell. It's the main reason I'm doing this.'

'I'd have thought it was the photography.'

'Well, yes, that's the job part. Isn't art really about communication? The camera is my preference. Yours is the brush.'

'Actually, it's pencil or charcoal. But I get what you're saying. I'm not sure that I'm enamoured of castles. Perhaps… perhaps you could share that passion with me.'

My heart jolted against my breastbone. He hadn't belittled me for what was a deeply personal ambition. For a few seconds, the bag weighed nothing.

'I'd love to.'

'I'll see you at Richmond then,' he said. 'Tomorrow?'

'Great. Bye, Joseph.'

TWENTY-ONE

Richmond

TURNER HAD PAINTED RICHMOND CASTLE. Sadly, I wasn't inspired enough by either his version, or what I saw around me. I abandoned the easel and paint box by the curtain wall. Something would spark, eventually. I leaned my back against the stonework and waited.

We hadn't arranged a time or an exact meeting place. It was assumed, given our previous encounters, that it would happen; in any case, Robyn had told me she was coming, and by the smile on her face, she wanted to "bump" into me again. I wasn't superstitious. However, the idea that she was following me had frayed my otherwise robust nerves because I had only her word that she was working for somebody. Perhaps she had seen me at Warkworth, a fleeting occurrence admittedly, then tracked me down and used the camera as an excuse. I searched un-Turner like skies, thinking that idea through and decided it was unlikely. Although I had started first, we were both following the same prescribed agenda. How was that even possible?

I shifted my shoulder off the wall and turned to face the keep. There was no sign of her. If she believed I was stalking her, then the proof was here to see. I was ahead of her, and she was following me. There was plenty of other things that differentiated our projects. I wasn't allowed to frame pictures or keep copies, and I was sending them by courier to Camilla, and then they were disappearing from there to some place else. I had no plans to form an attachment to them. It was important not to in my line of work. Robyn seemed smitten with her photographs, and she had told me as we walked back to the car, there were boxes and boxes of them at home. I wondered, given she preferred to collect images, whether she was pained at the thought of giving these new photographs away. Whatever motivated her, we weren't twinned by artistry. Something else drew us together and it wasn't the magic pull of castles either. Did she feel it too: the fragile connection of two lonely souls?

Sighing, I walked to the abandoned easel and picked up my things. There was one spot I could try, a terrace below the curtain wall where a garden had been planted and recently opened to the public. A garden within a castle was rather like a windmill on the walls of a fortress, something unusual.

My working day was long, so I typically started early, and Robyn – I was rather taken by the ambiguous name – was travelling from Darlington, which was reason enough for her tardiness. The weather had been an issue, and although my tent was packed into the back of the car and still a bit damp from the storm, today, I needn't worry about rain. The temperature had risen sharply, and the sun poked out between the wispy clouds. Ideal conditions for painting. And photography. The weather was a freakishly good omen. But, I wasn't superstitious.

I fiddled with a screw using my penknife and managed to get the wobbly leg to sit still. I hummed louder as I began sketching out the wall above and the garden below, flicking the pencil across the paper in sweeping lines. The colours drenched my thoughts, and I mixed this and that on the palette until the right one shouted out.

'Did you know they kept conscientious objectors imprisoned here?' Robyn emerged from the shadow of a bush with her camera strap looped around her neck and the sizeable bag knocking against her hip.

The rush of heartbeats steadied. She had that knack of stealth movement, creeping up or moving away, like she had done at Prudhoe. Was she aware of it?

'No, I didn't.' I tucked the pencil behind my ear.

We stood side by side. She raised the viewfinder to her eye and focused on a tall tower. 'You're painting the Gold Hole Tower?'

'Am I?' I examined the pencil lines. 'Was it the treasury?'

Her abrupt laughter bubbled away into a little fizz of amusement. 'No, not that kind of gold. You're painting latrines again.' She blushed.

I chuckled at her embarrassment. 'Well, I'm sticking to a theme, then, aren't I? What about you?'

I crouched down and flipped open the lid of the wooden paint box. Battered and tarnished, the square container had antique properties that dated it. Months ago it had belonged to an admirable friend, who gave it to me, knowing it would be usefully employed, and I had carried it all the way from the Ionian Sea. Inside, the contents were neatly arranged and clean. I selected a tube and squirted the paint onto the plastic palette.

Robyn continued my education. 'The prison block, which adjoins the keep. It started out as an armoury, built in Victorian times. I have to work both keep and block into the photograph.' She blocked out her face with the camera and scanned along the wall.

'You know quite a bit.' I added another colour, then picked up a brush.

'I've this antiquated guidebook written by a castle guru. He points out the quaint stuff like the conscientious objectors' graffiti on the walls of the cells. Pity I can't photograph them, they're out of the public eye.' The shutter clicked.

I hadn't read any guidebooks. I avoided postcards too. 'How frustrating for you. What else are you taking pictures of?'

She lowered the camera. 'This is my old film camera; I use the digital for Medici's list.' She fiddled with a setting, embellishing the procrastination. 'I'm not sure, to be honest. It depends on my mood.'

My confidence in her story grew. She was obsessed with something, and she didn't trust me enough to say what it was. I stirred two colours into one blend until it mirrored the hue of the stones.

'So you have some freedom?' I asked.

'It's mutually beneficial, yes. Kind of. I'm not into latrines or cell blocks. They don't make me feel anything.' She glanced away. Her voice had a despondent edge to it.

I had stumbled onto something. There was a weakness to her story, something she hadn't told me, and I was drawn to find out more about her. Now there was plenty I hadn't said, but bartering wasn't an option for me and I'd rather she opened up first. With a few nudges, and luck, she might just reveal what it was she was actually doing so far from home.

TWENTY-TWO

'**I HAVE TO GO,**' I said. 'The cell block awaits.'

'Okay,' he said, pausing mid-brush stroke. 'I'll be longer.'

'Yes.' I hung the camera around my neck. 'Are you staying in Richmond?' I asked tentatively.

'Outside.' He glanced in my direction. 'Farmer's field. You?'

'I've escaped Darlington.' The bickering couple were no longer amusing me. I had left the tiresome accommodation with a stronger appreciation of the bond between my parents. They argued, yes, but never to the extent it was part of their daily routine.

'Camping has its up and downs. The toilet facilities are trying.' He grinned; 'Cheap plastic and far from golden.'

'I don't want to imagine, thank you. I did manage to use the washing machine and so I feel thoroughly cleansed.' The mundane things in life had risen to a whole new level of appreciation.

The smile on his face disintegrated. He looked down at his splattered jeans. 'Oh. Yeah, well, I'm hoping the next place will have better facilities.'

I covered my mouth. 'I'm sorry, I didn't mean to make you feel awkward. I've gone over a week without a washing machine and it's so odd not to have one to hand.'

He dabbed his brush on the paper and colour spread upwards, mimicking the walls. 'I've travelled a lot and put up with worse.'

I wanted to know more, right there, but he was concentrating harder, and his eyes were scanning the stonework.

'I'm staying here,' I said, 'in Richmond tonight; it's close enough for Middleham Castle.'

The brush stopped moving. 'Middleham? And then you're going to—'

'Bolton?' Now our eyes locked together. 'Yes. The day after Middleham. It's on the list, remember?'

'Yes, I know. I just thought for a minute you were going to do your own thing.'

I laughed. 'What? Go off piste again, like you did at Easter?'

'Well, I had my wrists slapped for doing that. He wouldn't know, would he? How would he know? You needn't say anything. I mean, nobody's put trackers on mobile phones yet, have they?'

I flinched. I hadn't told him that Medici had the uncanny knack of knowing exactly where I was and what I was seeing.

'God, I hope not. Would change everything, don't you think? Stalkers' paradise. There'd be no escaping your enemies.'

Joseph dropped his brush and bent over to pick it up. His expression, on rising, was one of abject horror. Why? He didn't even own a mobile phone. The questions remained unanswered: who was following whom, and why were we so bound to the same list of castles, the same order and deadlines? Joseph might have doubts still about Medici's involvement in both our projects, but I was convinced. I was in the mood for another interrogation. However, David was holidaying somewhere, and as for Medici, David's injunction was still in place. Should I break it? In order to, I needed an internet connection.

He rested the brush on the palette. 'Let's do this properly. We can meet, have a nice cup of something, and get to the nitty gritty points. What do you think? I'll try getting hold of Camilla again—'

'No luck?' An earlier call to Yvette had gone unanswered so I had left a message, conveying a degree of urgency without the intent of alarming, or so I hoped.

He shook his head. 'She's damn hard to pin down at the moment. Could do with that tracker after all.' The laugh was decidedly half-hearted. 'Tea? Cake? You choose.'

I recalled the town below, and one pretty looking tearoom. I described its location and he agreed we would meet in three hours.

Which left me more time to kill. 'I'll go to the keep. It's next to the cell block.'

❖

'You bleedin' coward,' says the gruff voice. 'Bread and water, that's all you'll get. You should be fighting the Hun like my son.'

The clang of the door echoes. The cell is tiny and he's not alone. He squeezes himself against the icy wall and the damp immediately is sucked into his bones. He shivers, violently.

Slowly, using the edge of his pewter spoon, he etches a letter in the wall. The limewash crumbles. Character by character he writes his name. His fingers by now are numb with the cold.

He hears voices, some despairing, others crying out in anger. There's no escape. He's trapped in this hellhole and struggles to breathe in the fetid air. Time passes, he can do nothing but wait for his fate to unfold.

The candle flame flutters. There is graffiti everywhere. Pictures of zeppelins and aircraft and the battlefields below. A few verses of a hymn, the scrawled lines of poems; some sad words, some defiant. He continues to draw in the dim light. His dog. His mother's face. A crucifix. A grave with his body lying in it.

They'll probably shoot him soon.

I gasped for air and removed my clammy hand from the wall of the cell block. I never made it to the adjacent keep. The cries of the prisoners were all it had taken to freeze me to the spot outside a small high window of the locked building. And there I had stood like a statue, caught suddenly aware of sounds, enveloped by my own imagination and wishing my immersion into the past wasn't so abrupt.

I thought of returning to where Joseph was painting and seeking comfort in his company. But as I moved out of the shadows of the building and the sun warmed the nape of my neck, I felt the raw emotion of fear subside to be replaced with the customary sense of self-awareness, and my own foolishness. I was annoyed with myself. The guidebook said the conscientious objectors sang hymns, debated their political views, even played chess. They tried hard to boost each other's morale and survived their imprisonment. But I had found a dark, miserable corner of a cell and allowed it to torment me with another haunting daydream.

My skin prickled as if the air was filled with static electricity. Glancing around, I wanted Joseph to appear close by, smiling infectiously. However, he was still in the garden below, painting the latrines, and yet for a brief moment, it had felt as if he had been watching me, or somebody had.

❖

Joseph ordered coffee and ginger cake. I chose tea in a China pot with a silver strainer and doily. The service was appropriately quaint, and slow.

He had left his painting in the car. I asked him if he was happy with it.

'I did two, which is why I took so long. I often do two or three perspectives. I did a quick one of the gatehouse and the cell block you mentioned.' He stirred cream into his coffee.

I peered inside the teapot. The leaves were stuck at the bottom, the colouration weak, but I wasn't in a hurry. 'Is the campsite safe for your things?'

'Good enough.' He yawned and apologised.

'Bad night's sleep?'

'Cows.'

'Early mornings on the dairy farm?'

'It's a small campsite next to the cow shed. The wind, fortunately, blows the other way.' He sipped and grinned at the same time.

'You couldn't… you didn't use hotels?' I skipped over the missing word.

He was sharp, though. 'I can afford them, just prefer the open countryside. I camped extensively in Greece. And other places.'

And then he started, hesitantly at first, to open up about his travels. I listened, slightly envious, and saw the glee in his bright eyes. I also spotted gaps in his tale, the lack of personal information about family and friends, the lack of interest in his teaching job, and the haphazard approach to his artistic work.

'You've not found your niche then?' I asked.

He stared, and then slowly scratched the stubble on his chin. 'No, not really. I am getting closer. And you?'

I gave him an abbreviated version of my biography, missing out the tedium of hotel work, focusing instead on the photography and my interest in history. I omitted the time-warping visions. I wasn't sure how to frame them without the risk of him making a sharp exit. He had a pragmatic line of reasoning, and seemed to care little for spun out stories. However he didn't glaze over when I keenly digressed into the history of Richmond Castle.

'A true Norman castle, designed to crush the people of the North. It's position by the river is rightly intimidating, don't you think?' I could easily have imagined cannon shot pinning down besiegers. But I hadn't. Instead, I had been locked in a pitch-black prison cell, wondering my fate.

A batch of fresh scones appeared from the kitchen, and one was deposited on my plate. I smeared raspberry jam over it.

'Jam then cream… you're revealing your true self.' His smile was infectious, and I responded in kind.

'Okay, ginger cake man, your turn. What do you see when you're painting?'

'See?' He dabbed at the crumbs on his plate with his fingertip and licked them off with a slither of a pink tongue. It was done daintily without losing the masculine appeal of his face.

I felt a tantalising tingle across my scalp. I glanced away, briefly, then recovered my poise. 'As in what do you think makes a good composition?'

'Oh.' His shoulders slumped a fraction. 'I don't tend to go that deep when looking at things. I tell my pupils, young and old, just go for what looks easy to do.' Another nervous laugh.

At Prudhoe I had seen his work in progress, and he wasn't an amateur who fell back on the simplest views, and he had already told me he had sold some of his paintings. Plus, he had a reputation and an agent to keep him busy.

'A good photograph is also due to the choice of composition,' I said. 'In my opinion, of course. I'm not a painter.' I was just as nervous as him. The pair of us fiddled with teaspoons, sipped our drinks, and prodded each other with cautious questions, but as yet, we had exposed nothing that explained why we were working parallel projects.

Joseph sighed. 'I don't know what the connection is, Robyn, if that's what you're thinking about. I don't know why I was chosen. I can't get hold of Camilla, and I don't know who the paintings are for. Okay. I agree, it's a mystery, but I'd rather just get on with it. I have rent to pay.'

I retreated into the back of the creaky chair. 'I'm sorry, I don't want to pry into your life. I didn't mean… it's that you said we'd thrash this out, and so far, there's no obvious connection between us.'

He stilled. If I had to put an emotion on his expression, then it was disappointment. It lasted only a second.

'Perhaps we're not meant to,' he said, slowly. 'You're taking photos for a man, yeah? Somebody who wants to stay anonymous, which is the same for my client. We've both got go-betweens who are elusive, people we trust but don't really know?'

I nodded in agreement.

'So.' He pushed aside the clean plate and leaned on his elbows, narrowing the distance between us to an arm's length. 'We're introverts, in some ways, happy to work alone, unafraid of travel—' He held up a hand. 'I know you said this was your first big adventure, but take it from a seasoned one, you've got the bug. I would say we're ideal for the jobs we've been given.'

'True.'

'But,' he paused, sharpening his focus on my face, 'we're able to see, as you put it, different things when we work. What we create isn't the same. Somebody wants me to create a gift, an attractive collection of paintings for private exhibiting perhaps? Yeah? But your job is more functional, like illustrations, because they're precisely defined.'

'So,' I shuffled forward on my seat, 'we're not working for the same person?' Or Medici's scheming was more elaborate than I had thought.

'What if,' his voice lifted with excitement, 'we're working for people who know each other, and copied the idea off each other.'

'I don't understand. Why keep it secret?' The cream dripped off my half-eaten scone. Joseph, sparking off his ideas, filled me with confidence. What if I told him my secret and that Medici had some inkling of my visions and that he had this ability to know what I was photographing from… 'He lives abroad. Medici. Where, I don't know.'

'Oh.' The fire in his eyes extinguished. 'You think it's too far-fetched? Two people borrowing the same idea for different reasons with the exact same agenda, and… Yes, you're right, more likely one person.'

My intention to open up to him had ended as swiftly as it had begun. How could I possibly trust him? I barely understood my own motivations.

He puffed out his cheeks. 'I guess we'll have to persist with our contacts.'

I had already drafted a mental message to Medici. The next guaranteed opportunity to email him would be in York, which was days ahead. It was the beginning of August and my schedule didn't have me in a decent hotel until later. My next bed and breakfast was going to be another surprise setup.

The conversation fizzled out. Did he really want to go back to a farm and listen to cows moo, and was I ready to meet my next host? I searched for something to spin us out. I craved company, and I thought he might too.

'You said you've been to Italy? My gran spoke some Italian. We called her Granny Izzy. She was a little batty. She thought she'd been to Italy, but Mum is absolutely sure she hadn't.'

His face softened. 'No harm in letting her think that, is there?'

Unfortunately, such kindness was too late for Granny Izzy. 'I'd love to go to Italy.' I twirled a lock of hair around my finger.

I had given him an opening, and he took it. He spoke of Rome, the tiers of the Coliseum, and the terracotta roof tops of Florence. He painted with words the colours and textures of arid summers and dusty olive tree groves. He had a gift, I realised, for seeing things clearly in his head, like a photographic memory, and while my talent was to see a different time and embellish it with my senses, his was to reproduce exactly what he saw and breathe life into it.

I wished I could paint, then I would add those extra details I imagined, something I couldn't do with photographs. There was something to connect us after all. If I could capture the realistic fabric of castles, he could bring them to life.

'Ten-thirty, Middleham Castle,' he said, leaving a couple of ten pound notes on the table. 'I'll see you then.'

I gathered my belongings and, as we parted company on the doorstep of the tearoom, I couldn't help wondering what it would be like to camp under the stars.

❖

My arrival at the Richmond guest house was greeted with little interest. Nobody asked questions regarding the purpose of my visit, nor were there tales of deceased spouses, in fact there was no socialising with the owners, who disappeared the moment my luggage was deposited in the bedroom, and if I hadn't met Joseph, I might have ended the day depressed by their lack of inquisitiveness. The place was purely functional, the decor overly simplistic, and since I wasn't the only guest, the neighbouring floorboards creaked.

I was on the cusp of taking a hot bath when Yvette rang me back. As I relayed the events of the last few days, finally revealing the details I had kept to myself for fear Yvette might repeat them to my parents, she listened attentively, occasionally interrupting with a soft gasp or a request for me to repeat something. The quality of the line wasn't great.

'Don't tell them, please.'

'I won't, although why you're afraid is worrying. Has he threatened you?'

'No,' I said sharply.

'But you don't know if he's telling the truth?' Yvette punched through my dithering to the heart of the matter.

I blinked several times. 'I think he is. But he doesn't seem particularly concerned that we're working on similar projects.' I drew the curtains to block out the low sun before returning to sit on the edge of the king-size bed.

'You had to think before answering.'

'I'm not rushing to conclusions, that's all.'

'You want me to find out if he's genuine or not?'

'David has gone on holiday, and I don't think I can reach him.' I rather wished he wasn't so confident of my abilities that he had simply upped and left me to it. He had sent two weeks' worth of expenses in anticipation of his absence.

'He'll be back. He'll have dissertations to mark, and next term to prepare.'

My patience was threadbare. I had to have the answers now. 'I could try to reach Medici, but he's supposedly in poor health, or so David has implied.' David was blithely unaware of my dilemma and happy to absent himself. Was that because he knew I might ask awkward questions?

Yvette was equally reticent. 'I can try to reach the art history department's secretary, but if it's the same jobsworth from when I was there, then you'll not get anything personal out of him. My advice is to keep nudging this guy, and maybe something revealing will tumble out accidentally. Some clue that you'll pick up on as to why he's painting castles.'

'I suppose,' I said. 'He's adamant it's just a gift, a portfolio for somebody. Do you know an agent called Camilla?'

The line crackled, and Yvette's voice increasingly drifted into inaudible. The phone battery drained itself whenever faced with poor reception. I could ask to use the landline in the hallway, but I was half-undressed and loath to bother anyone. I pressed the device closer to my ear.

'…agents, I only know advertising ones.'

I guessed the rest of her reply. 'So you don't have any ideas. How did David find out about me?'

'…the exhibition, you mean… I can't hear you.'

'You encouraged me to go.'

'You got the assignment on your own merits. He didn't recognise me until I spoke to him.'

The line went uncomfortably silent. 'Do you think he considered anyone else?' I asked.

'You were the only photographer exhibiting.'

There was a weariness in her voice that mirrored mine. I thought it unlikely Yvette would uncover anything about Joseph. Although he and I were linked in some way, the person directing us behind the scenes had made sure David wasn't involved with Joseph. Medici's schemes remained a mystery, and the only way to get to the bottom of the secrecy was to plough on with the assignment, and keep a close eye on my fellow artist. The idea cemented in my mind. Frankly, the flagging project needed fresh excitement to keep me occupied fully.

Yvette slipped away with a whispered goodbye, as if she was floating out of the window into the distance.

Mum had sent me a text. I had ignored it until now, hoping that the emotions it forced upon me might lessen. Instead, the sense of guilt grew. My great-aunt, Granny Izzy's step-sister, had taken a turn for the worse. The timing was bad; the long expected event was due to happen in the coming weeks, and Mum wasn't prepared for Beryl's departure.

Mum's message was blunt.

I'm dreading the call.

We both were. Auntie Beryl had better cling on for a little longer for both our sakes.

TWENTY-THREE

Middleham

SHE SAT ON A NEARBY WALL and watched me paint. It didn't bother me. While I worked at a comfortable pace, she had darted here and there, snapping away, switching cameras and lenses. She finished within a couple of hours.

I didn't ask why she had been given the whole summer for this assignment. We tiptoed around the subject of patronage, not knowing where it might lead us. I loathed knowing the answers in case we exposed some malicious person, a mastermind of deceitful games and trickery. I couldn't condone working with somebody that unscrupulous, even one called Medici. I was unenlightened by the subject of our current location too.

Middleham Castle was another box, two in fact, with an inner keep and an outer shield of a massive wall. We were between those sandwiching walls in the shade, looking up at the towering shell of the keep. Away from direct sunlight, the sense of claustrophobia intensified. This wasn't where I wanted to be. I would have to relocate and move outside the walls and try again.

Robyn was unperturbed by the snare of walls and shadows. She had her guidebook, a hardback pocketbook with chewed corners and bleached cover, and was reading Middleham's entry aloud. My education of castles had begun.

The original castle was a wooden palisade and when the new one was built, the old was abandoned. The groundwork is still visible to the southwest of the current castle.'

She lifted her nose out of the pages. 'Ooh,' she said. 'I'll take a look in a bit from up there.' She pointed to the uppermost ramparts.

A shiver went along the ridge of my shoulders. Memories of grim passageways and concrete balconies, my fearless brothers jeering each other on, squealing with excitement as they lined up their missiles.

I remembered the screaming. God, the agonised screaming.

My head ballooned with pain. I gritted my teeth, said nothing, and dabbed a bead of mulch green onto the canvas. It dribbled in a precarious fashion. A small group of people stopped in the space between the two walls, which resembled a gargantuan roofless prison corridor. My concentration was utterly broken into pieces. I dropped down onto the grass and crossed my legs.

'Go on,' I said, plucking at the grass with a violent gesture.

She stared at the mingle of colours on the paper and pursed her lips.

'It's okay,' I added. 'I need a break.'

'Oh, all right.' She opened the book. *The stone curtain was added in 1300 and the castle, which had been in the possession of the Neville family, was granted to Richard, Duke of Gloucester by his brother Edward IV. Richard made Middleham Castle his principle base in the north of England, and home to his son and heir, Edward...'*

Robyn's voice trailed off, then rebounded. 'Odd to think of kids raised in a castle. On the one hand, it might be gloomy, and on the other, a great big adventure playground, lots of hide and seek. My brother probably would have found it fun.'

'And you?' I asked.

'Teeming with life is how I think of castles. I don't think I would ever have been lonely.'

She had never spent time in a mega block of council flats where being lonely while surrounded by people living on top of each other was entirely feasible and equally tragic.

She read on.

'Tragedy struck when he – that's Richard *– lost his young son at Middleham, dying of an unknown disease. The mourning couple were described as mad with grief, and their son's final resting place is disputed. Missing graves is something for which Richard became renowned: where did his nephews end up?'* Robyn licked the page and turned it.

'An infamous tale,' I said. 'I heard of the Princes in the Tower when I visited the Tower of London, yonks ago.'

'How exciting,' she said.

I wanted to say children dying was never exciting. Then realised she meant the tower itself. I sighed quietly to my pessimistic self. 'Go on.'

She resumed her reading. *The giant keep reveals how the floors were divided into different levels: kitchen on the ground floor, great hall on the second. The staircase ascends to the upper level, providing the visitor with excellent views of the surrounding countryside and village. It's worth the climb. Although the castle is imposing and threatening in its structure, Richard spent his childhood here and grew fond of the place. Upon his death on the field of Bosworth, the castle passed into the hands of his rival, Henry Tudor. From then on, Richard's legacy and reputation was like the castle, ruined by his successors.'*

'Do you want to climb up there?' she asked abruptly.

I shook my head.

'Oh.' She didn't attempt to hide her disappointment.

There was an easy excuse to hand, and I grabbed it. 'We shouldn't leave valuables down here. You can keep your camera bag here and I'll look after it.'

The offer melted the frown on her face. 'I'll just take mine.' She fished out the battered camera and scooted off in search of the stairs. She moved at a fair pace with slightly knocked knees. I was once again tempted by the idea of painting her, despite my dislike of portraits.

I ate a buttie. I was living on biscuits, garage shop sandwiches and, in the evenings, tinned soup, which I heated on a gas ring. The farmer, probably thinking I was destitute, gave me bacon rashers for breakfast and mentioned something about a local charity for the homeless. I didn't correct his misunderstanding. I had recounted the small episode to Robyn to illustrate how artists are always expected to be stricken with poverty, and she had latched on to it to tell me her own minor stories of misunderstandings.

While I had picked a spot for my easel, which I now realised was a poor choice, she had gabbled away about her experiences of B&Bs. I had smothered a grin as she recounted the discomforts, not so much the physical ones, but the awakening of innocence to a world she had barely seen. Death and sex, two necessities of life, and she seemed surprised by them, as if they had no place in the privacy of somebody else's home. Yet, she had remarked that her current guest house lacked personality and she missed the gentle elderly couple at Bamburgh. I suspected they reminded her most of her own home, the parents of whom she had fondly spoken, who lived in the town she thought was a dead end but where her friends waited for her to return, and where normality would resume after this digression into her ideal world of escapism. I understood, I got the same vibes out of travelling.

I had nothing to say, though. I had never lived on a quiet street.

She had reached the top of the tower. Up there, she was a dot, buffeted by the wind, and she clung onto a handrail, or something, and leaned her head over the side. Gradually, her upper body lifted, and for a second, I thought she was about to tumble over the top. I jumped to my feet, ready to shout, hoping my cries would echo upwards. Abruptly, she stilled, then slowly slipped downward and out of sight behind the parapet. The nature of that retreat was unnatural, alarming almost. I glanced at all the equipment – mine was not of great commercial value, but hers was, I couldn't leave it. I picked up the camera bag, admiring her strength as it wasn't lightweight, and hurried to find her.

TWENTY-FOUR

HAVING LEFT JOSEPH BEHIND, and while on route to the upper ramparts, I crossed the great hall. Like Kenilworth, the pillar stubs were lined up in the middle of the ground, but any other similarities ended there. While Kenilworth was exposed and well-lit by daylight, in Middleham's keep the sun was banished to the highest parts. At ground level, the only sunlight sneaked through the empty window slits. Where the beams struck, the walls were smothered with grey moss and lichen. Medici wasn't interested in the hall; his preference was the chapel tower, and the remnants of kilns and ovens in the outer chambers of the castle, practical stuff illustrating functionality, like the latrines, and windmill, the essence of his architectural treasures which I had obediently made crisp and delineated with my zoom lens.

I nearly made it to the wooden stairs, reconstructed for the benefit of visitors, when I heard a mumbling of voices. I spun, expecting to find somebody behind me, but there was nothing there. I turned several times, and each rotation sent me spiralling back in time in the hope of discovering the origin of the sounds. My vision was unfocussed and only sounds broke through: laughter, repetitious rhyming, blended singing; the odd burst of applause, and in the midst was the shrill voice of a child.

Bombarded in all directions, and feeling slightly nauseous, I closed my eyes, and then it happened, the unfolding of my imagination like the pages of a well-thumbed book.

Colourful banners, painted with symbols and scenery, hang from the walls. A theatre is installed, the decorated, raised platform stretching across

I opened my eyes and heard only a soft wail.

The sound came from above, and I followed it, climbing the steps, panting in my haste to catch up with the noise. The cries were of a woman, and they drew me to the apex, and the iron railings placed there to protect the visitors.

I gripped the bars tightly, struggling with the overload of information. The raw heat of the sun on the nape of my neck was unable to compete with the icy metal beneath my fingers. The bout of dizziness was overwhelming. I leaned into the railings and embraced the vertigo, hoping it would be swift. Throughout the battering of my senses, the heart-breaking cries of grief, a woman's lamentation, echoed all about me, but they seemed now to be below me.

I shrank down to the ground, covered my ears in vain and silently begged her to stop.

'Robyn?' The hoarse voice breached the weeping.

I jerked, believing for a moment that somebody from the past had bridged the gaping chasm of time and found me. The connection, though, was physical, the grip under my arms strong and forthright; I had little chance to protest.

'For God's sake, if you don't like heights, why come up here?' Joseph said. He hauled me towards the stairwell. 'I thought you were about to fall off.'

I wriggled out of his grasp. 'I'm fine. It was just a brief attack of vertigo. I got out of breath from the climb.' The excuse came easily.

'Let's go down before it happens again.'

He stepped cautiously, my camera bag wrapped around his body, and kept his gaze locked on the flagstones rather than appreciating the spectacular view of fields, church tower, and roofs. The wind picked up and howled softly, reminding me how high up we were. We stood abreast on the top step. I heard footfalls below. We would have to give way to others.

Joseph froze, his grip on the handrail unyielding and white-knuckled.

I nudged him. 'Joseph,' I hissed. 'Budge over.'

He started, as if woken, and moved to one side, pinning his back to the stone wall. I recognised the reason for his paleness and the beads of sweat on his brow. While my vertigo was induced by the intrusion of a vision, his was more commonplace. Given his heavy breathing and the panic etched into the lines of his face, he was terrified. However, to save him from embarrassment, I wasn't going to comment on his neurosis.

As soon as the new arrivals were out of the way, I grabbed his hand and directed him down. The rescuer became the rescued, and we smoothly transitioned into the roles. I led him down, keeping one eye on the steps, the other on his stuttering feet. Only when we reached the second corner did I let go of his trembling hand. We reached ground level, and he immediately brushed away the perspiration with the back of his hand. What passed between us was left unspoken. I had touched him, and he had touched me, and the matter was best left there.

We walked purposefully to the exit of the keep, passing the stone foundations of the pillars. I recalled the scene I had envisaged minutes earlier, and the information in Braithwaite's little guidebook. I was convinced I had heard the grief of a mother who had lost her son, and before that, some recollection of more joyful times, when the child had been entertained by jesters and performers. It fitted. It made sense.

I was relieved it wasn't a myth, and that I had conjured up something rooted in history, and not poems or legends. If what I had felt – my skin remained prickly – was verifiable, then I had encountered a real person's echo and it was as intense as Joseph's fear of heights. There had also been a notable absence in my daydream tableau. Richard, the maligned king, hadn't shared the "mad grief" which historians had described – where was the father when the son died?

Joseph stopped. The colour had returned to his face, the loss of control over and forgotten. He looked upwards, scrutinising something.

'It's bleak,' he said.

'I suppose it is now.'

'Do you think he did it?'

'Did what?' His quiet tone startled me. 'Who?'

The blush deepened. 'Richard the Third. You know, the Princes in the Tower. Did he kill the children?'

I tripped on a grass-covered flagstone. He grabbed my arm to steady me, and I smiled a small thank you. The stumble was as much mental as physical. I had told him my love of history and he had seemed indifferent up until now, but somehow following the episode high above he had latched onto my train of thoughts. I felt a degree of shame. I had in my arrogance assumed that the more castles I notched up, the greater my knowledge of the past. Yet, Joseph was just as capable of seeing things beyond the here and now, and had picked up on the irony in Braithwaite's benign commentary. The father who supposedly murdered his nephews to gain the throne of England had been denied his one son and heir. He had been punished.

I tried to sound nonchalant. 'Well, if Richard did it, he died a violent death. So maybe that was justice.'

'And if he didn't do it, and his allies hadn't turned on him, we would never have had the Tudors. Imagine that. No reformation.' He clucked his tongue.

'Unlikely, I think it was fate that a new dynasty came to power. I mean, once you start murdering children, self-destruction is inevitable, isn't it?'

He blanched again, the loss of colour more dramatic than the previous one. His eyes widened; I had shocked him somehow.

Given his response, I wasn't prepared to dig deeper, no matter how curious I felt. To compensate for his discomfort, I blurted a question with little forethought.

'Did you take history at school?'

There was a notable shifting in his demeanour from rigid to gently indignant, and the roll of his eyes was a swift rebuke. He added nothing else to it.

'Oh.' I nibbled my lower lip penitently. I was good at misjudging Joseph. Ever since we had met, I had downgraded him because he dressed like a scruffy street dweller. He was a teacher, and probably more qualified than me. In any case, he didn't need to study history to know things.

He softened his expression to one that was less critical. 'I'm sorry. That was unfair. I did study it, although I wasn't a star pupil, I managed to listen from time to time, and I rather liked the scheming kings in the War of the Roses. Although not Shakespeare's versions.' He manufactured a long yawn.

I laughed in sympathy.

Out in the open, we returned to his easel. Nobody had interfered with any of our things. I took back the camera bag, which he had carried with apparent ease, even when hoisting me upright. He examined his half-finished picture and sighed.

'I'm sorry, I'm going to have to move and pick a different spot. It isn't working for me down here.'

I said nothing, because I agreed with him. The painting, although technically brilliant, was dark and foreboding, and placed the viewer in a pinioned position, as if the walls were closing in on them. The castle had that effect on the inside, but up above, as I had discovered, it was remarkably open and inspiring. Perhaps Joseph had realised there was more to Middleham than the imposing walls.

I waved my hand to a hill on the other side of the village. 'I'm going to pick somewhere outside the castle to take a few scenic shots.'

He followed the direction of my pointing finger. 'Yes, there, or maybe the old earthworks.'

'You go there, and I'll meet… we'll meet up later, won't we?'

He turned and brought his hand up to shade his eyes. 'Where do you suggest?'

I searched his face for a hint. Even with the shelter of his arm, the sunlight caught his eyes and when he looked directly at me, I spied an animated sparkle. In coming to my rescue, he had exposed what he had in turn attempted to hide: his fear of heights. If he could take a risk, so perhaps, could I. Dare I tell him what had really happened up there? It would be nice to have his trust, to know that what inspired me was more than an interest in history and the camera in my bag.

The guest house wasn't appropriate for meeting up. The answer rattled off my tongue with surprising ease. 'I've never been camping.'

He had no idea I had just lied. Once upon a time, I had been a Girl Guide and nearly burnt a tent down with a match in the middle of the night. But I needed a toe in the door, and this was, sadly, the best chat up line I could muster.

I giggled, childishly, and to my delight, Joseph smiled too.

❖

Joseph had moved to a different campsite, one with better facilities and an on-site shop. He had purchased a disposable barbecue, sausages and buns for our evening meal.

I found the campsite after driving up and down several narrow lanes. The caravan park was busy with squealing children chasing balls, while their drowsy-eyed parents lay on sunbeds under colourful awnings. On the other side of a tall hedge, the campers occupied tents of various shapes and sizes, scattered like rose petal confetti. Joseph had chosen a corner pitch and I parked my car next to his aged Ford Focus, which was crusted with mud around the wheel arches.

He greeted me with a stubble-free face. He had lost five or so years in the transformation and revealed dimples in his cheeks, which pitted when he smiled.

'Decent showers and a washing machine.' He sniffed his armpit. 'I smell like a florist's.'

I held out the bottle of ginger pop. 'For the ginger cake man.'

He laughed. 'I should dye my hair red to go with it.'

I fetched the picnic blanket from the boot of my car and spread it out in front of the tent. I had expected a shoebox size tent, but it was large enough to accommodate two people, including a stooped man of Joseph's height. The zip was down, though.

He had been working on one of his paintings. The easel was up, the box opened up and brushes scattered on a cloth. The picture was of Middleham Castle, but not from the interior. He had gone out to the old earthworks and painted the castle from the higher vantage point.

He cocked his head to one side. 'Better? I'm just finishing it off. Then I'll send it tomorrow.'

I stood next to him and admired the delicate brush work, the hazy colours and ripples of cloud in the sky. 'It's really good. I can see how it might have looked in its heyday. The palatial size of the keep. It must have been an incredible sight for miles around. Brilliant.'

'Thank you.' He picked up the brushes and bundled them up using a cloth wrapping. 'I'll finish it later.'

I stretched out on the blanket and watched him turn the spitting sausages. The deluge of two days ago had had little impact on the hardened ground beneath my back. The sultry summer continued unabated.

There were damp socks pegged to the tent lines. 'An improvement on the last campsite?'

'Yes,' he said. 'Washing machines come at a higher price. But I don't have to put up with cows.'

'It's getting busier. I noticed that today. Harder to get clean shots without people strolling into view.'

'Summer holidays in full swing. At least I can just ignore people.' He slit open a bread roll, then handed me a bottle of ketchup and two plastic tumblers.

I gave the bottle a brisk shake and unscrewed the cap. I was starving and we happily ate in silence. The fizzy drink tickled the back of my throat. I relished the mini barbecue for what it was: simple and tasty.

' He passed me a paper napkin. 'I found a phone box, but unfortunately it was out of order. So I've still not managed to call Camilla.'

I dug into my handbag and retrieved my mobile. The signal strength was one bar. 'You could try using this.'

He had the number written in a little notebook. He thumbed through the pages, licking his fingers as he went. The reception was poor, and he walked about the field, trying different locations. I tracked his frustrated movements while sipping on ginger ale.

He returned with visible furrows on his forehead. 'I think I've managed to leave a message on her office phone. The personal one didn't connect.' His frown deepened. 'I suppose she could have changed the number since I last used it.'

'But you are sending the pictures to her? She must be receiving them.'

Given the alarmed look on his face, I'd touched upon something he hadn't considered. 'I send them recorded delivery to the office. But I've no means to check if they were signed for.'

'You've not spoken to her recently?'

'I know she's got the earlier ones from the Easter break – Bamburgh, Alnwick and Dunstanburgh. But we haven't spoken since I left London.' He handed the mobile back to me. 'Sorry, I've eaten your battery life somewhat.'

'Don't worry. I'll charge it tonight.' I dropped the useless thing in my bag. 'Perhaps she's gone on holiday with David.'

I was joking, but it gave me ideas that put a different slant on how things might pan out over the next few days. Abandoned to our own devices, we were unfettered by agenda and the constraints of our assignments. What if we merged them into one and established a timetable that suited us both?

'You haven't reached the professor either?' Joseph asked.

'I set my spy on to him.'

Two neat eyebrows lifted quizzically.

'Yvette, my friend.'

'What about your Medici?'

'Ah, well, I could try to email him. I thought I might try the "Wow, isn't this an amazing coincidence" approach. There's this bloke painting *your* castles, just like I'm doing using a camera. *Crazy*, I know, but do you think you might know him? Yeah, I think that will be my non-confrontational approach.'

Joseph occupied the other half of the blanket. He leaned back on his elbows and crossed his bare ankles then wriggled his toes. 'I would just come out and ask him if he's my client.'

'I'm trained to be polite and diplomatic, and only when things turn nasty am I authorised to harden my tone.' I echoed the "customer is always right" mantra of my bosses.

'You're not in a hotel now. You should assert yourself with this guy.'

I rolled onto my side and the gap between us shrank a fraction. This close, I could see the dark pits of his pupils and the tint of his eyelashes.

'I know he's not my boss. Yvette sold me this idea of having a patron. A benefactor who supports my work. Hence I'm paid expenses. It's a mutually beneficial arrangement.'

'Is it?' Joseph grimaced. 'I'd prefer not to be tied to one person's sponsorship.'

'It wasn't a big deal, not knowing his real name. Now I regret not insisting.'

'Perhaps he's famous. You said he lived abroad.'

I pursed my lips. 'I don't know. His English is excellent, like a native speaker.' Except, I had never heard his voice, only read his words. My heartbeats pattered noisily, mirroring my racing thoughts.

Joseph touched the back of my hand and swiftly withdrew when I glanced down.

'Camilla is hiding from me, and your Mr Medici has kept his motives a secret. We're both in a bit of an awkward situation.'

'So do we stop? Abandon the game—'

'Game? This is work for me—'

'Sorry. I didn't mean to imply it wasn't. I just meant as in how we're being played. Work should have clear targets and a process to follow, shouldn't it?'

'Maybe in a hotel, where there are managers, but we're freelancers working on a commission.'

'I have a contract.' With David, I didn't add.

'Mine is with the agency.'

We stopped there, perched on the edge of some uncomfortable precipice of uncertainty, too scared to upset each other's sensibilities.

'I don't like it,' I said, finally. 'I've been amateurish. Naive. Now I feel I'm stuck.'

The second time his hand settled on mine, it reassuringly stayed there. 'But are you enjoying yourself? I thought you were happy to travel?'

An electric tingle shot along my arm. 'I am happy. I think that's why I don't want to ask questions, or send that email. What if it he ends the agreement? What if he wants the camera back?' I looked over to the boot of my car, where everything was locked away. Things I considered my own, but weren't if I didn't fulfil the criteria of the contract.

'I can see your dilemma and it's similar to mine. Perhaps we should just go with it until your friend gets back to you. Or maybe this professor guy?'

'Tomorrow I'm at Bolton Castle.' To the west, so I was staying put in Richmond for the night.

He sighed. 'I'm going to have to take a rain check.'

I sat up, slowly, my hand slipping away from his.

He smiled. 'Don't worry, nothing to do with you. I've paintings to package up, which is complicated, and I need fresh supplies. I can get them in Richmond. I might reach Bolton… but I doubt it.'

Tomorrow was Friday. For the weekend I had other plans involving an abbey. 'So I might not see you again?'

'Oh, I'll catch up on Saturday. Then I need to move on.'

I braced myself. 'Back to London?'

He shook his head. 'God, no. I'll soldier on. Far as I'm concerned nothing has changed. I'll paint Bolton.'

I stood. 'You love being out and about on your own.' I stepped off the blanket. 'I get it.'

The shadow descended on his forehead; the sun was moving below the tree line. The timing couldn't have been more poignant. He rose and dusted the loose grass from his spotless jeans.

'I never anticipated company, Robyn. It's been a pleasure getting to know you…' He fumbled with his pockets.

I had come to the campsite with the clearly unrealistic ambition of revealing to Joseph what I had actually experienced at Middleham Castle, and instead, we had retreated behind our ramparts.

'Why did you come up to the top of the tower?' I asked.

He stiffened. 'I thought you were in trouble.'

'But you could barely stand being up there. And I wasn't exactly in trouble. I felt dizzy… I get dizzy when I…' I shrugged. 'It doesn't matter.'

'What doesn't matter?'

'If I told you, you'd definitely wouldn't want to follow me to Helmsley, or Pickering. They're next on my list.'

The snatch of breath was audible. 'They're on mine too. You know they are.'

'But you're on the verge of saying goodbye—'

'You implied I like being on my own, and I think you do too.'

I inched back onto the blanket. 'I can wait for you to catch up. I'm going to Rievaulx Abbey this weekend. I've always fancied seeing it. You have your own route planned… so…'

'Honestly, I don't mind. I'm not that much in a rush. I'll go to Bolton, and we can meet up on Monday. Is it Pickering or Helmsley next for you?'

'Er. Helmsley and Pickering. Then I've booked a few days by the coast at Scarborough. Just for a break. Then York.'

'York.' He scratched the invisible stubble. 'I guess I can hold off going to York after Pickering. Have you ever been to Whitby?'

I shook my head.

'The abbey there is a good place for photographs.'

We were face to face, searching each other's faces for clues. I had lost track of my own emotions. The last few minutes had been a rollercoaster of excitement combined with trepidation of not knowing what to ask him, or tell him. As it was, I had achieved nothing, and Joseph was equally defensive.

The smoke from the barbecue billowed in a death throe, its dying heat brushing against my bare ankles. I had forgotten what kicked off this rapid exchange, but Joseph hadn't.

'What doesn't matter?' he asked. 'You said something doesn't matter. But clearly it does.'

'It's nothing to do with the project.'

'But it made you feel ill, up there? Was it like a flashback?'

Yes, I nearly said, but I realised he didn't mean what I read into that term. He was thinking of traumatic flashbacks, the PTSD kind. I recalled the ashen pallor of his face, the tremble of his hand and stumbling feet barely able to move. He was referring to himself. He was the one who dreaded telling me something.

'No,' I said, carefully. 'It was a funny turn, that's all. I should have taken my time on those stairs.'

I had lied again. It was starting to become a habit.

TWENTY-FIVE

Rievaulx

THE ABBEY PROVIDED ME with an essential break, as if I was a weary traveller in need of sustenance. It possessed everything I required to combat my throbbing headache and calm the rapid pulse of my heartbeats. Yesterday had been a tedious blur and even though I had lingered at Bolton Castle, Joseph hadn't caught up with me, assuming he had tried.

That niggling little doubt clung on to me through a restless night, the last one at Richmond, and during the hour-long drive to Rievaulx I nursed it until it triggered the tension headache. Regardless of our timely encounters, there was no reason why we might see each other again and for all I knew, he could be going out of his way to avoid me; he hadn't seemed keen on the idea until I had pushed back at him. We hadn't exactly made any firm plans for meeting on Monday and twenty-four hours later, having reassessed his reticence, I decided he was going to slip away.

Described as the perfect example of a preserved medieval castle, the privately owned Bolton Castle had failed to both inspire and distract me. For the first time my photography permit had been scrutinised at length. The experience unsettled me further, and I had struggled to fulfil Medici's precise criteria due to the exuberant antics of children. They had swarmed like newly hatched flies. I eventually found my quarry – the spiral staircase that twisted anti-clockwise, supposedly unusual, but I had seen plenty of examples in other castles, and wasn't sure it warranted special mention or the price of the ticket and permit. The trip steps – steps of uneven height designed to send an attacker head long down the stairs – were also one of his little foibles, but weren't one of mine. But

Medici decided… I had sighed and huffed a great deal while I waited for people to move out of shot.

By the time I had finished there was no hope of a quiet spell; even the pleasant gardens laid out below the walls were teeming. I ticked off Bolton, irritated at its failings, which were really entirely my fault. I was in a bad mood.

Rievaulx Abbey, thankfully, came to my rescue the next day. Although busy, the dense ruins had plenty of space to explore and also offered me sanctuary in the form of nooks and crannies amongst the broken stonework. There, safely out of sight in a roofless chamber, I embraced a pleasant level of calmness. The baking sun couldn't reach my shelter, and the shadows cooled my sticky forehead. I clutched my camera to my chest and heaved a sigh of relief. Looking up, the cloudless sky, still so unexpected two weeks into my journey, was aquamarine, as if the sea and sky had swapped places. A bird spiralled upwards on a current, dipping then diving before climbing again. Its long wingspan, black against the sky, was that of a hawk or buzzard, and it attracted the crows, who in turn mobbed it. I watched, mesmerised by their persistence. Eventually, they moved out of my limited view, and I was alone again.

I listened, but heard nothing out of the ordinary. No chants or murmurs of prayer, nor the bells calling the monks to their choir stalls. Given the purpose of the abbey, silence was appropriate, and I abandoned that sense and sought another route. I inhaled through my nose and held my breath.

What scents would have greeted me if I had been here, centuries ago? The herb garden, surely? Or maybe the hops in the brewery? My nostrils wrinkled with displeasure. Urine. Hot reeking piss. I gathered my things and hurried away. I had been sitting in the tannery.

But I was relieved. I still had it, whatever it was and, just as I preferred, my daydreams were rooted in historical facts, and not myths or unknown events. It wasn't long before my senses snared me again. In the refectory, I was engulfed by the aroma of burnt wood, perhaps carried in from the warming room, the one place the monks were allowed to light a fire. But as I backed against the cold wall, the smell intensified until I sneezed. I crouched, and hugged my legs. The burning was like that of a bonfire. Was the abbey being attacked? I knew marauding Scots had stormed it and stolen from the sacristy. Or maybe it was an echo of the destructive Reformation, when everything was stripped out and sold, including the land.

I closed my eyes, and there was nothing but blackness, heaps of it, piled up and around me, smouldering and filthy. I watched as a solitary man piled more and more of it into the space in front of me.

He coughs and staggers under his load. The stench of burnt wood follows him into the undercroft.

White eyes, bloodshot, filthy snot streams out of his nostrils. Dust. Spittle. Heavy breathing, as if death is close by and waiting. His lungs are bursting, and the daggers of pain sharpen with each sucking inhale. He carries a burden on his shoulders. It presses him down until his knees are close to buckling. With a sob, he stumbles and lands on his hands and knees, and crawls on the hard flagstones, still carrying the load on his back.

A light glimmers, dangerously close; the naked flame dances.

A voice calls out, demanding and authoritarian. The weary man ditches his load on top of the still smouldering pile and with bowed shoulders lurches toward the light. His face is illuminated. A young man, his lips are cracked and the whites of his eyes are glazed with tears.

'Robyn!'
The fading figure turns to look back; his expression of despair magnifies.
'Robyn?'
He staggers beyond the candlelight and the darkness swallows him, burying him in the shadows.

Somebody touched my shoulder.

The involuntary jerk started a wave of shivers and I struggled to tolerate the daylight. The man crouched until his face was level with mine. The stubble was evident again, the squareness of the jaw familiar. His eyes were unhooded and wide as full moons.

'Are you okay?' he asked.

'Yes, of course,' I said, quickly.

'You were staring into space, like a zombie.' Joseph stood and held out his hand. 'Can you stand?'

My legs were jelly. I heaved myself up using the wall for support. If he touched my hand, he would know how fast my pulse was racing and feel the cold clammy palm.

'What are you doing here?' I asked, dusting grass cuttings off my skirt.

'Having finished off at Bolton, I took a chance you might be here, and hot-footed it over.' He pursed his lips. 'What were you doing just then? You were so lost in thought, staring into space. Did you not see me wave? I called your name.'

My name. I had heard another calling a name. And why were my eyes open? I was convinced they had been shut.

'Did I look kind of… catatonic?' I kept my back lodged in the protective stone blocks.

He shrugged. 'I suppose. Do you have seizures?'

I stiffened, unprepared for such a sensible question. It had never occurred to me that the visions were symptomatic of something far more worrying. This time, when he held out his hand, I grasped it.

'God, you're so pale,' he said. 'And cold.' He drew me towards him.

His breath was warm, so close, and mingling with mine. Not yet, I wasn't ready. I needed more time to know for certain, so I hesitated, just long enough for him to register the reticence in my face, and he let go. My hyper-aware acuity remained sharp and needy, as if searching for an outlet. I saw details that weren't important: the outer edges of the print on his t-shirt were peeling away from the cotton; the pierced ear lobe; the necklace of gold pressed against his throat. Was this the first time he had worn it? A Saint Christopher pendant hung between his collar bones.

I touched it with my fingertip. 'Did you wear this especially for today?'

His chin lowered. 'It was a gift. From someone who takes these things more seriously than me.'

I sharply withdrew my hand and looked up into his eyes. 'I didn't come here for that kind of spiritual enlightenment.'

His shoulders stiffened. 'A ruined abbey is much the same as a ruined castle. I wasn't implying your reason was anything other than that.'

I took a step back. 'I do like the tranquillity.' I manoeuvred around him, and he followed me as I stepped out of the shadows into the sunlight. I blinked several times. 'It's perfectly located, isn't it? A flat valley, the river, grazing land and trees for…'

I stopped so abruptly, he nearly collided with me. 'What? Are you having a funny turn again?'

'No.' I frowned. 'I wasn't having one in the first place. I'm not epileptic. I just realised something.'

He glanced at his wristwatch. 'It's nearly closing time.'

I gaped. 'Really? I've been here that long?'

He smiled. 'I managed to finish off Bolton this morning, drive here and find you, and you've been here all this time?'

'I had a bit of a lie in.' Followed by a late breakfast, and a fruitless conversation. My request for access to the internet had been met with a bemused look by the woman at the guest house. 'Most of our working guests have laptops. We have a connection point in the sitting room,' she had said in a busy voice. I regretted not asking for a laptop from David.

'I've taken lots of photographs.' Two whole reels of film. 'And a picnic lunch.'

The soft smile spread across his face. 'You really do have a passion for these kind of places. I'm actually jealous.'

We walked toward the kissing gate. 'Don't you feel anything while you paint?'

'See, now feel? Still seeking my motivations?'

'I'll tell you mine if you tell me yours.' I grinned.

The expression of mirth fell off his lips; I'd done it again, thrust him into a place of deep discomfort. The time and location weren't appropriate for revelations, but I was determined that if we were to understand what had brought us together, one of us had to come clean.

'What are you doing tomorrow?' I asked.

He waited for me to swing the gate, and only when we were both on the same side again, did he answer. 'Nothing special.'

'There's a white horse cut into a chalk hillside. Do you fancy looking at it?'

'Where are you staying tonight?'

'Thirsk.'

He nodded, musing on my choice. 'I'm moving, too. But closer to Scarborough. I'm on the way there now.'

I was too far away; my idea wasn't sensible. 'Perhaps we should just meet up on Monday, at Helmsley Castle?'

'Sure.'

There was no mistaking the tone; I flinched. 'I'll see you there then.'

We parted company by the gift shop. Joseph strolled away, unperturbed by the last part of our exchange. I went into the shop and brought a book on the history of Rievaulx. Sitting in my car, I flicked through the pages and found what I was looking for. Once again, I had managed to imagine something of which I had no prior knowledge. And there was another odd coincidence. Joseph had been present, as he had been at Richmond and Middleham, and he had witnessed me drift away in a nightmarish recreation. My waking dreams were becoming claustrophobic and intense, and I was suspicious of why.

Mrs McDougal had no qualms about giving me access to her computer. The redoubtable lady with flaxen hair and raspberry skid marks down her blouse, was eating a jam sandwich when I arrived at the Thirsk B&B. She carried my suitcase upstairs like a miniature lumberjack. I didn't ask if she was still married or a widow. There wasn't a ring nor a shadow of one. I concluded she was also unlikely to have nocturnal callers, and thankfully, since my stomach was growling, she was happy to provide me with dinner – she offered me steak pie. She paid no heed to my camera equipment. At the mention of checking my emails, she waved me out of the bedroom, and I followed her downstairs.

'Ye've lovely hair.' She poked at her bun. 'Mine's twisted like thistles. Canna get it tae hang straight.'

I sympathised wordlessly.

'Gin ye fancy a wee dram, then help yourself.'

I had noted the whisky bottle next to the kettle.

'I put ane ivery room. It's my wee welcome tae ye.'

Having struggled with the Geordie dialect, I was having to concentrate even harder with the diminutive Mrs McDougal's native tongue.

'You've not lost your Scots,' I dared to say.

'Ay, sae people like tae say.' A jovial smile fractured her face. 'The Edinburgh folk like tae stay here. But ye're a southern lass.'

'Midlands.'

'Ay, south.'

She showed me into her cluttered front room. The keyboard was overwhelmed by magazines and knitting patterns. She bustled and cleared a space for me on the chair. 'There ye gae. Take ye time.' She paused by the door. 'Dae ye like your tatties mashit?'

I replayed the sentence a few times. 'Yes, please.'

The door squeaked.

'An yer gravy wi onions?'

My fingers stilled on the keys. 'Yes, please.'

'Ye're an easy lass. No fussy.'

Finally, she left the room.

I composed two emails. The one that went to Medici had an assumption of continuing mutual trust:

I'm not alone in my endeavours. A young man is painting the same locations, supposedly for an agent – Camilla Brooke – do you know her? Small world! I supposed there is no harm in us working together, just a bit weird that he has the same list you gave me.

I hesitated over the send button, and impulsively added a few sentences at the end:

I saw, heard, something at Middleham and it felt so real. I might be going a little crazy. Hopefully not affecting the quality of my photos. Memory stick two on its way. Hope it reaches you okay. Did you know David had gone off on his holidays?

Of course he should know, but I wanted to make a point that I felt abandoned, and that he should feel responsible for me; he was my patron.

With David I expressed my concerns with a demand:

Did you commission an artist to paint exactly the same castles as me? Do you know an illustration agent called Camilla Brooke? She's the one he's dealing with. I'm understandably spooked. We have talked about it – his name is Joseph – and agree we're being kept in the dark. Is there a purpose to what we're doing and why is Medici so secretive? Would like some answers.

And if Joseph was working indirectly for my patron, so would he. Buoyed with energy, I felt invigorated by my newfound assertiveness. If the emails failed to draw the pair out of their shells, I would have to withdraw my services and hope that a half-finished project was sufficient a threat. Medici might find another photographer to complete the assignment if he wished, but I doubted he would get one by the end of August. There was plenty of money resting in my account and I planned to milk it while I enjoyed Joseph's company.

Before I logged out of the account, an email bounced back:

Professor Carmichael is out of the office. Please contact the faculty office for further assistance.

There was no date provided for his return. Deflated, I went for a walk around Thirsk. I didn't take a single photograph. My lack of focus extended to the camera lens; I didn't know where to point it. I nearly dropped the phone on the pavement when it beeped. The text from Yvette capped my unproductive day with fresh worries.

No response from David. I contacted his faculty. He's not expected back after his holiday. He's retired.

Retired! Talking to her wouldn't alleviate my concerns. I was utterly alone, abandoned, it seemed, to my own devices, and worse, I wasn't finding one jot of comfort in photography.

I stuffed the memory stick in a jiffy bag along with a scrawled abbreviated index of the photographs, and tossed the envelope into a post box. There, David, do what you want with it, assuming you're bothered.

TWENTY-SIX

Helmsley

I HADN'T TOLD HER A SUBSTANTIAL THING about myself, not really. I considered this an insurance policy just in case things took a wrong turn. I was adept at reversing myself out of dead end relationships. Dad once said I was a quitter, like Mum. He knew how to hurt me. It wasn't said out of hatred, only fear, the fear of losing all three of his sons. I had fought against him for a while, refusing to visit, then one day, I turned up on his doorstep with a pack of beer. The walls of the sitting room were bare. He had removed the photographs and the one painting I had done of my brothers when they were last together. We watched the football on TV, sprawled on either end of the sofa, as if the two of us could comfortably share those kinds of moments. We hadn't, and we never would. But I kept turning up even though he had nothing to say to me.

Robyn has no skeletons in her cupboard. At least not the kind that gave you nightmares and flashbacks. But something troubled her in a different way. She had gone pale when I mentioned what had happened at the top of the tower. And then I had witnessed something equally odd at Rievaulx Abbey when I found her amongst the ruins looking like she'd had some kind of seizure. Given the state of her, she couldn't blame me for thinking that she was scared of something, and the tremble of her lips only added to my suspicions. Should she even be driving if she had fits? The car wasn't hers; it was a lease or something. Perhaps she had lied to get it?

My car was filthy, inside and out. I had to keep the canvas safely apart from the camping gear. Dried mud flakes covered everything from the water container to the boot liner. The painting stuff I stored on the back seat, but dust moved, especially after a few rainless days. Fresh water was a problem. I had two containers, one for drinking and washing, the other smaller one just for my brushes, to avoid contamination. Fortunately, spending a few summers in hot countries had prepared me for this heatwave. Perhaps Robyn struggled to cope with the oppressive, unnatural heat, and hence the dizzy spells.

Arriving at Helmsley Castle, I scanned the car park for her little red car; it wasn't there. She had to drive up from Thirsk, which wasn't an easy road – winding and steep, one of the steepest roads in the country. I considered waiting for her, but I had to press on. I packed my rucksack, then hooked my fingers around the easel like a claw crane, and walked briskly to the ticket kiosk. I had become efficient in what I carried; a beast of burden drawing on hidden sinews. Even so, the easel knocked painfully against my thigh, adding to the bruise already there.

The diffuse sunshine and gentle breeze were a welcome change of weather. The heat was there, but not sticky and humid, which was the benefit of being on the edge of the North Yorkshire Moors. I paid for my entrance ticket, another expense I had to cover until my final fee, and smiled and answered the usual questions about what I was going to paint, and why, and would I sell it, blah blah. I lied copiously. In fact, I made up a different story every time. I was an adept liar, a habit of my upbringing; it helped to be someone different and not have your identity known.

Today I told the ticket man that I had lived in Paris and studied at the Sorbonne.

'Really, I lived near there for a few years. Which street?'

My adeptness quickly fell apart. I mumbled something French like, and took the ticket out of his hand.

'Must get on,' I said, cocking my head at the ruins. 'Light and everything.' Most non-painters assumed light was critical, but a canvas wasn't film, and a brush didn't need light meters and filter lens to compose a picture. If necessary, I could artificially brighten a painting, or darken it. I had some imagination with which to play. But for this project, the criteria was to be as natural as possible, whatever the weather.

Having dumped my burden in a discreet location, I circled the castle a few times, following the curtain walls. I tried to take a leaf out of Robyn's book and embrace the history of the place rather than see shapes and patterns, the spaces between the walls. If I unintentionally picked latrine chutes again I was going to be ribbed no end by her. I smiled at the thought.

The ideal vantage point for making a choice should be on top of a tower. It wasn't going to happen; looking up and beyond to the skies and church beyond rather than down to foundations and ditches was fine with me. I had actually had Camilla add a clause in the contract that prohibited the necessity to climb to roof top level. Writing it down in her notebook, she had tut-tutted at the condition with a lop-sided smirk on her face; I regretted telling her why I was afraid of heights. We hadn't spoken much since. She could be a bitch sometimes.

Thinking about Camilla only added concern to the stream of inexplicable emotions that had begun the moment I had woken up in my tent. Best policy was to put my agent out of my mind. I fetched my gear and chose my spot. With everything set up, I picked up the finest pencil and touched the paper.

'Hello!'

I clutched my chest and nearly stabbed the pencil point in my neck.

'Jesus. You can't half creep up on somebody.' I turned to face her.

Robyn beamed from ear to ear. 'Revenge,' she said. 'You did it to me at Rievaulx.'

'I thought you were ill.'

She shrugged. 'Well, I wasn't.' She was determined not to talk about it.

There was another matter to discuss, one that she was bound to ask me. I decided I had to go for a pre-emptive strike.

'I haven't got hold of Camilla. Still no answer.'

If I had to describe the emotion on her face, the way it drained of warmth, I would paint it as fear.

I wished I'd kept my mouth shut.

TWENTY-SEVEN

MY **MOUTH OPENED** and shut like a guppy fish. What the heck was going on? Joseph spoke with the pretence of nonchalance, but his pensive expression said otherwise. Glancing away, he opted to examine his shoes. I felt utterly dejected. I had checked that morning before leaving Mrs McDougal's cluttered establishment and neither Medici nor David had replied to my emails, and now Joseph had had no contact with his agent either. It had to be the same person, and that control freak had silenced his agents, leaving the pair of us in the dark. But why?

I lowered the camera bag, its weight too much to bear on top of the hurt that gnawed away at me. How many possible ways could this project go wrong before I jacked it in? Joseph's hooded eyes dimmed further into the shadows. He carefully rested the pencil on the easel and moved toward me. I should have instinctively stepped back, but I didn't. The gap closed but he didn't touch me. I looked over my shoulder to the scene Joseph had picked. It was good, encompassing several features, and full of potential unlike my bizarre lists of architectural quirks.

'Robyn?' He spoke tentatively. 'Don't be angry with me.'

'I'm not.'

He retreated back to his easel, brushing something off the surface with an agitated flick of his finger.

'Sorry,' I said. 'I was hoping one of us would have answers.'

'No luck with your emails?'

I shook my head. 'We're on our own. Do I go on?'

He stiffened, ramrod straight. 'What?'

'Or go home.'

'Why? Surely this is only a temporary breakdown in communication? You said yourself he's on holiday.'

'But Camilla—'

'Is a self-centred bitch when she wants to be. She's probably cosying up to her next customer,' he said bitterly.

'So… we should just plough on?'

'Yes,' he said. 'If we'd not met, you would be here taking photos, not worrying, wouldn't you?'

He was right. His "so-what" attitude helped, especially as my anxieties were born out of meeting him. I licked my dry lips. If I wanted to be a professional, I had to acquire his calm, business-like approach. There was money in my accounts, and a car and camera in my possession. If David wanted them back, he would have to find me, and I wasn't going to make it easy for him. As for Medici, my hope that he might be some kind of informative mentor had trickled away. He was playing a game of hide and seek, and I was damned if I was going to jump to attention whenever he decided to pop his head out of the rabbit hole. I puffed out my cheeks and blew away the tightness in my chest with a lengthy exhale.

'I'll get started.' I crouched and unzipped the bag.

'What's on today's agenda?' Joseph's voice had lifted a tone or too.

'Odd things, as usual.' I rose and hung the camera strap around my neck. 'I like what you've chosen.'

His shoulders relaxed further, and an elastic smile spread into his cheeks. Somewhere underneath the stubble, there were two dimples forming. 'Good.' He seemed genuinely taken by my approval. 'No latrines?'

I laughed. 'No. You're okay. They're windows.'

Some narrow, some rounded with arches; there was a hotch-potch of everything on the East Tower. It was the lack of symmetry, the variety of structure that drew my attention deeper into the stonework. In contrast, I had the impression Joseph hunted for something that emanated outside the buildings, between them almost. Whatever the weather, and it had been excellent to date, he always overlaid an airy complexion to his paintings, as if he was a special effects artist, and the technique ensured the contrast of dark and light remained balanced and colourful. I focused my zoom lens on one spot to test it, then wandered off and left him drawing his pencil lines.

Helmsley Castle was a sprawling ruin with extensive earthworks and robbed out walls. Joseph had chosen a corner spot and settled into his task easily. I thumbed through Braithwaite's guide. He had dedicated two densely packed pages of enamoured information on Helmsley. Reading it again, I felt little inspiration; the passages lacked his usual hubris and whimsical insights.

Out of Joseph's sight, I dropped down onto a low wall. The list was scrunched somewhere in the bag and torn in two. I pieced the halves together and smoothed the sheet across my lap. There were four areas to photograph. Medici hadn't given me precise locations. There was a carved corbel and a jutting oak beam for starters, intricate design features, practical architectural stuff. I criss-crossed the bailey in my hunt for each one. The light was problematic due to thickened clouds. I made adjustments to the shutter speed until I thought I had the right balance of shades. The breeze ebbed, sending my fringe in all directions. In between shots, I occasionally glanced over to Joseph. When he looked across, he waved and I waved back. After my last sequence of photographs, I checked again and he was gone, having left his easel behind. I spotted him halfway to the Great Hall and hastily intercepted him.

'Taking a break while a layer dries,' he said, upon my approach. 'Time for my tour.'

'Oh.'

He grinned and purloined the camera bag. I didn't mind the intervention as my arms ached badly.

'We agreed. My education is wanting.'

Hardly true, but I buzzed with a burst of energy all the same.

'No little guidebook?' he asked.

'I'm getting tired of it.' We were outside the Great Hall which had been converted into a Tudor house with glazed windows and timber interior. I explained the beginnings of the castle.

'The same family behind Rievaulx,' he said.

'It's only a few miles away.'

I walked him around the expanse of earthworks including the square ditch surrounding the curtain walls. There was no central keep, only the rugged leftovers of looming towers. 'The East Tower was demolished during the English Civil War.'

The rubble still lay in the ditch. We stared in turn over the side, Joseph briefly leaning forward, then stopping. I held onto the wall, noting the rumbling beneath my feet, a vibration that massaged the soles.

'Bombardment destroyed the castle?' he asked.

'Too well defended.' I battled my senses. This wasn't a convenient moment.

Joseph, fortunately, had his back to me.

'There was a siege.' I closed my eyes. Why were my emotions so intense when I was near him? It was as if his presence alerted me to things my camera failed to see.

'I like the scale of the fortifications,' he said. 'Reminds me of Dunstanburgh. The same vastness but without the bleak coastline.'

A rotten taste laced my tongue. I heaved, nearly vomiting as if I had eaten something revolting. The reference to Dunstanburgh heightened everything I felt. The icy blast of wind carried with it the smell of burning flesh and I wished I couldn't hear the moans of the dying, like a horrible tinnitus. Again, the world of the past was too vivid, too close, and sadly unwanted.

'They starved to death,' I said, hoarsely.

'Who? Oh, you mean during the siege?'

The breeze dropped into nothing. I opened my eyes just in time to catch him pivoting to face me.

He grimaced while those sharp eyes of his narrowed into slits; he was studying me too closely. Before he spoke, he cleared his throat nervously. 'Poor sods. Not a nice way to go. Something to be said for a swift...' He blanched, even his lips were tinged with whiteness.

'What?' I was still hyper alert, a sponge waiting to soak up his feelings and feed off them.

He sighed. 'Nothing.'

I nearly asked, but the hesitation lasted too long. The moment was lost again for both of us.

The easel had gathered an audience and he hurried to protect it from overly eager prying.

'Best finish it,' he said over his shoulder.

Rather than shoo away the small crowd, he slipped past the semi-circle, said something that triggered smiles, and returned to his brushwork, quietly persevering while staying the centre of attention. The concentration on his face bloomed with each second and he hunched his shoulders over the easel, cocooning himself from intruders, practising his art without a hint of doubt at his abilities. Envy struck me hard. He was content, and certainly not bored.

Was I suffering the slow erosion of my long-held fascination with castles? The self-serving passion was perhaps doomed to failure when faced with reality and not imagination. My visions hadn't augmented my understanding of castles, instead the vivid daydreams unnerved me, and along with their vague origins and links to events I could not possibly have anticipated, they had negatively impacted my journey in a way I had not anticipated before I left. My dream of visiting every castle was curtailed to just these fifteen, and the limitation no longer felt disappointing. It was realistic. Satisfactory. Manageable.

In the distance, the small figure of Joseph, now alone again, standing over his easel sharpened into focus through my zoom lens. I snapped one indulgent shot of him on my personal camera. There was a man content in his work, confident of his skills and indifferent as to its execution. Whatever passions he embraced, he held them tight to his chest.

Jealousy bit again, for his freedom, his stoicism. I wanted to know what he felt, crack him open and rob out that hardened shell he wore so robustly. An unlikely prospect given we would soon go our separate ways.

My love affair with castles was drifting, rudderless and confused. My feelings for Joseph were equally unresolved.

❖

On the menu was another sizzling barbecue delight: burger in a bun, and while Joseph fussed over flipping the burgers on the disposable grill, I told him about my latest accommodation.

'It's just outside Pickering. I literally threw my stuff in the room and skedaddled to here. Oh, thanks for the map, it helped no end.'

Joseph had drawn the location of the campsite on a scrap of paper and without it I might not have found the place. I'd had enough trouble finding the B&B. Having arrived there, I had been greeted at the door by an elderly gentleman in a tartan dressing gown and matching slippers. He peered at the suitcase by my feet and yelled over his shoulder.

'Malcolm, there's somebody 'ere. She thinks she staying 'ere.' He frowned expressively. 'Are you his girlfriend?'

There was a large B&B sign above the door. I had pointed to it. 'I'm here—'

'God, I am so sorry.' The new arrival, a middle-aged man, had calmly deposited the old man to one side and, leaning forward, had whispered, 'He's got dementia. He keeps forgetting we're a B&B.'

The family introductions continued: a drowsy-looking wife, three children with chocolate smudges around their mouths, two dogs and a rabbit in a hutch. The youngest child, a freckle-faced ginger, had insisted on showing me the rabbit, which cautiously hid in a pile of straw. I had sneezed several times.

Joseph handed me a bun. 'And one granddad?'

I bit with gusto then licked the scalding juice from my finger before answering. 'Mm, tastes good… It was his house, according to his son, and when his mother died, they moved in to help him, and opened the B&B for extra money. It's a huge place with rooms in the attic for the kids. I felt a bit bad for running out the door. They seem like a nice family.'

We sat side-by-side on the picnic blanket in front of his tent. The site was surprisingly quiet.

'Popular with hikers,' Joseph said, noting my curiosity. 'The ones closer to Scarborough cater for families.'

The campsite was amongst the moorland shrubbery, fringed by thickets of heather and gorse, and heavy with flies. He swatted one away.

He shifted to sit cross-legged. 'Could do with rain. There's a hosepipe ban down south.'

The ground around our feet was cracked open and rock-hard underneath.

'Do you sleep on an airbed?' I asked.

He squirted ketchup on his burger. 'Oh yeah. I'm not one for scrimping on comforts.'

He still hadn't shown me the interior of the tent.

A lengthy pause was necessary as we ate and avoided dripping fat onto the blanket. The breeze, which had kept us cool at Helmsley had dropped to nothing, and even up on the moors, the humidity drenched the air as if it had rained. I thought back to the conversation with Dad and his demands that I took Wellington boots. A parasol would have been more appropriate.

'What's the smile for?' Joseph asked.

'Oh, just a memory.'

'A nice one?'

'Yeah. Dad.'

'Do you miss your family? Home?'

He offered me a box of tissues and I wiped my chin. 'I've tried not to think about them too often. I am twenty-five.'

Saying my age, I couldn't believe how quickly life had accelerated since leaving school. There had been a few years working in retail, plus weekend jobs. A legacy of hits and misses, including two weeks at a garden centre, which had been an undeniable disaster; what did I know about plants?

'Tell me.' He nudged my arm with his elbow.

So I told him my employment history, how I had gone from one job to another, never settling in or making lasting impressions on anyone. Craig had been one such failure, but I didn't mention him to Joseph.

'And now a hotel receptionist. Nothing to do with castles,' he said.

'No,' I said, scrunching the tissue into a ball.

'Sorry I can't offer you an ice-cream. I do have a tin of fruit. Or an apple?'

'An apple would be nice.' I accepted the Granny Smith and bit into it. More juice dribbled down my chin. If he wanted a portrait of genteel manners, it wasn't drawn on my face.

He handed me another tissue.

'What about you?' I asked.

'I'm good.'

He thought I meant the apple. Should I push him, play a game of quid pro quo? Truth or dare? He seemed content to lie on his back and examine the mottled sky with its luminous evening clouds and hints of red. Tomorrow promised to be another scorching day of sunshine.

Without warning, he jumped up. 'I know, coffee. You okay having coffee in the evening?'

I wasn't, it would keep me up all night. 'Sure.'

He boiled the tin kettle on the stove and shovelled a generous spoonful of granules into a mug. What with barking dogs, shrieking kids and an infusion of caffeine, I was doomed.

'You're smiling again,' he said, glancing over his shoulder.

'Am I?'

He sat opposite me this time. Face to face, I saw lines under his eyes that weren't related to age. He had caught the sun on his forehead and flecks of his hair were bleached. I touched my cheeks, wondering if they too were golden or tinged with sunburn.

'You get lost in thought. I noticed it at the castle.' He wore that uncomfortable pensive expression again.

'I have an overactive imagination.' The truth. I itched to say more, but he was leaning forward, approaching me for another reason.

'I envy you. I copy things, that's all.' He continued to shuffle closer. The angle of his chin rose, and he tilted his head to one side.

'I don't think so,' I said quietly. 'I think you're really talented. I wish I could have those paintings.'

A slight blush spread to the high bones of his cheeks. 'You have your photographs.'

'I have lots of photos. I don't have paintings.'

He shrugged. 'Whoever gets them will probably sell them.'

'They're a gift, I thought.' I licked my lips. He hadn't retreated; our noses were inches apart.

'I think we both know that we're working for somebody who plays games. So who knows?' He swiftly cupped my face with his delicate fingers and stopped me looking away. 'And who cares, eh? Just enjoy the… process.'

'Meaning?' There was a warmth to his hands that spread into my cheeks. I held my breath, praying that I didn't bottle.

'Us. The process of getting to know each other.'

There had been many kisses in my life. From the friendly peck on the cheek, where contact is barely established, to the embarrassing indulgence of the grandmother with wrinkly dry lips. Craig had typically smothered me with his mouth. Because of his shameless tonguing technique, I had thought he was fantastic kisser and assumed long snogs were therapeutic.

I had been so wrong.

Following the eternity of hovering, not knowing whether to touch or not, Joseph kissed me without applying awkward pressure. Rather he caressed with his lips, nudging my mouth open and embracing it with his own, and it generated a lovely warm feeling. The excitement caught me in the throat, a constriction of nervous pleasure.

It was delicious. The aroma of strong coffee drifted out of his mouth. I closed my eyes and was about to offer a soft moan of delight when he broke off. Staring at him, I couldn't fathom the need for quizzical eyebrows. Something had gone wrong. Embarrassed, I leaned away. Nothing between us seemed to happen right, as if we were icicles waiting to melt in the midst of a frozen tundra.

'I'm sorry,' he said. 'We're going too quick.'

For him or me? More frustrating vagueness and the mellow moment was ruined. I had done nothing to imply I was hasty. He had initiated the kiss.

'What's wrong?' I asked.

'Perhaps I'm just tired.' He looked anything but tired with his bright eyes.

I brushed aside my roaming fringe with a jittery hand. 'I should go. I'm sure they'll expect me back before it gets dark.'

He rose. 'Tomorrow? Eleven o'clock at Pickering Castle?'

'Yes, of course.' I slipped on my jacket. Everything had gone suddenly cold. We needed a breakthrough opportunity, so I threw one in his direction. 'After that, I'm going to take a breather, and spend some time relaxing. Since nobody seems to care where I am, I'm going to drag my heels.'

His slow nod was of the sympathetic kind and not in agreement. 'I've got to keep to my schedule. I've lessons to plan... Evening classes start up, too.' He wrung his hands into a knot and stopped there.

Go on Joseph, make it happen. I stared right into his eyes, forcing him to blink. 'Whitby? It was *your* suggestion.'

A nod of a different kind. 'Yes, you're right. What the hell. It's still early August. We'll go to Whitby.'

'Good, because I want to tell you something when we're there.' My heartbeats accelerated; had I just committed myself?

With his back to the dusky sky, a shadow framed his face, and he seemed to disappear into a tunnel of darkness. What I couldn't see, I heard in his voice.

'If it's important—'

'No, no. Nothing bad... I'm waiting for the right moment.'

He turned and the low sun lit up his face. 'I understand,' he said, with such feeling, almost relief.

Something had to happen and not while visiting Pickering Castle, which was just a ring of stone on a hill, but later. Perhaps the ruins of an abbey on a cliff would give us the motivation to finally tell each other what bound us to the same path.

We said goodbye. We didn't kiss again, neither did we hug; we'd not planted roots to a romantic relationship, only the hope of one.

By the morning, after a night of dreamless tossing and turning, I was on edge, and also optimistic. I tracked down my host. He was laying the dining room table.

'Could I use your computer to access my email account? I promise I'll be quick.' The question was met with a swift glance over the shoulder to the noisy kitchen where his wife was cooking breakfast.

'Well, you see, a friend of mine manages the website. We don't have a computer. My wife thinks the electromagnetic waves will kill us all. Please remember to keep your mobile switched off.' He blushed and hurried away.

Glancing out the bay window, the evidence of rebellion was suddenly obvious in the regimented rows of an organic vegetable garden, and in the next room, there was the ancient television that was probably never switched on and next door, in the kitchen where there was the gallery of crayon pictures pinned on the walls, extolling the importance of protecting the planet from lethal bombardments of the unknown kind. They were a lovely family, but the precautions were ridiculous.

I walked down the road until I was out of sight of the house, and then checked my mobile. Nothing from Yvette or David. In fact, I realised something more worrying. Mum and I hadn't texted each other in two days. I hadn't even noticed. If that proved anything, it was that I was focused on other things. Was that so bad?

TWENTY-EIGHT

Whitby

I OPTED TO STAY WITH THE COSY FAMILY in Pickering rather than move to the touristy bedlam of Scarborough. By ignoring their bizarre beliefs, I accepted the family were, in their own way, happy. They were wonderfully energetic with their noisy banter and homespun activities and the kids were polite with their curiosity. Only ever home-schooled, which was seemingly limited to the boundaries of their house, they spotted the equipment I had unpacked on the bed and asked questions. I showed them the difference between the digital and film camera until the mother heard the word computer, then she encouraged them to leave me alone. The grandfather shifted from lucid to confused in a twinkle of his grey eyes. He had plenty of random memories to tell, and was tolerated by his son and daughter-in-law with tired patience. Over breakfast he chuntered away merrily.

Pickering Castle came and went in a blink without any visionary incidents. Perhaps that was due to my levels of concentration, and fear that any strange behaviour on my part would be witnessed. How swiftly I had gone from uncaring to self-conscious with regard to my daydreaming. Joseph and I worked separately, but not independently. When I wasn't playing with my tilt lens, I ambled over to him and admired his progress. I wished I was Mary Poppins and could jump right into his wonderful landscapes.

Because Joseph thankfully hadn't embarrassed me by mentioning our abridged kiss, I had set my heart on revealing to him the real nature of my "seizures" at Whitby. At least if he backed off after that, I would know destiny had other plans for us.

Fate played a lot on my mind. I doubted the architects and builders of castles ever envisaged them lying in such ruins, so I had to be equally optimistic that Joseph was here for a long-lasting purpose. Whatever Medici had intended with his parallel projects, I had decided it was no longer going to be photography that motivated me to finish mine. I was too reluctant to test the waters to find out if Joseph felt the same way about his project.

❖

Having agreed he would drive to Whitby, he picked me up the next morning, an already cauldron hot day. The children, their names impressively old-fashioned – Mungo, Fred and Elsie – waved from the attic windows.

'They look like prisoners,' Joseph said scathingly, while reversing out of the drive.

'Oh, don't. They're really sweet and happy.' I waved back.

'Looks are deceiving,' he said, grimly.

I brushed aside the dark commentary, the hints to the even darker places in his mind. I decided if I came clean, then he had no excuse not to open up. But not during a car journey.

I navigated with a road map, but he didn't seem to need the instructions.

'I came a few years ago,' he said. 'On the way to Hadrian's wall, I took a detour.'

The reference to years left me wondering; I had no clue to his exact age. He could be anywhere between twenty-five and thirty-five.

The journey took half an hour, sufficiently long to engage in a meaningful conversation that didn't stray into uncomfortable topics. We compared, in a neutral fashion, the art of photography versus painting. By the time we reached the outskirts of Whitby town, we'd agreed that the crafts were different, but the outcome was the same; a picture that captured a moment in time whether it was the scene itself or the occasion when it was painted. We never mentioned the exact destination in Whitby, as he rightly assumed it would be the ruins of the monastic abbey on the cliff top. It certainly was my preference. The popular abbey was the famed windswept location of Bram Stoker's *Dracula*. However, with skies clear of foreboding cloud and the sun already creating swirling mirages on the road surface, we weren't visiting the misty set of a horror movie.

The abbey car park was heaving. We spent time finding a space. Joseph had left most of his painting stuff behind at the campsite. But my idea of taking a break didn't mean I wasn't going to use the camera. I had dispensed with the digital one, which was back at the bed and breakfast, and stuck to my faithful film one. I had stocked up on reels of film. Joseph carried the tripod, casually resting it against his shoulder; it was much lighter than his easel. I bought a guidebook. Joseph read the placards dotted around the site. Side by side, we walked from one end to the other, through the skeletal remains of the abbey church.

He circled a pillar. 'I like the way it's a cluster of mini columns glued together.'

I took a photograph.

'Do you have paper in that bottomless pit of a bag?' he asked.

I rummaged and found part of the Medici list, the first sheet, which I had already completed. The back of it was creased, but he didn't mind. From out of his back pocket he retrieved a stubby pencil. I offered him the guidebook and he rested the paper on it for support. While he sketched the pillar, I took snapshots of him. He didn't seem to mind. A few minutes later he showed me the result of his scribbling. The sketch used understated pencil strokes yet still managed to capture all the elements of shape with a hint of shade. The absence of sandstone colour didn't matter.

Moving on, he pointed out the Saxon grave markers, then the tracings in the stonework that masons had carved. I read aloud snippets from the guidebook. We continued to move together through the ruins. The previous day at Pickering Castle, we had been busy with our own tasks; mine prescribed by a tatty list, and although he had the freedom to choose he sought my approval, which touched me deeply, more than I might have anticipated. After I had finished photographing Pickering Castle I watched him painting. I had missed the sketch stage and the application of the background wash. He worked on texture with a finer brush and darker mixes of paint, and I had enjoyed the hypnotic process in reverent silence.

Visiting Whitby released us from the constraints of professional detachment. Now I could see no reason not to speak of other matters. However, the weather kept me procrastinating. The breeze, which felt like the oven door had been left open, dried my throat and I gave up reading aloud. Joseph crouched in the shade, and I joined him. The water bottle was nearly empty; the remaining liquid brackish and tepid. We rested, letting the sweat seep through our cotton t-shirts. I wasn't ashamed of the perspiration. I considered it an emblem of my stubbornness that such discomforts were tolerated. If, as Dad had predicted, it had rained for days on end, I would have grown accustomed to a different kind of wetness and considered that acceptable too.

Slightly sleepy, I drifted, allowing my imagination to roam freely.

A boom echoed. I started, and looked up at the blue skies, half expecting to see something fly through the air. But it wasn't coming from the sky. The blast was repeated, this time, I was sure, I heard it out at sea. I shivered, alarmed by the abrupt onset. The stone behind my back shook, as if an earthquake had struck. I pressed my palms onto the ground to anchor myself.

'What's wrong?' Joseph asked, leaning over me, concerned.

Cocking my head to one side, I listened. The explosive sound faded quickly until there were just the voices of people and the squawk of seagulls.

He handed me the water bottle and I pressed it to my lips.

'I get the impression you're an incorrigible daydreamer—'

I spluttered. 'You do?'

He pressed his palm against mine and held my hand. 'It's okay, you know. If you don't want to talk about it.'

'But I do.' I wove my fingers between his. 'I'm scared to tell you.'

The tension in his square jawline amplified. He spoke softly. 'Is it something you've done since you were a child?'

I blinked. Why had he said that? 'Yes, kind of. But more recently, they've become intense and frequent. I hear and see things in my mind that take me back in time.'

He pursed his lips, chewing them slightly. 'It's just at Rievaulx, you seemed, how can I put it, too far gone. Like out of it.'

'I guess it can look that way. But I'm not unconscious or having a seizure. I'm just elsewhere. How did you know?'

He released my hand. 'Oh, kids at school sometimes have that faraway look when they're bored.'

'I'm not bored,' I said adamantly. 'Quite the contrary. I'm connected, like a conduit, to other… people… places.' I ended limply, hearing the craziness of what I was saying.

He smiled. 'And you see stuff?'

'Yes.' I cringed. 'But no hallucinations, if that's what you're inferring.'

'No. Daydreams is what you said.' He inhaled and rested his back against the wall. His hair was damp with sweat. 'Is it happening everywhere?'

'Mostly at these kinds of places. Ruins especially.' Only the fragmented remains of the past; broken pieces and, I realised, broken people too, going by the recent ones.

'What did you see just then?'

He was paying attention, the artist at work, observing and reporting back. Instead of answering, I flicked through the guidebook and showed him a page. He read it.

'The bombardment of the abbey in the First World War.'

'Yes. I heard the explosion. I felt… I imagined vibrations in the walls. The sound came from out at sea, where the battleship was.'

He examined the text. 'Did you know this before—'

'Yes. I just read it. So it's just my imagination going wild a bit. Except…' I swallowed the lump in my parched throat.

'What?' He closed the booklet.

'At Rievaulx I saw a man carrying a load into the infirmary. It was dark and filthy, the air choked with soot. I couldn't work out what I was seeing. So, I bought a guidebook, like this one, and it turns out, after the Reformation, the abbey was used as an ironworks and the charcoal was stored in the undercroft.' I bit my lower lip.

Joseph stared at me blankly and said nothing. I was close to panicking; that the thing I feared – him walking off – was near at hand, but I continued talking, feeling compelled to tell him more.

'I'm saying I didn't know that stuff about the ironworks. And at Dunstanburgh, I had a vision of a cavern, and a knight, and I heard a horn blowing, and it turns out that was based on a myth. I didn't know that either.' The heat was almost unbearable, burning me, and yet I was trembling as if icy cold.

He slowly uncoiled himself, drawing straighter and embellishing his inquisitorial height. 'How did you find that out?'

I took a shaky breath. 'I asked Yvette, and she told me about a poem, Sir Guy the Seeker, and when I contacted Medici, I told him, and he knew the poem. He quoted it straight back in an email.' I dug into my bag and retrieved a small notebook where I wrote down the details of each photograph and other important things. I read the lines to Joseph in a brittle voice, spoken through parched lips.

"That horn to sound, or sword to draw,
Now, youth, your choice explain;
But that which you choose, beware how you lose,
For you never will find it again"

'So you see, I think he knows, somehow.'

Joseph stood above me, looking in the direction of the car park. That was it, he was going to abandon me in Whitby.

'Come on, daydreamer,' he said, and held out his hand. 'We'll go find a nice cup of tea and something to eat, and you can stop shaking like a leaf.'

'You don't think I'm crazy?' I allowed him to ease me up onto two wobbly legs.

His lips twitched with amusement. 'No. You've got a wonderful imagination. I'm jealous. I've tried to paint like that, and I can't. I can only recreate a version of what I see in front of me.'

I hesitated, letting myself feel the relief wash through me like a joyous wave. Joseph wasn't judging me; he was actually jealous of my over-active imagination. Months ago, the old lady at Ashby-de-la-Zouch had called it a gift, and I had taken to the idea. Then, as I'd travelled and experienced things that unnerved and confused me, I'd lost faith in her philosophy of pursuing my fantasies. Daydreaming myself into a catatonic state had become a nuisance and it had begun to destroy what I enjoyed. After all my angst, revealing my secret and unburdening myself, was it that easy for him to dismiss my ability as simply nothing more than an over-active imagination?

We moved out of the shadows into the bright sunshine. Dazzled, I slipped on my sunglasses.

'What about Medici?' I asked. 'Knowing the same obscure poem?'

'I don't know, Robyn. It could just be a coincidence. He's a history buff, isn't he? So he probably just knows these things off the top of his head.'

'Yeah,' I said, unconvinced.

Joseph led me out of the abbey grounds. I followed, my reckless nerves quickly calming. The deed was done. I had to wait now to see if he was going to reciprocate and reveal what he had kept secret.

TWENTY-NINE

I DIDN'T HAVE THE HEART TO TELL HER what I was thinking. I was too concerned about her mental wellbeing. It had obviously taken some courage for her to describe what was going on in her head. I wasn't into the supernatural or apparitions. There weren't any fantastical figments of the past projected into my mind, at least while I was awake. I was pretty good at holding my very real memories at bay.

I rationalised. I had to. I was under-prepared, and not sure what the appropriate response was for a fast developing, somewhat immature relationship, which was becoming like the kiss, so sweet and adolescent in its execution. What I felt towards her was urging me onward, evolving rapidly, and dependent on something more than chance or an interfering busybody who had thrown us together for no obvious purpose than his entertainment. Robyn had opened up to me, as I hoped, and now I was obliged to reply in kind. Like me, she was a natural observer, and had the potential to dig deeper behind my fractioning veneer and find my soul. I struggled to hide things from her, and the incident at Middleham had given her cause to suspect I was harbouring a secret.

Should I tell her? Did I have the courage? And when was the right moment? Thinking ahead to the next few days, the last three castles: York, Spofforth and Conisbrough, I had an inkling of how things might play out. She was yearning for a connection, and, oddly, I was too. I couldn't remember the last time I had felt so needy and aroused. But then what would happen? Was I prepared to take the risk? Yes, if she was. However, it probably didn't matter. What we had started would surely have to finish and become nothing more than a summer affair, the kind of tragic fling portrayed in a movie that left the audience with tears in their eyes.

Having hidden the camera under a blanket in the back of my car, we walked away from the abbey into town. An ice-cream perked her up and she was once again the confident Robyn who had confronted me only days ago and caught my attention so effectively. I much preferred this assertive version of Robyn. Thinking it through, she was right, there had to be something triggering her episodes, but it wasn't going to be anything like my baggage. Tomorrow, all being well, I would take her to Scarborough and the beach; no cameras, no ruins, nothing to distract her, and then I would know for sure that my suspicious were correct, and that she could control this thing that went on inside her head.

We walked along Whitby's steep streets, visited the harbour walls and paddled in the shallows of the sea. The afternoon was too hot. My clothes had stuck to my skin, and Robyn's face glowed amber. It felt like there was no escape, no means to build on what I was feeling inside, the ache of wanting her.

'Joseph,' she said, 'do you have air-conditioning in your car?'

'Yes. It only blasts cold air, nothing temperature controlled.' I followed her train of thought. 'If we moved it to somewhere under a tree, it would cool down super quick.'

'Mm.' She looked up at me, and her smile provoked an immediate decision. We were on the same wavelength.

'We can drive somewhere,' I said, as nonchalantly as possible. The moors would be a perfect location.

THIRTY

I HADN'T DONE ANYTHING like that in a long time. It probably showed, given how it had started. The silly adolescent spell of kissing on the back seat of his car in a remote lane somewhere on top of the moors had rejuvenated us. It was merely the prelude, the warm-up, because as the outside temperature started to drop, my body had warmed. I had no doubts that Joseph, given his roving hands, felt the same way. He quickly drove us back to the campsite.

I forgot about the conversation in the abbey. The way I had acted, all pathetically nervous and coy. The original issue that had brought us together, my mistaking him for Medici, then accusing him of stalking me, seemed irrelevant and overblown. The whole mystery of why we were together had lost its fascination because we had gone that one step further.

Many steps further.

Thankfully, the airbed was durable. And thank God, we managed to keep quiet when it mattered. And heavens, it was a relief that he found me attractive after that sticky hot day, because I'd had no time to return to my lodgings to freshen up. And blessed Jesus, they might shun computers and mobiles, but my unorthodox hosts had a landline and I had their number, so I called them, and told them I was visiting a friend, then hung up before they could ask awkward questions or overhear Joseph's suggestive whispers in my ear.

As for my feelings for Joseph, I had crashed through some invisible barrier and discovered an important thing about myself that I hadn't known. I had the capacity to love somebody without reproach.

He had apologised between energetic spells for the cramped conditions. The sleeping bag, unzipped and spread out like a duvet, barely covered us. It didn't matter, the muggy night trapped the lingering heat inside the tent. We added body warmth to it, and only in the middle of the night was I sufficiently cold to snuggle under his arm and spoon myself around his still form.

Then, in the darkness, he began to speak, without any prompting from me. And I listened, and immediately I felt guilty for having provoked him into thinking this unmasking was necessary. I had bartered my problems, and he had offered me back memories that were costly and more life changing than the things that troubled me.

❖

I woke early and extracted myself from his loose embrace. He purred softly, still deeply asleep. The necessities of life forced me to dress in yesterday's limp clothes and hurry over to the amenities block. Relieved of the discomfort, I returned and crept back into the tent. My phone lay next to my camera bag. I hadn't switched it on since the call to the B&B. To my surprise it had a strong signal, and there were messages, an abundance of them, all sent in the last couple of hours and from Mum. The last text told me all I needed to know.

Hospice called. She's slipping away fast. Please come and say goodbye. I really need you. Richard can't get back.

Beryl was Mum's best friend. She wasn't a blood relative; Beryl was Granny Izzy's step-sister, the offspring of another marriage, and younger than my late grandmother. But Mum didn't care to distinguish the 'step' part of sisterhood, which had been dropped years ago.

I cradled the phone to my chest and thought of poor Mum. Having lost her own mother to a long illness, now she had suffered the same fate a second time with somebody who had acted in a similar capacity. Beryl was fifteen years older than Mum and

191

consequently had been a substitute mother when Granny Izzy's mind truly failed.

I hadn't the same affinity for my surrogate great-aunt as my mother. In the last few years I had spent little time with Beryl, who had opinions on everything, and in my teen years I had not taken well to being told what to do – what teenager ever did? Having parents blow hot and cold over your decisions was tolerable, but a busybody aunt who claimed to fill the shoes of your beloved granny had not won me over. However, regardless of the strain between us, she had been part of my life far more than my own grandmother.

Joseph stirred. Soon he would wake and want to know why I had tears in my eyes, and why I would have to go home. From what he had told me in the middle of the night his family had been ripped apart, destroyed by one awful event, and the relationship with his father was held together by a single thin thread of loyalty. The callous way his mother had abandoned him as a small child only added to the hurt. He hadn't wept, or showed much emotion, other than bitterness and disgust at the fallout. Hounded was a word he used, but without explaining exactly what that meant.

'You were a child,' I had whispered in the darkness. 'Traumatised.' The enormity of what he had told me wouldn't sink in. I simply didn't want to imagine the grief of the other family involved, the bereaved mother's anger and the waste of such a young life.

'I failed to stop them. I told the police everything that had happened. My brothers blamed each other, but in doing so they kind of exonerated me.' It was the only point at which Joseph's voice had come close to breaking apart.

'Were you fostered afterwards?'

'Briefly, for a few weeks, but they couldn't find a reason to keep me there. I came home but... never did in my mind. Dad was supervised for a long time by social workers. It might have helped if things weren't already fucked up. Art was my escape. Dad eventually realised that; it's the only thing... the only means of escape I have left to me. The open spaces, you see, are what I crave. But from the ground up. I can't bear the fear, the idea of falling.'

Or failing?

What had nearly broken me was when he had rested his head on my breast, snuggling in for comfort and I had stroked his hair and wooed him to sleep like a dedicated wife.

Now, with birds chirping merrily, I was about to leave him at a crucial moment, and it would probably appear to him that I was running away. With the temperature inside the confined tent rapidly rising, he opened his drowsy eyes. They quickly sharpened when he saw I was dressed and holding my phone.

'What?' he asked, sitting bolt upright.

'I have to go.'

The lines on his forehead relaxed a fraction. 'I'll take you back to the bed and breakfast, of course, then—'

'No, I mean I have to go home, to Coalville. Just for a day or two, probably.' I dropped the phone inside the bag. 'Mum wants me. Auntie Beryl is in a hospice and, well, it's not good news. I should go and hold Mum's hand.'

He adopted a sympathetic expression and nodded gravely. 'I see. Then let's get you to the B&B and you can head off.' He threw off the sleeping bag and reached for his jeans.

'I'm sorry—'

'It's hardly your fault.'

'We can do Scarborough when I get back.'

He had one arm in a sleeve and stopped there. He peered over the top of the shirt. 'I'll be in York. There's no point me going to Scarborough alone.'

'But… You're going to carry on with the painting?'

He yanked the t-shirt over his chest. 'I have to. I need to think ahead to later in the month.'

'Oh.' I had no idea if I would be back tomorrow or the day after, however, it made sense for him to go to York. 'I can meet you there instead.'

He ran across the field to the amenities block leaving me to scavenge for water from a nearby standpipe. Gulping down a cupful, I tried not to think too much about what he had said last night or wonder if his haste to complete the paintings was a symptom of regret. We hadn't mentioned what I had told him at the abbey; my so-called "gift" now seemed insignificant compared to his troubled life.

In the car, I interrupted the unpleasant quietness with a nervous cough. 'We're okay, yeah? We're going to see each other again?'

He glanced in my direction. 'Yes, why not? Didn't we have good time last night?'

A good time sounded like something I might say about a trip out to the cinema. I had given him so much of me last night, and a "good time" wasn't what I had felt as he moved over me. Bloody brilliant was more like it.

I turned away and looked out the passenger window at the scenery flashing by. 'You'll wait for me at York?'

'Yes, I said would. You'll go straight there?'

'As soon as Mum has the support she needs. Beryl has a younger brother who lives in France, and I suspect he'll come over and help. Dad too.' Dad was good with practical stuff, but he wasn't the best person at dealing with emotional outbursts.

'That could be more than a day or two.' He overtook a tractor with little room to spare.

I winced, shrinking into the back of my seat. I battled nausea and gripped the overhead strap. 'I suppose. I can't really say until I'm there.'

'Look,' he said as the car approached our destination, 'I know you're taking your time with the photography and it's not as if you have to get back to a job—'

'True, but this is work—'

'A paid hobby really, isn't it? My commission is a job; it pays the rent.' He pulled up the handbrake.

Through the open car window I heard the three siblings hollering to each other somewhere in the garden. I struggled to loosen my seatbelt, fumbling with the catch in my haste.

'I see,' I said curtly. 'Then I can't possibly stand in the way of you and your job. I'll let Medici know we're parting company, shall I?'

'What the hell has he got to do with it?' Joseph opened his door and threw out his long legs.

I retrieved my camera bag from the boot and faced him. The silence between us stretched until I couldn't bear it.

'He means nothing, obviously, since he's given up on me too.' I grabbed the tripod out of Joseph's hand.

'And there lies your problem, Robyn,' he said, carelessly. 'You need to stay focused, get a handle on this *condition* of yours.'

'Condition? You mean like I'm psychologically damaged? That's rich coming from you, given your obvious need for counselling. You're still traumatised, blaming yourself, and now you won't commit to me either.'

He slammed the boot door shut. 'I just offered to meet you again.'

I opened my mouth, prepared to push back further, and I couldn't say the words. What happened last night was never in my mind going to be a one night stand, and I had to hope he felt the same. The children's voices were louder. We had little time to heal the rift.

'I do want to meet again,' I said. For the second time that morning, tears baited my eyes, but I refused to shed them.

He sighed, and with the hooded crook of his elbow shaded his eyes and the rest of his unfathomable features. 'I have to keep painting, keep the momentum. It's a fluid process for me. If I pause too long, I stopping seeing… what's there,' he ended, with an uncharacteristic stutter.

'I'm there, with you.' My lumpy throat restricted, painfully.

He nodded weakly. 'I know. So, look, I'll keep going. But don't worry.' He stepped forward, lowered his arm and touched my wrist with his hand. 'Hopefully, we'll see each other at York or the one after. I'll not rush, just plodding my way forward, like I have up to now, okay?' He faked a reasonably good smile before leaning forward to peck my cheek.

I smiled warily, equalling his lack of commitment. We were two peas in the same pod, afraid to commit to what might come next. Where would we end up - London, Coalville? How would we maintain a long distance romance so far apart? What would we do about my so-called condition and his ugly past? We had been dealt an awkward hand of possible outcomes, and I suspected Medici had shuffled the pack. Was my anonymous benefactor conniving with the devil or playing at God?

'We had a good time,' I repeated, slowly.

Joseph, pale-faced and suddenly gaunt, nodded again.

The sentiment of doubt left me cold and afraid to ask what he meant by the phrase we had both used. I knew that it wasn't enough for me.

PART FOUR

'Too much knowing is misery.'
Lorenzo de' Medici

THIRTY-ONE

Coalville

'TELL ME ABOUT HIM,' Yvette said.

I had crashed on her stylish sofa just after midnight, having left Mum asleep on our settee at home. She had cried herself into that state of fatigue. I had arrived home too late; Beryl passed away while I drove along the motorway.

Dad had rung the undertaker, sorted out the death certificate, and contacted Richard. He was immersed, as I suspected, in practical things, which meant I had to navigate Mum away from Beryl's bedside and keep her supplied with tissues. I had cried too. Death had left such a pale pallor on a well-remembered face, so much so, I hardly recognised my poor aunt with her chiselled cheeks and hollowed eye sockets.

Mum had insisted on going to Beryl's poky flat. There, sniffing loudly, she touched things, tidied the ironing away, and talked about her childhood as if it was yesterday. Beryl was woefully disorganised and what Mum wanted was bank accounts and her pension book. I had told her it could wait. But had Mum latched on to the need to search and wouldn't let go. I let her because it stopped her crying and gave her something to do. It was in the back of a drawer that she had found a bundle of tatty airmail envelopes covered in faded ink. The stamps were missing the queen's head. I had managed to wring the letters out of Mum's hands and told her that was enough; we would look at them tomorrow. I had dropped her off home before escaping to Yvette's house. I needed to air my grief away from Mum.

Yvette was sharp though. She deduced my sadness wasn't simply due to the predicted death of a great-aunt. We hadn't chatted since

Middleham, which was only four days ago, but it felt like a lifetime. I had revealed that Joseph was my mysterious stalker but little else. However, she had pieced enough together to know that we had progressed considerably since our last exchange of texts.

I clutched a suede cushion to my chest and rested my chin on it. 'I don't know if I'll see him again.'

'You can contact him, give him a call.' She read my face perfectly. 'Oh.'

I stared at my friend gloomily, feeling embarrassed by my failings. 'All I know is he's a teacher. Christ, why didn't I find out his surname or telephone number? What was I thinking?' The argument outside the bed and breakfast was so unfortunate, and pointless.

'Go on, what else?'

'Oh, he told me his mum had left when he was a little boy. He's not seen her in years.'

'That's tragic.'

'You would think so, but it gets worse.' I shuffled myself upright. I should feel exhausted after the drive, finding Mum distraught, Dad running on automatic mode, and myself, swamped with conflicting emotions, but I was beyond sleep and tanked up on frustrated energy.

'Worse?' Yvette frowned. 'You don't have to tell me.'

I blew out a stream of air through my pursed lips. 'He has issues. I noticed he's scared of heights. Turns out he gets flashbacks.'

'Flashbacks of what?' Yvette fetched her laptop.

'His brothers, Jake and Ben. Twins.'

I told her about the incident as Joseph called it; it certainly wasn't an accident, at least the killing part wasn't. There again, I only had the information Joseph had told me. Two young boys, their lives ruined by an act of stupidity born out of boredom. Joseph was firmly opposed to boredom. He kept himself occupied by juggling two, sometimes three jobs at the same time. I saw his motivations far more clearly curled up on Yvette's immaculate sofa than I had lying in his tent.

Yvette's face was perfectly still. 'Robyn, darling, you don't remember any of this?'

'What?'

'The reports in the national papers. On the news? Everything you told me fits with what I remember.' She opened the laptop and began typing.

I unfurled my arms and put the cushion to one side. I had cared little about life beyond Coalville, and my interest in the national news was minimal; I had stacked the newspapers in the rack at the hotel reception but rarely read them.

'But this happened years ago,' I said. 'I would have been the same age as the twins.'

'That doesn't stop the papers; they refer to it still, like some ghastly horror story.'

Hounded, Joseph had said, and he'd suffered the consequences for years. 'Do you know the brothers' surname?'

She nodded. 'You're not going to find it helpful. Have you never heard of the Smith Twins? The Tower Block Killers?' She turned the laptop screen toward me.

I gaped in horror at the headline. 'They were nine years old, Yvette. You make them sound like gangsters.'

'Not me, the papers did that. His name is what I'm trying to tell you. It has to be Joseph Smith. You'll struggle to find him: it's a hell of common name, I should think, especially in a big city.'

'He said he had suffered hell because of his brothers' actions. I just didn't think to ask him what surname he used.'

Yvette put the laptop to one side. 'Oh, darling, what will you do? You clearly feel something for him. You slept with him?'

If I had been in a jovial frame of mind, the cushion would have bounced off her head, instead, I clutched it tighter. 'Uh. That obvious?'

'My expertise is observing, looking beneath the gloss of an old masterpiece to the message behind it.'

I did manage a small smile. 'My sun-drenched face?'

'Your lips are sad, but there is desperation in your eyes. You have to find him.'

'I know. He said he'd wait for me. But I think I'll have to spend some time with Mum before I can go back.'

'Understandable.' She rubbed her eyes.

I wasn't ready for bed yet. Other intriguing things had come to light in the last few hours.

'We found some letters, old ones, in Beryl's house. They've got a foreign stamp on them.'

'Interesting perhaps. But you should go home. Try and get some sleep.'

I dragged myself up onto two heavy legs. Yvette gave me a swift hug. My head cleared in preparation for driving the short distance home.

'Oh,' I said, suddenly remembering a multitude of things. 'Did you track down David?'

'Ah. Well, you see, he's more than gone on holiday; he's spending time in Italy at a friend's house. He's living there for now.'

'Living?'

'According to one of his research students — I had more success with the students than staff — he's taken a lengthy sabbatical. Retired or holidaying, it doesn't seem to matter what, he's incommunicado with lots of people.'

I slumped against her shoulder. 'Those damn castles… do I keep photographing them? I've three left.'

'Far as I'm aware, he has fulfilled all of his existing obligations to the university and continues to mark dissertations and receive his post, so what you've sent is probably being forwarded. I say incommunicado, but it might be that he's being picky.'

And I wasn't on the right list, obviously. 'Medici is off the radar too.'

'Forget about him. Three castles, so close to the finish line, darling. Just bloody well do them and put this all behind you.'

All of this meant Joseph. I wasn't ready for that finality.

THIRTY-TWO

York

YORK WAS A DISASTER.

The day started well with washing clothes at a laundrette, followed by topping up on supplies, and posting the two paintings I'd finished. I added a note for Camilla – **was she aware of somebody else working on a similar project to me?**

She never answered her damn phone, and when I checked my email in an internet cafe, I discovered my inbox was full of junk mail and bureaucratic updates from the school, but nothing from her. Robyn was right about the lack of communication with our contacts. I regretted not taking her concerns more seriously. But it didn't end there. I regretted everything I'd said outside the bed and breakfast. A good "fucking" time, was what she had obviously heard. Why had I acted like a schoolboy? I wasn't afraid of falling in love, but clearly expressing my true feelings was now beyond me. I had learnt that lesson too well.

By referring to her "condition", what had I done to her confidence? I'd spoken to her as though I was some expert on maladaptive daydreaming. She hadn't a clue what I had been referring to, and why would she if she believed there was nothing wrong with her? I had only come across the disorder after researching it during my teacher training – the excessive need to fantasise was an excuse for not paying attention in lessons.

Waking up that morning in the tent, seeing her forlorn face, I had blithely demonstrated my selfish nature. She had been thinking about her family, and I had rushed her to make a decision about us, and now, sitting in the car park next to the Clifford Tower, I was regretting plenty.

She had a phone and I had brushed the hint aside. Why hadn't I asked her for her number or her home address? Even her surname would help me reach out to her. Well, I knew why I hadn't. She would have asked for mine, then once she had thrown that name at the internet, added some extra choice words, she would have found out the extent of the vilification, the persecution of my dad and me as we moved from one council house to another, and why I had hidden in the garage pretending it was my safe zone.

She had accused me of lacking commitment. I resented the accusation; I always did. However, it was exactly why I was alone. All Robyn had really found out about me was that a childhood prank, briefly referenced, was the reason why I was afraid of heights. I'd built such a successful barricade around myself, she would have to arm herself with a pickaxe to smash it. I wondered if she knew how close she had come to reaching me.

My bitterness had followed me to the city centre.

Painting Clifford Tower, the last remaining medieval edifice of York Castle, was challenging. The tower-topped mound was next to a museum and situated in the middle of a city car park. I tried to work from a park across the road, which at least added a church spire to the backdrop, but due to excessive prying by onlookers and my woeful lack of concentration, all I had managed was a sketch, then I'd given up. Robyn would have dashed here and there, energetically carefree, whereas my foul mood left me with one option. I bought a disposal camera, took photographs, and decided to paint the tower at a later date, probably in the comfort of my flat.

I had nothing else to do but sit in my car and wait for her.

THIRTY-THREE

Coalville

THE NEXT DAY I grew multiple arms and heads as I juggled tasks on behalf of my parents and myself. The funeral was likely to be in ten days. I calculated that still gave me time to finish off the last bits of photographs and be back for the service. While Mum wrote an obituary for the local newspaper and Dad tried to find a will in the hope of stemming arguments, I caught up on emails, laundered clothes, and reminisced with Mum.

Another disgruntled email to David bounced back with an out-of-office reply. I couldn't describe the hurt to my mother as she was dealing with something far more painful. The email I had sent to Medici wasn't even granted an automated reply. I worried he was either so ill that he wasn't capable of reviewing my photographs or had decided they were so bad they weren't worth the effort of a reply.

The negativity extended to my separation from Joseph. I tried to push him to the back of my mind, which left me fretting over who else I could trust. Yvette had no insights into why someone like David, an eminent professor, would associate himself with a trickster and pass him off as genuine.

A bad seed planted itself in my head, and grew – why should I finish off the project? I had enough money from the expenses to cover my credit card bill, and the new camera, and when the lease finished, the car could go back too. But my pride, my dignity, would suffer. I felt duty bound to deliver on my end of the bargain. And there was the castles, just fifteen, hardly my original of dozens. However, they were representative of my ambition, and if I couldn't manage fifteen, then what did that say about my resilience?

If Joseph hung around at York, even for just a couple of days, I might see him again. The idea fuelled itself; all I needed to do was stoke it with practicalities. Hope replaced disappointment.

The main problem was Mum had glued herself to me emotionally, and I shouldered the grief by her side, present-minded, and glum-faced. I kept her topped up with tea and biscuits while she rang this person and that, arranged flowers and donations to the hospice, debated over which wood to choose for the coffin and the hymns for the funeral.

'Mum,' I said, 'you've got plenty of time. Nobody is hassling you, and the crematorium isn't available until next week.'

She wiped her nose and inspected a well-thumbed address book.

'I had no idea she was this popular. Look at all these Drake cousins – I thought they hated Beryl.'

Beryl's past was something of a mystery to me, especially the relatives dotted around the country with loose connections to her. The likelihood of hawkers had motivated Dad to hunt for a will.

'She could be a difficult person,' I said.

Mum sighed. 'True. And stubborn. Do you remember…'

And so we continued chatting through that day and into the next, a stagnant Saturday. Rain was desperately needed. The garden was a mortuary of wilted rose bushes and honeysuckle.

The letters, tied up with frayed ribbon, which Mum had left on the dining room table in amongst other documents and photo albums, finally reached the surface the following morning at breakfast, two days after I had said an awkward goodbye to Joseph.

The blue paper was as thin as tissue, the writing in the faded ink of a fountain pen, not biro. I selected a random envelope and inspected the date stamp on the postmark.

'Mum, look at this. They're old.' I re-examined each one. None of them were addressed to Beryl.

She read over my shoulder. 'Isabel Drake.'

'Granny Izzy. That's her maiden name, isn't it?'

The writing was somewhat spidery and childish. The address, I didn't recognise, although I knew the village was close to Coalville. 'Do you know the house?'

'No. It would have been where your gran grew up. She married Colin, your grandpa, the year I was born, when she was eighteen.' Mum blushed crimson on Izzy's behalf.

I squinted at a stamp. 'Italian, perhaps.'

I sorted them by date stamp, which was hard, many were smudged. The first letter wasn't easy to read, most of it was in Italian and the handwriting was characterised by big loops. Many English words were often wrongly spelt. As I turned over the paper, what caught my eye was the name, Lora. An Italian friend? I checked the postage date.

'Nineteen fifty-two. How old was Granny back then?'

Mum calculated on her fingers. 'About eleven.'

'Sweet, she had a pen pal in Italy; the postal address is Potenza, Basilicata.'

Mum shrugged. 'Ever since she was little, she was obsessed with Italy.'

'Why?'

'Oh, obvious, her mother, your great-grandmother, Catherine. She lived out there before the war, when Mussolini came to power. Catherine was a political activist.'

'For or against?'

'Oh, against. She made posters, wrote propaganda and journal articles, according to my grandfather,' she said, ending on a bitter note.

'You mean Nigel.'

Nigel Drake was my great-grandfather. Remarkably, he was still alive, somewhere. Ancient and forgotten, he had abandoned his family because of the scandal of Izzy's shotgun marriage to Colin. The last we heard, having been widowed for the second time, he had settled in New Zealand.

'So, Izzy was writing letters to an Italian, da-dah.' But Mum didn't smile. Too soon, perhaps for a return of humour. She had the look of someone lost in the past, something I easily recognised. Granny Izzy liked to reminisce too, but she often couldn't tell the difference between fact and fiction.

Mum's train of thoughts was elsewhere. 'It got her in trouble... Catherine. She nearly ended up in prison, so she had to leave Italy. She was a talented artist. Then suddenly, she stopped painting, too.'

I flinched at the word painting. I hadn't known. Nana Catherine had died in an air raid in London not long after Isabel was born.

Mum spread the letters out. 'They're in Italian and English, a bit of a mix, some strange symbols, too, like hieroglyphics. Everyone thought she was joking when she said she could read Italian.'

'Izzy?'

A big sigh from Mum and I detected regret in the accompanying murmur. 'Apparently, she could.'

I picked up a letter and read it aloud. '*Dearest Isabel. I am in good health. Father has allowed me out to play. My leg braces hurt. But I must not take them off.* Lora's English is good.' I found the last letter, according to the postmark. 'Dated 1958. Granny Izzy would have met Grandpa by then.' An obvious conclusion because Mum was born in 1959.

'Your gran married so young.' The laughter died on her lips 'Nigel had lost Catherine and by then had married again.'

There were widows and widowers a plenty after the war, and two such people had met. Nigel, single father with young Isabel, married lonely mother of two, Carole. The two families merged under one name, Drake, and the union gifted Beryl and her brother a step-sister, Isabel. Years later, Colin had snatched Izzy from the cradle of this family, and there had been a notorious, somewhat acrimonious wedding. I couldn't remember much about my grandfather, Colin, other than he favoured beer and didn't like Nigel, hence the estrangement. He died a few years before Izzy passed away.

I was about to fold the letter away, when with a thump of my heart, something in the last paragraph sharpened my attention. 'Listen. *Does she suspect we are writing? We must be careful. If my father finds out, he will be angry. He says I must never mention Mama's name. My memories of her are long gone. Perhaps you could send me a picture, you must have photographs?* Whose mother is he talking about?'

Mum's lips pressed tighter together.

'Mum?'

'Rumours, just family gossip.' There were fresh tears in her eyes.

'What rumours?' I led her to the settee, and she sat, cradling the letter I had read in her hands.

'That Catherine had a lover in Italy before the war.'

'But you don't believe it?'

'Izzy, when she was in that psychiatric hospital, talked a lot. But you know we thought her memory wasn't reliable, all those silly things she said.'

I fetched another letter, and opened it. 'I wish we could read the Italian.' I screwed my eyes and deciphered a name. 'Beryl – look, that's definitely Beryl. Why would Lora know about Beryl?'

'Izzy must have told her about her step-sister. I mean, there's only three years between them...' She wiped an eye. 'And they were both teenagers at the time she was writing. When Izzy met Colin, Beryl was jealous of them; she had formed an attachment to your gran, and Izzy... well, she was suddenly married and pregnant, and not interested in her younger step-sister.'

'This Lora,' I said cautiously, 'do you think she's Catherine's daughter?'

Mum brushed the letter off her lap with a defiant gesture. 'Water under the bridge. This all happened years ago. I don't remember.'

I picked up the flimsy sheet and tucked it back in the envelope. The pain was too much for my mother. Dad wasn't likely to help either, and Richard was a vacuum when it came to family information. The untranslated text, and strange squiggles, might reveal the true nature of the relationship between Lora and Isabel.

Yvette spoke some Italian.

While Mum returned to funeral arrangements, I excused myself, gathered up the letters without her noticing, and left to visit my friend.

THIRTY-FOUR

York

FOR TWO DAYS I hung around the Clifford Tower, paying out for parking tickets, eating sandwiches and drinking black coffee, listening to the radio or experimenting with colours on my palette to fill the time.

The parking attendant probably thought I was some pervert. If he had asked me why I was there, I couldn't have explained my irrational need to know one way or the other if I had made the right call. Trusting somebody new in my life was tough. I had just a few friends, and even with them, I hadn't told them personal stuff, like my real name.

By the end of the day, Robyn hadn't appeared at York Castle. Perhaps she needed to stay longer in Coalville than she thought. But then, I might be totally wrong about her. I could be falling in love with a fake. But the little I knew about Robyn didn't match with that image of heartlessness. So wherever my feelings took me, hurt followed on swiftly, but this time the taut knot in my stomach wasn't due to anger or fear.

I turned the key in the ignition. Let her find me; the tactic had worked before. Next stop was Spofforth Castle; the penultimate ruin and hardly the best place to spend a lonely day.

THIRTY-FIVE

Coalville

YVETTE EXCITEDLY CLAPPED HER HANDS at the sight of the bundle of letters. 'A scandal, delicious. In the absence of pictures, what's better than letters? Art historians find them useful for provenance.'

We sorted them, and while I pottered in her kitchen rustling up coffee and a bowl of crisps, she tried to decipher the writing with the aid of a dictionary.

I walked back into the sitting room and nearly dropped the mugs. 'What?'

'Put those down and sit here.' She spoke firmly, but her face was flushed.

'You're scaring me.' The mugs rattled together; I was grateful for the coffee table.

'It's not the letters, per se. They're two kids writing to each other. They're secretive. I can't crack the code.'

'Code?'

She smoothed out one sheet on her knee. 'These symbols are unintelligible. The Italian is basic, school level, fortunately for me, and Isabel. Her pen pal writes of her family, and calls herself Lora, but in the first letter, when she introduces herself, she uses her full name.' She ran her finger under a line. '*My name is Loretta di Matteo.*'

Now I knew why she'd asked me to sit down. My eyes clouded over, the dizziness swept me back into the seat, and I crashed there. 'Loretta. Lora.'

'Yes.'

'Di Matteo.' I said, but thinking de' Medici at the same time.

'Yes.'

'L. D. M.'

'Are you okay?' she asked.

'Yes. I think.'

'You understand—'

'I do. Yes. And I thought she was a man. Why didn't David ever correct me? And an Italian too. Are we related? Mum brushed off the idea.' The blurriness cleared. I needed clarity of thought not emotional reactions. As for David's lies, I would have to wait for those answers when I finally contacted him.

Yvette squeezed my hand. 'She claims in this first letter to be your grandmother's half-sister. Born in 1937. She starts writing to Isabel in 1952, when she was fifteen. How she found out about Isabel isn't clear.'

'She found Izzy's address? There had to be a record of it somewhere, perhaps in papers Loretta's family kept. Maybe when Nigel married Catherine, she contacted Loretta's father. But would you want the father of your love child to know you were getting married?'

Yvette selected another letter from the pile. 'Isabel, unsurprisingly, didn't believe her at first, because Loretta writes again, pleading with Isabel while acknowledging the lack of evidence. She wrote a name: Catherine Maynard. Familiar?'

I nodded. 'My great-grandmother. After she married Nigel, she became Catherine Drake. She was in Italy before the war. The timings fit. I already suspected she was Loretta's mother, she has to be. And she abandoned her?'

Yvette skimmed through a few pages, and I waited, schooling my impatience as she looked a few words up in a dictionary.

'Neither family approved of the relationship and hushed it up,' she said eventually. 'Loretta is illegitimate – must have been a scandal back then.'

Another scandal in my family. We seemed to attract them. Was I about to manufacture one with Joseph? A hard lump formed in my throat.

'There are references to leg braces,' I said quietly.

'Yes, some kind of disability. Perhaps she was born premature. Maybe she couldn't travel?'

Medici wasn't able to take the photographs herself – David had told me this upfront. Numbness struck my mind dumb. I had to accept that the person responsible for Joseph and I meeting was connected to my family.

Yvette continued. 'Catherine returned to England, kicked out of Italy by the sounds of it, and Loretta's father, Giuliano, was married off to another woman.'

'Mum said Nana Catherine was involved in political activities against Mussolini. That would have made her unpopular there, but not here, so why not bring Loretta home to England?'

Yvette pulled a face. 'Imagine the disgrace of being a single woman fathering a child with a man from a country allied to the Nazis.'

'Oh God. I see.' Loretta, though, had been an optimist. 'They kept writing. She hoped to meet Izzy one day.'

A smile washed over Yvette's frown. 'It's rather lovely, I think. Ignoring the grown-ups, they became good friends, well, on paper. I think these strange little symbols are some secret code. Without seeing what your gran wrote back in reply, it's hard to decipher. I think Loretta made it up, not your Gran. They couldn't risk being found out.'

'Why? Catherine was long dead by then.' I paused to think. 'Do you think Nigel, Izzy's dad, knew about the secret daughter, because if he loved Catherine, surely he would've helped her trace Loretta? But… I don't suppose they had much time together after they married; they had Isabel, the war came along, and Nana Catherine died in the air raid. What if Colin found out about Loretta after he married Izzy and she wasn't allowed to write – the letters stopped about that time. She was barely an adult when she married Grandpa and husbands back then…' A bitter taste formed on my tongue. I would give my dad a big hug the next time I saw him; I was sure he would have helped find a love child and even adopted it as his own.

'I think,' said Yvette carefully, 'Loretta, Lora, knows she has family somewhere near Coalville. But the trail had gone cold: Isabel moved house to be with her husband, and changed her name, then your mum also married, and her name changed too. It must have been impossible to trace the family without marriage certificates. Loretta must have asked David to find somebody local to the area to photograph castles, and she wanted, perhaps hoped to find you, or some relative.'

I shook my head. 'Nah, it's just too ridiculous. Why a photographer, why castles?' I stopped there because though the link was tenuous, it existed in my lineage: Catherine had been an artist, a painter and journalist. But how had Loretta known I existed and followed in Catherine's footsteps? Medici's emails now seemed more relevant than ever to my unanswered questions, especially their references to "seeking". Was that supposed to be me? Seeking out what though? What else had I missed in those brief messages?

There was a long pause; Yvette continued to read more of the letters, working her way forward in time. 'Oh, according to the last one, it looks like some of Isabel's letters have been sent back unopened. And they both agree Beryl is behind it.' With Izzy married off, Beryl had cozied up to my mother as an alternative, and she never married or had kids of her own.

'Beryl thought Gran was mad, and it would suit her to have everyone believe it. Let's suppose, given she was only fifteen when Izzy married, perhaps out of jealous spite, she uncovered this secret half-sister and hoped it might put Colin off marrying Izzy…'

'Go on, why are you smiling?' Yvette nudged my arm.

I laughed half-heartedly. 'Isabel deliberately got pregnant so she had to marry Colin. Beryl was side-lined completely.'

'Granny Izzy wasn't really crazy back then, was she?'

I lowered my eyes, realising how Beryl had twisted the past to suit her agenda – stealing Mum's affection away from Isabel. 'I know the family teased Granny Izzy and it seems we were all wrong. I wish I knew more about Catherine too, why she left her daughter behind in Italy. That's the thing… the…'

A heavy weight landed in my stomach as the ping of the lightbulb moment sent my mind into overdrive. Why had I not seen the big picture until now?

Yvette poked me again. 'Robyn?'

'David is in Italy. I have a secret great-aunt in Italy who is called Loretta, who likes history, castles especially, and—'

'Joseph—'

'Stayed in Italy, somewhere.' I snatched up a letter; Lora's address – was it still valid all these years later? 'But why would Medici... Lora go to such lengths to find me but keep her identity secret?'

Yvette rolled her eyes. 'Got me there. Do you think Joseph is in on it?'

I studied the handwriting, the odd words of childish affection, the hope that they "might meet one day". I read through the smattering of English, and couldn't imagine Joseph knowing this story and acting the way he had with me without revealing a hint of foreknowledge. He was mired in his own past; somebody else's would be meaningless.

'Joseph needs to know, though. If he has met Lora in Italy, then that's the connection between us, and something might have happened out there that explains why Loretta di Matteo plotted for us to meet.'

'Where are you going?'

I draped my jacket over my arm. 'Back to York. He's got a head start.'

The letters disappeared into my handbag. 'I'll send Medici... Loretta the last photographs, and add a picture of me and Joseph together, see what she has to say to that. Just because she might be my long-lost great-aunt, she doesn't get to play God without a bloody good reason.' I paused to collect the letters. 'Can I borrow your Italian dictionary?'

THIRTY-SIX

Spofforth

ON THE ROAD TO SPOFFORTH CASTLE, I allowed myself to recall the words of wisdom spoken not by my father, or any of my kinder friends, but the one woman who had told me that I had what it took to be an artist and to keep faith that there was such a thing as good fortune. I wished I was back in Italy, sketching in the converted barn, taking Tony's mother for a spin in her wheelchair. I missed Tony and his little family with all my heart.

I smudged paint, blotched and splattered it over the canvas in an uncharacteristic display of modernism. The portrait of the Spofforth was that of dereliction and emptiness, the space vast and now meaningless. I hadn't filled it and I knew I never would or could fill that void on my own.

I tried to stretch every second, to give Robyn time to find me. Had she left Coalville? If her mother needed her, she might not be able to escape a second time, and if she decided not to finish the project, would she come at all? What if she gave up on the idea we were fated to meet and turned her back on our scheming patron. My attitude hadn't helped. I had insulted and cheapened her, called her an amateur when I was little better. And what if she didn't care enough to even try to find me? One amorous night under the skies, passionate and kindly in its simplicity, wasn't sufficient to kindle a lifetime of love. I knew deep down it took more than that.

The "what ifs" stacked up.

As I mixed a dull grey colour I saw him again, the old man, accompanied by a black Labrador, aimlessly walking the grounds, occasionally glancing up. Dressed in an overcoat, as if it was

December, he crossed and recrossed my perspective, and I nearly added him to the painting in the form of a ghostly shadow.

I wondered what he thought was there, because his craggy face sometimes had that same expression I had seen on Robyn's. The old gent had discovered something transcendent to admire, something I couldn't see. Robyn wasn't the only person in the world to have ever fallen in love with a particular place and time. Had I hurried to label her visions as a psychological disturbance when in fact she had harmlessly used her imagination to make such ruins as this exciting to visit?

I tossed the brush on the ground in a fit of pique. If I had any hope left in me, I had to take action and not mope. My "fly by the seat of my pants" style of life wasn't going to work this time. I had to devise some plan of action. I made a quick decision. I would leave a message for her at the ticket booth and keep my fingers crossed she would get it, and then choose to contact me.

Bending over to pick up the brush, my back aching from the soft hotel mattress, I cursed. There was nothing and nobody, except the wandering man, at Spofforth Castle, not even a damn toilet to piss in. I would have to venture on to Conisbrough Castle and try there instead.

THIRTY-SEVEN

York

YORK WITH ITS IMPRESSIVE MINSTER, narrow Shambles, museums and tower on a hill, should have satisfied my desires beyond measure. But it wasn't going to be; I was already disappointed. I weaved the car through the perils of unfamiliar roads, dodged the lazy pedestrians, and focused on the location of the Clifford Tower, the site of sieges, rebellions and mass deaths, and where I knew Joseph had been, but wasn't any more.

I had arrived in York too late. No amount of delaying could justify him waiting when his clock told him to keep to schedule. Time ticked, silently and relentlessly, punishing me, too. I had less than half an hour before closing time, and had only made it to York from Coalville by flooring the Corsa's accelerator and driving somewhat recklessly. The car would never forgive me; but it wasn't mine.

I flew around the innards of that bombed out Tower, the last remnants of a giant castle keep, with a vigour that was nothing to do with energy. I was desperate to finish my side of the bargain. Bamburgh and Alnwick were a lifetime away. Those leisurely days of submersion, allowing myself to drift and see deeper to another time, seemed as distant as the miles between Joseph and me. I left Braithwaite's book in the car, unopened.

The inside of the tower resembled an oversized dovecote. Pigeons cooed, perched on the shelves of fireplaces and embrasures, or what was left of them. The last visitors of the day thinned out as I released the camera shutter, meticulously zooming in on tiny architectural details.

The person responsible for my haste was Loretta di Matteo, Medici that was, and I wondered if she had thought that by now I had either thrown in the towel and given up on the project or expected me to have discovered who she was, and why I was here, yet still doing her bidding. I had managed half of the enigma, the who, but not the why. Lassitude and a lack of inspiration afflicted me. My own camera was filmless. What brought me to York was especially apparent when I climbed to the top of the tower and looked across at the city. Joseph would have stayed in the car park, attempting to build a picture from down there, perhaps afraid to pan out and go beyond the panorama, preferring to keep himself in the here and now of life. I had the advantage over him in many ways. With my bird's eye view, I saw what was in front of me – a path to another life. I sensed nothing else, only this one man.

I was the last person to exit the turnstile. However, with the sun dipping behind the tops of the buildings, there was no point dashing to Spofforth. I resigned myself to a run of the mill city hotel and a fretful night of impatience.

❖

Under the chilled waft of the room's air conditioner, I laid out the letters and armed myself with the dictionary. Having allowed infatuation to influence my emotions, the thought of hating those passionate hours I had spent with Joseph was too much to bear. Logic told me not to dwell on Joseph, a man I had only met two weeks ago, and instead, dig deeper into my family's history.

Yvette had concentrated on the first few letters, which were mostly in Italian, and the last, and there were a couple of dozen between those ones that she had barely touched. Dated in the mid-fifties, and always from the same address in southern Italy, I began to piece together the life of my patron, my great-aunt. After Isabel's initial wariness, she had embraced her secret sister. The mutual affection was obvious. I discovered Italian words for many terms of endearment befitting to their relationship. The letters were also insightful. There was plenty of unenviable parental control, and the influences and obligations of an Italian society still marred by war and oppression. Loretta described poverty and the migration of people from her native south to the north. As a teenager approaching adulthood, she desired to join the wave, but couldn't. The reason why was increasingly apparent in each letter.

As they taught each other to read and write a foreign language – I could guess from Loretta's comments that Isabel was not a quick learner compared to herself – Loretta alluded to her physical disability. She acknowledged she suffered with spasticity, and that movement was difficult to control. She struggled with speaking, often stammering, and understandably shunned lengthy conversations.

I prefer the pen and paper. But I cannot write neatly.

The spasms explained why her handwriting remained childish into adulthood, the speech impairment was why she used emails to contact me. As I delved deeper, I read how two young people lost interest in rock music and Hollywood movies, and wrote of their aspirations. Izzy wanted to travel, and yet, she had married at eighteen, which rather threw cold water on my idea she had deliberately got herself pregnant. I suspected it might have been the other way round, and the marriage was imposed by Nigel; he had rescued one unmarried mother, and a war-widow, and probably felt honour bound to put his daughter on the right path. Colin, perhaps, having not expected it, resented Nigel, forcing his father-in-law into exile.

As for my great-aunt, her wish was buried in one passage – to follow in her mother's footsteps. Fortunately, the sentences were in English

Thank you for sending me the obituary. I did not know she won an award for photojournalism or that she lost her life photographing the Blitz. A brave woman. We should both be proud of her. It is sad we do not remember her.

I blinked back tears. My great-grandmother had been a photographer, too. And now I knew why she had died in a bombing raid.

I cannot take pictures or paint. My hands shake too much.

An abrupt hiccough of grief hit me then; in that one sentence she had unknowingly explained so much to me. Loretta had commissioned me to do what she could not, and even though I was still none the wiser as to the purpose of the photographs, she had wanted to do them herself, and that was evident in the stringent details, from the vanishing points she had dictated to the angles of the shot. A photographer at heart, it seemed.

I blew my nose on a tissue and resumed my deciphering, caring little that it was long past midnight.

What Isabel had written was something of a mystery. I only had Loretta's replies to questions and her perspective of my grandmother. Over the years, the use of symbols and codes had increased to the point I suspected they were fundamental to their communication. Had they plotted to meet up? Was Isabel on the verge of running away to Italy, just as she claimed later in her life? Whatever was missing from the letters, she hadn't anticipated Colin marrying her. Right up to 1958, there was barely any mention of him by Loretta, just a cursory reference to the man Isabel had met and had thought funny and good company. Loretta had warned her to be careful.

How could I, a twenty-first century woman with different values and upbringing, criticise Izzy's father for pushing through with the ill-fated marriage? My mother's life was born from that marriage. I sighed, and it turned into a yawn. I was surrendering to sleep when I spotted a familiar word in among the Italian phrases: Ashby. My grandmother had visited Ashby-de-la-Zouch Castle several times.

There followed a feverish few minutes of thumbing back and forth through the dictionary, piecing together odd words, until I framed a rough translation of what Loretta had written.

You think you see other places, like Italy? I think I can too. Or I listen to them in my mind. When I am still, I travel because my body cannot. What I see are the fantasies of a paralysed young woman. I will try harder. If you can, maybe I can.

The wafer-thin sheet of paper floated on cooled air before resting on the worn carpet. My eyes blurred and one solitary tear escaped. Isabel hadn't been crazy, and neither was I. Whatever condition Joseph had conjured up in his mind to explain what I saw and felt, it wasn't unique to me. And if it ran in the family, surely it was a gift to embrace, not run away from in fear? But how could Loretta have known I had it? We'd had no contact before David had introduced us. Nothing in the letters shed light on her motives.

I faced a dilemma in the morning. Did I push on and catch up with Joseph, a man who had in a short space of time captured an essence of my heart, or go hunting in York for an internet point and email Loretta, tell her I had read the letters, that I believed I knew who she was, and ask her bluntly: had she gone looking for me, or was it pure chance that she had found her great-niece? And why, oh why, had I been put on a collision course with Joseph?

THIRTY-EIGHT

Spofforth

THERE WAS NOTHING AT SPOFFORTH, not even a toilet, but at least the castle grounds were open all day, allowing me to arrive half an hour after an early breakfast in York.

Banks of cloud drifted across the sky, shielding me from the relentless heat of the sun. The t-shirt formed a second skin, plastered onto me by the weight of humidity. Such a summer as this was unprecedented. The Yorkshire Moors were turning into bonfires, filling the sky with plumes of smoke.

Light picked out the reddish colour of the stonework, the unique randomness of the blocks, the patterns of wear and weathering. As I climbed up a stair turret, I ran my hands along the cool stone and felt each ridge. It helped calm my nerves before I reached a level where I could photograph the great hall from above; Loretta continued to require the unusual, macabre vistas and angles, the bespoke images and minutiae that would only fascinate a keen architect.

Why was this particular castle on her list? Less castle, more hollowed out manor house, it held no fascination for me. With a gentle breeze on my back, the only respite from the heat, I leaned forward and held my breath. Waiting, and… there was perhaps a wisp, a brush against my bare arm, a weird sensation of something floating close by, but looking behind me, there were only tiny flies hovering above the cool stone slabs.

Perhaps there was nothing here for me to conjure up or imagine. My reaction to its absence was ambivalent: horrified one moment, relieved the next. Maybe my reticence since Whitby had more to do with my change of plans, or something else had fundamentally changed me; it felt as though I was waiting for the right occasion and lonely Spofforth wasn't substantive enough to engage me and, consequently, I was holding back from finding out what I needed to know. Seeking Joseph was more important to me than indulging in imaginary medieval dreamscapes. Maybe his absence was affecting me more than I realised, and without him, I lacked the emotional triggers to drift away.

Back below, on the ground level, the camera resting on the flat of my palm, I peered through the viewfinder.

'I'm not alone then.' The deep voice came from behind me, and I nearly jumped out of my sweaty top with surprise. He walked around to face me.

I was in the company of an elderly man with a gnarled walking stick, slate overcoat and a traditional flap cap. He was dressed as though it was the middle of winter and not a shimmer of perspiration on his brow.

'Sorry?' I said, politely.

He smiled a near toothless grin and his wrinkled skin looked as if it might shatter with the effort. 'I don't like walking about here on my own. Good to 'ave thee company.'

A local man. In the distance, a black Labrador was barking frantically. 'Here! Robbie, get here!'

The dog bounded over to him at such a pace I was convinced the excited animal would send his master toppling. Instead, the dog skidded to a halt by his feet and licked the man's boots.

'Why don't you like being here on your own?' I asked.

'She fell.' He pointed to the walls with his stick. 'From there parts.'

'Who?'

'Lord knows,' he said. 'Just half of her. She be blue.'

'Blue,' I repeated.

'Thee ghost.' He nodded.

'Ghost?' I examined the height of the wall. 'What did you mean by half of her?'

'That's what she looks like. Half a body. Just her upper half,' he explained. 'Blue, she is, jumping to her death from on high to ground. Terrible, falling like that.'

'You've seen her?'

'Nobody has for nearly three decades.'

'Oh,' I said, disappointed, and raised my camera to my eye.

'Except me,' he said proudly. 'This 'ere is where I wait for her. I close my eyes, and she jumps.'

I nearly dropped the camera, tongue-tied, and very aware of what he was referring to. Was it truly gone, this gift Loretta alluded to, which had condemned Izzy to some false diagnosis of madness and, if I hadn't lost it, was this going to be me in years to come – senile and unchaperoned, lurking at the bottom of a wall, waiting for an endless loop of fate, played out for my satisfaction and nobody else? Izzy, me and a few others, had this condition – or whatever Joseph might call it – and since I had allowed it to control my aspirations for too long, it was beginning to feel like a curse again.

He tapped his walking stick on a stone. 'Can't seem to stop her,' he said, frowning. 'I don't like coming here on my own, even with Robbie.'

'I can understand.' My throat was dry.

The old man broke into a beaming smile. 'She might land on me.' He patted his leg. 'Come on, boy.'

He wandered off chortling, the dog bouncing by his heels.

I tried to not to believe him, but as I continued to explore the ruin, a coldness descended. I had been unperturbed by my surroundings until his description of a blue ghost, now it felt as if icy blueness had crept into my bones and frozen them solid. It struck me how terrifying loneliness could be. Throughout my summer trip, I had, with only a few exceptions, discovered little about what drew people to visit castles. Instead, I had shared my time with myths and ghosts, battles and death, and even the nicest people I had met I had kept at a distance while I sought excuses to avoid speaking of my assignment, as if embarrassed by its objectives.

I missed my friends at the Hare and Hounds pub. Even my shifts behind the reception desk had provided more conversations than the last few weeks, and what company I had accepted during my stays at the bed and breakfasts wasn't for my benefit. I had tolerated my hosts, even the eccentric ones, but I'd learnt little from them given my limited experiences of life beyond Coalville. The truth sank in. I had abandoned a good job to take photographs in the vain hope of capturing my perfect castle, when what I actually needed to do was carve out a proper career, like my great-grandmother, who had achieved so much in a short lifetime.

I wasn't crying on the outside, but inside I was heartbroken. For a brief while, I dreamed of a different future, one that might merge with Joseph's – assuming I had judged him right. My last chance for taking this different path remained Conisbrough Castle.

Would he wait for me? Then it dawned on me why he might not. In my selfishness and relentless focus on daydreams, the successful twinning of Medici and Loretta, I had failed to appreciate his own fears and doubts. He might not wait if he thought himself not worthy.

THIRTY-NINE

Conisbrough

I CARRIED THE EASEL, hating the damn thing. The paintbox rattled, a reminder of better times.

Whenever somebody walked in front of me, interrupting my view, I wished it was Robyn. But nobody crept up on me. The castle was the easiest to transform into a painting: rounded hillock, ditches, circular wall and preserved keep. Robyn would love the white stone keep with its angled walls and vaulted ceiling. Which lords and ladies had sat beneath those carvings, feasting on their hunts? I bet that her Medici would get her to photograph it. I started to see what appealed to Robyn; or maybe I wanted the location to be a perfect romantic setting for a reunion.

After I finished painting, I wrote a message on a notepad and tore it off. The woman in the ticket kiosk had taken convincing; I had given her a believable sob story. My phone was broken and my friend was due the next day. Or perhaps the day after that. Could she pass this on to her? I folded the sheet and wrote *Robyn (photographer)* on it with a pencil.

The lady, austere and unamused, fanned herself with a guidebook. 'Storm coming,' she said, frowning.

'Will you keep an eye out for her?' I held out the note. 'She'll have a permit for photography. A big camera bag. Short hair.' I touched my neck.

'Can't promise; lots of visitors on these hot days.' She rifled through a drawer behind the counter. 'I'll put it here for safe keeping.' She dropped it inside and slammed the drawer shut.

I had delayed and wasted as much time as possible, but nothing could alter the fact that we were so out of sync it was unlikely

Robyn would catch up with me, assuming she ever intended to. I guessed not. Fate had played its hand; I had scared her off, and who could blame her. I had too much history and faking a different name had never wiped the slate clean. Eventually, somebody had the knack of piecing fragments together, and the ones that were especially hawkish always seemed to know the details as if it had happened yesterday and not fifteen years ago.

'You're one of the Smith brothers, aren't you?'
'Those evil boys, Christ, how do you sleep at night?'
'What was it like growing up with them?'
'Were you there when they did it? When they killed that baby?'

So yeah, I could see why Robyn hadn't appeared.

FORTY

Spofforth

I **HAD NEARLY MADE IT TO THE CAR** when I had an idea. I dumped the weighty bag in the boot, locked it and ran back to the castle. By the time I found the old gent, I was dripping with perspiration.

I leaned over, resting on my hands on my knees.

'Are you quite well?' he asked, pulling the dog on its lead.

I rose and steadied myself. 'You haven't seen a man with an easel, painting here?' I was panting so much I could barely talk.

He pondered, drawing his grey lips into a crumpled pout.

Oh my God, what was I thinking? This was a man who thought ghosts jumped on him. 'It's okay. Forget it.' I hung my head.

'Scruffy. Could do with a shave if you asked me. Don't like these young chaps with their whiskers.'

I clapped my hands together into a prayer position. 'When?'

Please make it today.

'Yesterday, I think. Not today. Quieter today. Too hot, I think.' The buttons on his heavy coat rose up to his chin.

Which meant Joseph was at Conisbrough. 'Thank you,' I yelled, running in the opposite direction.

It took an hour and a half to drive to Conisbrough due to an accident on the motorway. I fumed, fretted, and cried in frustration. Time ticked, always moving on, taking me with it, kicking and screaming in its wake. So much of my life I wanted to go backwards, to the past, now I merely wanted to stay here, in the present, where the action was actually happening.

I couldn't see his car below the castle, but he might have walked from the village. I was willing myself to believe anything.

In the ticket kiosk, I waved my membership card. 'Have you seen an artist painting today? Scruffy guy with stubble?' If a description worked, use it.

Slowly, a pair of eyes, hidden behind bottle top glasses, focused on my face, followed by a leisurely scratch of the nose. 'Sorry, not seen anyone like that today.' The man behind the counter continued sticking price tags on pencil sharpeners.

'Are you sure?' Had Joseph decided to skip a day and come back tomorrow?

'Well, now.' He paused. 'It's possible. I only work afternoons.'

'Was anyone here earlier, somebody else on duty?'

'Margaret.' He adjusted his spectacles. 'She's gone home.'

I nearly slithered onto the floor in tortured agony.

'I've only been on the desk an hour. I suppose if he came earlier, he might be somewhere—'

I bolted out of the little shop and charged up the earthworks into the open space of the inner bailey. If he was here, then this is where I would find him, painting the limestone keep against a backdrop of trees and sky. But there was no sign of him anywhere.

I couldn't blame him for not waiting and it didn't matter what I thought of the relationship if he wasn't feeling the same way as me. I had scared him off with my silly tales of visions. That night, he had simply comforted me, and I had reciprocated in kind, hoping that was a good a display as sympathy as I could muster, when in reality, I had fallen far short of understanding the burden he carried. Ours was a summer's love affair that had blossomed in one night, then died the next day like a mayfly.

I mechanically photographed the vaulted ceiling, absorbing nothing of interest. On any other occasion, I would have soaked up the history of Conisbrough. It was the perfect castle and surrounded by beautiful countryside. I would have worked my way through everything, the buttressed keep, the crumbled remains, and imagined all the intrigue and plots until they came alive. Instead, I performed a perfunctory duty. There wasn't enough time left to do anything else. The sun, dodging the clouds, sank to the tops of the trees, and the shadows stretched from one wall to the next. In the distance, towards the north, an electric fork of lightning criss-crossed the blackened skies.

The man with the disappointing news waved to me from the gatehouse. I picked up the tripod and walked over.

'Sorry,' he said. 'It's closing time.'

I was the only visitor still on site.

As I drove off, I saw the same man walk with some haste along the road behind me, as if chasing me off. He waved, holding a tissue or something white. Strange man – I seemed to be attracting them over the last couple of days. I wasn't in the mood to wave back, so he shrank into a tiny figure with the castle looming high above him.

❖

I arrived home late in the evening, feeling grubby and hollow with hunger but unable to stomach food. Mum wasn't on the settee waiting for me, nor was Dad. They had gone out, according to a note, to the pub for a meal. I suspected my father was behind that decision.

I showered, put on pyjamas, and pretended to show an interest in the contents of the fridge. Weakening, I slapped two pieces of bread around a slab of cheese. There was one last thing to do: write up the final list of photographs, and post the remaining memory stick to wherever David was hiding. Bloody coward.

Thinking about David and his deceptions, I decided to send him an email in which I would tell him I knew everything, and that the secrecy was no longer necessary. Medici could unveil herself fully and tell me the truth – why was I taking photographs for her? Waiting for the laptop to fire up, I cracked my knuckles over the keyboard. To my surprise, there was an email from David.

> **Dear Robyn.**
> Sincere apologies for not replying to your emails. I have had internet problems at my art gallery - a new venture for me which is why I have been absent for so long.
> I understand your frustration at the secrecy, and under any normal circumstances, I would not be party to it. But I made a promise, and you must believe me when I tell you that I have honoured it out of love for a dear friend.

The same day as Beryl.

My heartbeats stuttered as I read on. He was telling me my
great-aunt had died, but he didn't appear to know that I was
related. He was referring to his friend as Medici, and telling me
how she had succumbed to a long illness, and I knew exactly
what that illness might be, and why she had struggled for so long
with it.

Was there any point in revealing the connection between
myself and Loretta? It seemed that what David had done on
Loretta's behalf was entirely due to a favour born out of some
deep-seated respect, and that extended to continuing to mask
the gender of my patron, something only now I realised was
evident in all our correspondence. I had acted as if we still lived
in a medieval patriarchal society; and for that, I had only myself
to blame. So what difference would it have made if I had thought
Medici had been a woman? Unless... Loretta had wanted to stay
anonymous – why, I still couldn't fathom – and she had latched
onto my mistake as provident, and David had helped by
deliberately maintaining my preconceived stereotype of a patron.
I read on to the last sentence.

Heavy eyed, too tired to even weep for a woman I'd never met,
I decided to let it go. I had my expensive camera, tons of
photographs to review, the motivation to finally find a job and the
courage to leave home to seek it. I had made love, briefly, to a man
who connected with me in some strange way, and I didn't care how
contrived that connection might be, my feelings for him were
genuine. And I supposed, given how vivid and intrusive the visions
had become, I might at last be free to daydream without losing
control of my faculties for it seemed nothing visionary had
happened since Whitby. I was locked into reality. When Joseph and

I had parted company, I had lost more than I had thought possible. My strange natural ability to envisage past events seemed also to have gone.

As for my parents, my mother in particular, there seemed no reason to tell her that I might have found her long lost aunt. I realised I had no proof that Medici had wished to be identified as Loretta Di Matteo, quite the contrary, she had reinforced the mystery to an extent that blinded me to the truth. If Joseph had met Loretta, then I might find the truth that way, and the only hope of finding Joseph was in London where he had witnessed the death of an infant at the hands of his brothers.

PART FIVE

'The more she is denied to him, the more desire
inflames and stings his smitten heart.'
Lorenzo de' Medici

FORTY-ONE

London

A CAR RUMBLED PAST, then another, followed by red double decker, its wheels heading straight for a puddle. I stepped back. Noisy, relentless London was an alien place. I stood on the pavement, clutching my portfolio case to my chest, trembling from head to toe, feeling those annoying rogue stomach muscles tying sinews into knots. But for a good reason this time. I'd just been offered my dream job.

It might be happening too fast. I was still playing catch-up with the fallout from recent events. A productive spell of planning had kept me occupied in the two weeks that had passed since Beryl's funeral – nearly four since I had last seen Joseph. With the help of Yvette, I had rebranded, transforming myself from hotel receptionist to professional photographer. I had written numerous resumes, some of which had been binned, and sent the best off, mostly to agencies. One keen agent, having given me two days' notice, sent me to London for a job interview. The company then put me on the spot and offered me the job there and then, and I accepted it without considering any alternatives. So what, I had thought; I was no longer afraid of throwing myself headlong into a challenge. The real challenge was the one month in which to find a place to live and relocate.

After several frozen minutes, my legs rediscovered movement, and I walked, and walked, my insides still buzzing with a constant stream of adrenaline, which had saturated my nervous system from the moment I had woken up at dawn, then kept me company on the train down to London and all through the intense interview.

What had won them over was the portfolio I carried in my aching arms. A collection of photographs from Bamburgh to Whitby – there were none beyond that day. I had selected them carefully, picking those images that best represented architectural features. It wasn't difficult. Loretta had primed me, taught me to see what an architect saw, and I had learnt over those sweltering weeks of summer how to present features both artistically and usefully.

I still didn't know what David had done with the digital versions. I had fretted that my prints would be substandard given the age of my film camera, but the team who interviewed me weren't bothered. They were architects and renovators, specialists who preserved old buildings or built replicas from scratch for film sets.

Was I prepared to travel across the UK and Europe? Yes, I had nodded enthusiastically.

Work independently? Yes, I had proof.

The questions had piled up and I batted them back with surprising ease. Loretta had prepared me well.

Having walked nearly a mile, I began the process of spreading the good news, to my parents, Yvette, and a few other friends. I texted or rang while sat on a bench in a green spot under yellow fringed leaves, my hunched shoulders buffeted by a gentle breeze.

I wasn't in the heart of London, but somewhere in between the suburban towns and the congested West End. My geography was limited to the underground network. But I wasn't worried by the thought of living here because I would be on the road, photographing before and after shots for marketing purposes, or working with surveyors on new projects. Best of all, if there was a lull in my workload, I was permitted to carry out freelance projects. I could continue my own quests.

One of the interviewers probed me about the castles, why I had picked them. I referred sparingly to my commission, and touched on, a little red-faced, my aspirations. Or what I thought they had been.

'Don't give up on it,' she had said. 'I think it's a remarkable idea – a distinctive collection of photographs based on a personal journey, and it shows dedication and perseverance. We like that here.' And then they offered me the job of architectural photographer.

There was no chance to celebrate; I wasn't catching the train home yet as I had one other personal mission to complete before returning to Coalville. But it could wait until the next day. Mentally exhausted by both travelling and interviews, I happily checked into the Travelodge, collapsed onto the bed, and fell into a deep sleep. Only when I woke in the morning, aware of the traffic outside, did a renewed sense of trepidation force me to face the day's task.

I hadn't found Joseph. As Yvette anticipated, Joseph Smiths were common. I had checked art galleries for listings of painters, some schools, but nobody was going to reveal confidential information on staff, and I also tried to locate Camilla Brooke, and her more unusual name. However, if she was in London, she wasn't advertising her services. No agency had her listed, at least those that gave out names. I was left with one course of action, the one I had scrupulously avoided.

Back at home, and between preparing for my interview and this fruitless project, I had slept little, eaten in small quantities, and dreamt of voids and stone walls, the kind that stood in your path and refused to yield. A kinetic ball of nervous energy had kept me bouncing about the house, annoying my melancholy mother and rousing my perplexed father into asking personal questions a father might reluctantly ask his daughter – had I met somebody?

Out of necessity, I had told them about how I met Joseph, but without referencing Medici's scheming. I maintained our coming together was a remarkable coincidence. As for the night in the tent, I had glossed over it with awkward phrases, inferring things that Dad grunted at and made Mum blush. They understood, though, that I was keen to find him, and because of that need, I had to tell them why he was hard to find. For like Yvette, I had trawled the web, and discovered old newspaper articles, digitalised ones because the event predated the internet. Yvette had been right – the newspapers had perpetuated the story for a long time, when now and again the ugly details were dredged up and compared to other crimes. The most recent reconstruction was two years ago. That article, one that at least wasn't sensational with the forensic details, referred to the location, the tower block where Joseph had lived as a boy. It was to this address that I headed, armed with my A-to-Z of street names and an umbrella.

The summer ended on the day I left Conisbrough Castle and drove home. The dark clouds that chased me down the road followed me. Storms erupted volcanically across the country, bringing down withered trees. Rainwater poured into the maze of cracks and swollen rivers, flooding the fractured lines of dusty fields. The service at the crematorium had been lit up by hair-raising lightning, and while other mourners considered the storm an unfortunate addition to the "beautiful" eulogy, I thought of how Beryl had interfered with Isabel's life and considered the angry thunder appropriate.

My expose of Joseph's past had troubled Dad. He found it hard to believe that Joseph wasn't the delinquent the papers had once described.

'A leopard doesn't change his spots,' he had said gruffly.

In rebuttal, I pointed out, heatedly, that Joseph never had the wrong spots; it was his brothers who had caused the accident. Mum winced at the word accident. I had no defence to the argument that what had happened was manslaughter, or as the gutter press called it, a callous killing. However, my parents had mellowed over the last few days, and accepted that I wasn't giving up hope of finding him, and even though he hadn't waited for me in Yorkshire, I needed proper closure, and a valid reason to let him go.

On Saturday, I checked out of the Travelodge, lugged the overnight bag and portfolio case to the station and squeezed them into a locker. With the key safely in my coat pocket, I set out to find a tower block in a sprawling estate located south of the river.

It was ugly as hell, an example of the brutal architecture of the seventies. It should have been demolished, but the council had patched it up, replaced the windows and added a few decorated murals. Lowering my umbrella, allowing spits and spots to peck at my face, I stood beneath it and craned my neck. It was higher than

I had imagined, and terribly grim with its grey concrete and rows of identical balconies. A few residents had tried to improve the aesthetics by adding hanging containers of plants. I counted up to the seventh floor, where Joseph had lived with his brothers and father.

I pictured Joseph leaning over the side, the horror on his young face as he saw what lay beneath – the pram on its side, the mother screaming, the crowd gathering, raging with anger and pointing up to where Joseph stood. Then, he would have heard the stamping of feet as the police ran along the passageways hunting down the two boys. The pleading of a father, begging people not to hurt his sons, and the baying crowd, held back by yellow tape.

What had Joseph said? How had it started? They had made water bombs out of paper. Joseph had helped fold the paper. He was the oldest, eleven, nearly twelve, while the twins were nine, and already out of control. Ever since their mother had abandoned them, the family had struggled to cope. Their hardworking father had gone out shopping and left them to their own devices; it wasn't ideal; he was a proud father who hated asking for help. Sometimes he came home and found the twins making trouble in the streets or at a neighbour's flat. Occasionally the police rounded them up and sent them home. Joseph had tried to keep tabs on his brothers. But he wasn't responsible for their behaviour. Nobody was, it seemed.

The twins had thrown the water bombs off the balcony. Joseph had warned them to be careful. They had giggled. Joseph told me their high-pitched squeals still infiltrated his nightmares, which I guessed were frequent enough to trouble him. God, I could just imagine the racket they made. I closed my eyes briefly, and I was sure I could hear it above the sounds of nearby traffic.

The neighbours had heard it, too, but hadn't bothered to look out of their windows. Their excuse was the usual one, it was just those awful twins, and they washed their hands of any responsibility.

There, I heard it again, this time clearer: childish laughter.

I glanced over my shoulder, but nobody was there. The rain pattered on my umbrella, mingling with the shrill sounds of children at play.

This couldn't be happening, not now, not after I had resigned myself to stopping. I had thought that I had it under control, and now, suddenly, I was slipping back, losing myself to a past event that was part of history as much as any other. I blinked hard, remembering what Joseph had said to me weeks ago in the tent.

Jake had been the naughty one, inconsequential and careless, while the sly Ben liked to egg him on. Joseph had watched by the balcony door, which had been propped open with a brick.

A reddish lump of dried clay.

I swayed, my vision flickering. One moment I was looking up to the balcony, the next I was looking down over the edge, battling nauseating dizziness. I had found Joseph. He was in my mind, where he had been ever since I had started to follow his trail, and he had led me to this place.

❖

He backs away from the edge. 'If you get caught—'

Another water bomb explodes. Ben smirks. 'Gonna snitch, Joey?'

Little sod.

There are cardboard boxes of rubbish on the balcony. Joseph sits on one and waits for them to get bored. It doesn't usually take long. He hates the pokey flat. It's cramped and smelly. There is no space to breathe, to do things. He hangs out on the balcony because he can see far away to the park and trees. He likes going there, but the twins wreck things. The last time, somebody had reported them.

Ben kicks the brick aside and uses another box in its place. Jake picks the brick up, a red one that their dad had found on a building site. He'd carried it home and put in on the balcony, just to use as a door stop, nothing else, he'd said.

But Ben has an idea. 'Drop it.'

Jake laughs.

On the box, in the corner, Joseph sits and shakes his head. 'Don't be daft.'

Ben picks his nose and flicks something at Jake. 'Go on, twerp. Drop it. I dare you.'

Jake is giggling uncontrollably. Two chubby cheeks flecked with grime wobble up and down.

Barrel-shaped Ben jumps on the spot. 'Go on, go on!'

They won't do it. They're not that stupid. Joseph fiddles with the edge of the box, head down, and stares, working his way up from the undone shoelaces to the big hole in his trousers. A bony kneecap sticks through. He's hungry.

'Go on, baby face.' Ben pokes Jake's back.

Jake spins on the spot. 'Get off me.' He lifts the brick onto the top of the balcony wall.

Too close to the edge! Joseph stands, then sits. Jake's just teasing. The pair of them do it all the time.

'Coward.' Ben's piggy eyes sparkle.

'I'm not!'

Jake pushes the brick with both plump hands. The brick tilts, wobbles on its edge, then it's gone.

'Kowpow!' shrieks Ben, like Batman.

Joseph leaps to his feet, pushes aside the exuberant twins, and leans over and looks down, daring himself, hoping that the only thing there is a smashed brick.

The screams rise up the side of the building. Such wretched sounds, the unforgettable cries of distress.

So high up, his eyes need to be like a hawk's. Down below, little figures surround an overturned pram. The mother is on her knees, grasping at something. The ground spins, circling upwards, bringing everything closer.

A door slams shut behind him. He's stuck on the balcony, alone, and the world is turning and turning…

The dizziness was overwhelming, and I nearly vomited onto the pavement. As I retched, my connection to Joseph was broken. I had found him here, but not today. I had found an echo of him from long ago haunting his own grey castle, one that rose high to the sky and trapped his memories inside, out of sight for eternity. The visceral emotions I felt weren't mine but his. This daydream wasn't bound to an urban myth, and how I wished it had been. What I had done was force together Joseph's traumatic memories and my lurid imagination. It was horribly gratuitous and cruel of me to come here. While I had hankered for excitement, he ran away from it, seeking quiet places. This wasn't where he lived now; I hadn't found him. Instead, in visiting this waking, vicarious nightmare, I had discovered a relic of him.

And thinking back, there had been other echoes of Joseph throughout the summer of the castles. Unknown to me, they had been the macabre pattern of my visions since Bamburgh. All those vivid daydreams were like hauntings, reflections of Joseph's subconscious, drawing on the legends I assumed them to be. The Pink Lady, who fell to her death, so similar to the ghostly tale at Spofforth where I had nearly succumbed to a vision, was a manifestation of Joseph's fear of falling. I encountered, at Dunstanburgh, the knight who called for help with his horn instead of fighting back – Joseph, like the knight, ended up trapped by his past, and not rescued. When I thought I saw a bouncing ball, tumbling down the stairs, it was not the brick, but it might have been something thrown, carelessly. At Middleham, I had heard the mourning mother crying for her dead child, and I wondered in hindsight, that high up there Joseph had felt something too. He had been terrified. What was worse was the repeating themes of bombardment at Bamburgh, Bowes and Whitby, even the sickly smell of death at Helmsley. They seemed to mirror the torments Joseph suffered, as if in the aftermath of the baby's death, when all he wanted was peace from those who hounded him, he was surrounded by the echo of other tragedies. Even in the most tranquil of abbeys, Rievaulx, I had unearthed a dark place, the charcoal store, where no man wanted to dwell for long, and witnessed one man dragging his burden into the shadows, out of sight. Was it possible that before I had even met Joseph, at Kenilworth, the corruption of my dreams had begun when the frenzied antics of the riotous guests had nauseated me? I might not have met him, but Loretta knew his story, and she had communicated with me, somehow.

And, somehow, I had broken through his defensives and unearthed the ruins of his childhood. This grotesque tower block vision had to be the last, my visions were no longer benign excursions.

My phone rang and I took cover from the rain under a nearby bus shelter. The caller was Polly, another receptionist at my old job and somebody I trusted enough to have my mobile number. Wiping my face with the back of my hand, I wondered if I wanted to hear the latest hotel gossip, but then I remembered Polly was one of the sensible ones, so I pressed the phone to my ear.

'Hi,' Polly said, breathlessly. 'I know this is going to sound strange. But I've just had this man turn up with a sketch of you, you know, like the police use for identification. He was dressed pretty smartly. You're not in trouble are you? I was too scared to give him your number, thought he might be a stalker. Did I do the right thing?'

The phone nearly slipped out of my wet fingers. Was it David? No, that made no sense, he had my number. 'Is he still there?'

'Oh, no. He's gone. But he left…'

Her voice broke into unintelligible monosyllables.

'What?' I nearly shouted.

'And his address. Do you want his phone number and address? The card says his name is Joseph Smith, freelance artist.'

I had to ask her twice for the address. I had thought she was joking the first time.

FORTY-TWO

AFTER TWO FRUITLESS SATURDAYS of badgering hotel staff in and around Coalville, I admitted defeat, and drove home. Perhaps there was a higher reason for my failure: destiny, and all that. Or more likely it was due to our collective thoughtlessness that she and I, partners for a brief while, had lost each other. Trying to find her was as ridiculous as my pathetic excuse for hunting her down: following a photo shoot, she'd left an expensive camera in my possession by mistake.

'Really?' one guy had said, his eyebrows arched in disbelief. 'Why not hand it into the police?'

He hadn't recognised Robyn anyway.

The truth was important for Robyn. I hoped she would see it as a sign of trust that I had printed new business cards using my real name. I had left one with each hotel, asking them to keep an eye out if anyone matched Robyn's description; I'd received some very odd looks when I showed them the sketch, the incredulous kind that marked me as either a pervert or some secretive private-eye. I saw at least one person drop the card in the bin as I walked out. Hardly surprising, I was acting suspiciously.

One heavily made-up receptionist repeated her name, slowly, like she was spelling it out, 'Robyn.' For a second I'd thought there was a flash of recognition in her eyes. Then she shrugged and put the card to one side. 'I'll ask around.' She'd spoken as if Robyn was a lost dog, but when she'd reached for the phone, staring at me warily, I panicked and bolted, not wanting to face a police inquisition.

What other clues did I have? A friend called Yvette, who worked somewhere. A professor who had gone walkabout. A patron whom she might admire but was faceless. And me, a casual acquaintance who somehow had fallen for her without actually knowing who she was.

Yeah, I should be laughing. But I wasn't. I was miserable. Nothing had felt right from the moment I had returned home from Conisbrough.

The outstanding payment had arrived in my bank account. Just like that, without prompting from me. Camilla had thanked me for the pictures, including the one I had painted in the studio using photographs and my memory cache. However, the message was left on my answer machine, and when I returned the call, it rang forever. I kind of hated her now. If I had slept with her, like she wanted me to, I would have regretted it in a way I never would with Robyn.

I had walked away from Robyn too quickly, allowed dark thoughts to shove out the nicer ones and, in hindsight, I knew I had allowed my past to infect me with doubt, and I had seeded my fears, however subtly, wherever I went. My biggest regret was giving up on her. If Robyn had really wanted to reject me, she wouldn't have stroked my hair and whispered caresses into my ear that night in the tent. So, buoyed with rekindled optimism, I had driven to Coalville with a list of hotels and the silly ID sketch. I had even bought a pair of smart trousers and a new shirt, and shaved.

Driving home, I wondered what to do next. I had school and evening classes to teach, although I had reduced my commitments once again in the hope of filling the extra hours with freelance stuff. A good portfolio was needed to boost my sales. The collection of paintings I had done, all fifteen of them, was out of my hands; I only had sketches and outlines left in a pad. I wondered about recreating them from memory – not too difficult to do as I had copious mental notes stashed away. But I didn't want to dredge those weeks up and remember Robyn. It was probably best if I forgot her.

Trouble was, my memories, good or bad, had a tendency to fester, especially if they stirred up unwanted emotions. I could never forget her.

Sketching Robyn's portrait had been somewhat cathartic. I created several versions including profile and face on, mostly in charcoal. The one I took to Coalville was simplistic and drawn in thick pencil. I wanted to put a smile on her face, like the one I had seen inside the tent, but instead I created a passport style representation that highlighted her lightness, cropped beeswax hair, and the sheen of her skin. I might have lengthened the eyelashes and plucked her eyebrows, lifted her chin a fraction. Call it artistic licence.

I would paint her properly, I decided, as I drove around the north circular road. And I would continue to pester Camilla, whose latest response to one of my stern emails was to quote the secrecy of the contract, as if she had signed some Italian code of Omerta. She must have been paid a small fortune to keep her runaway mouth shut. I swore at the invisible Medici, if he was the man behind everything, because having finished his game of chess, he had left key pieces on the board and walked off without explanation. But there again, if he had intended for Robyn and me to meet, he had achieved his goal. The end game perhaps didn't belong to him.

My journey home reached its end early evening. I parked on the street, grateful that this quiet side-road had achieved sufficient infamy that shoppers from the nearby high street shunned parking on it. The reputation wasn't anything to do with me, for once, but due to the suitably spooky graveyard. Abandoned long ago, the most recently interned corpse was probably a hundred years old. The bad reputation was perhaps, and occasionally, justified. Junkies climbed over the rusty metal railings and dropped needles behind the crooked gravestones. I wasn't tempted to slip into that shitty world again, once was enough. The police sometimes stopped by and raided the forgotten cemetery. I was perfectly safe behind the stone walls of my home.

On the outside, my little cathedral – Dad had called it that on one of his rare visits – had suffered badly from neglect. I hadn't painted the flaked woodwork or mended the fence as it wasn't my job. The perpendicular windows, which weren't as grand as Dad thought, were invaluable for light, and why I rented the place. The landlord was the absentee type, and that suited me fine. He had bought the old Methodist chapel with the view of turning it into smaller flats, then ran out of money. The lack of a modern kitchen and missing partition walls never bothered me. I moved seamlessly around the place, unhindered by brick walls. The upper horseshoe tier had been boarded up to reduce heating costs, and the enclosed gallery now functioned as a vast attic. An ideal place for storage. My favourite spot for painting was under the arched window that once lit up the altar. I had a view of trees through the unstained glass, and early in the mornings, the birdsong outperformed the grumbling car exhausts.

The front door key jingled in my hand. Chapels, unlike parish churches, weren't blessed with porches, so I suffered the rain for a moment while I forced the deadlock cylinder to turn anticlockwise.

'Joseph?'

I dropped the key. The clatter filled the gap where my missing heartbeat should be. I froze on the spot, drenched less with rain and more with disbelief. She couldn't be here. My imagination had conjured up her voice, like an echo. There was no way she could have got from Coalville to London ahead of me. So If I looked, and she wasn't there, I would know I always wished it otherwise.

My throat closed, trapping my held breath in place. Slowly, I turned.

She had done it again; crept up on me.

FORTY-THREE

I BENT AND PICKED UP THE KEY, and held it out to him; I couldn't disguise my trembling hand. The tips of our fingers touched, a brief second of reunion, then he backed away. It seemed like a bad omen, but his face said otherwise.

I tilted the umbrella down. 'Can I come in?'

He nodded. This time, he managed to unlock the door.

My breathing wasn't back to normal. 'I didn't mean to scare you. I dashed from over there, on the other side of the road. I've been standing under a tree for an hour, waiting for you.' Like he might have done in York.

He held the steel door open, and I shook the rain off the collapsed umbrella before crossing the threshold. I followed him through what must have been the little entrance hall into vast space of the old chapel.

'Wow!' The word dropped like a stone out of my mouth and immediately echoed. 'Joseph, this is perfect. It's no wonder you love it. When you said studio'—I twittered on while eyeballing the stone architrave of the windows— 'I wasn't thinking of this.'

He cleared his throat. 'It's convenient.' He placed the key on a low table. Next to it was a chewed settee, one that a dog must have once favoured. Joseph had kept things minimal, right down to the kitchen that had obviously been cobbled together from bits and pieces out of a household tip or charity shop. Everything was clean, yet also shabby and used too many times to be worth anything. There was no television.

I rested the umbrella against a whitewashed wall. Above my head, inlaid into the wall, was a memorial plaque to the dead of a war. Very little had been done to hide the chapel's origins other than to strip out the wooden lecterns, railings and pews. Beneath my feet, a patchwork of Hessian mats covered the creaking floorboards. A cast iron radiator rattled. I touched it and flinched.

'It's heated. There's water, and a bathroom through there.' He pointed to a door at the far end. 'Just about the only thing that isn't original.' He switched on the kettle. 'You found me.'

He was speaking almost too softly. I edged closer to where he stood next to the makeshift cupboards.

'Yes. Polly called me. She recognised the picture. It was where I worked. She didn't say anything to you, because... well...'

'She was being perfectly sensible. I'm grateful she rang you.' He nearly smiled.

My lips twitched. What now? I couldn't say what I wanted to say.

'You're dressed very smartly,' he said, filling the silence.

I had forgotten. 'I've got a job.' I popped my handbag on the settee. 'Went for a job interview and they offered it me then and there. A small firm of architects who specialise in historical buildings. I'm going to be the company photographer.'

He hadn't moved. 'Congratulations. It's sounds perfect for you.'

'So... I'm going to have to find somewhere to live.' I bit on my lower lip. Now I sounded cheap. 'I'm going to be travelling a lot.'

'It's what you wanted.'

The steam billowed around him as the kettle whistled. 'Tea? Have you eaten?'

My stomach wasn't rumbling. If I was hungry, it wasn't for food. I shook my head. 'No. Not yet. I was going to wait another hour then... go.'

He turned to face me, the teabag crushed under his hand. 'I shouldn't have given up on you in Yorkshire. Trouble was, on my own, I got to thinking about what I'd told you about the twins. I thought it was for the best to go home.'

'I thought you might have... I rushed back to York but it's not your fault we missed each other. I didn't really expect you to wait more than a couple of days. But I needed to say goodbye properly. So I'm staying in London, booked into a hotel. And I went… I went to the tower block where…'

His turn to flinch. The tea leaves scattered on the stained Formica worktop. 'Why?'

'To find you. Silly really, because obviously, you're not there.'

'I've not been back there in years.'

I wrung my hands. 'Stupid thing to do. Rake up the past when the future,' I said carefully, believing that Joseph was responsible in all likelihood for the content of my summer of visions, 'the future is where I'm going.'

He finally shifted his feet, leaving behind the untouched kettle. 'Oh?'

'Yes. No more maladaptive daydreaming, and yes I did look it up and maybe that's what I suffer from.'

The gap was no more than an arm's length. I wasn't sure if my pulse could take much more; it thrummed in my temples so hard it was deafening.

The colour returned to his cheeks. 'I'm sorry, that was my fault. I should never have implied—'

'You were right. They might have been entertaining daydreams, but now they hurt me.' I stopped. If I talked about the letters, Loretta and Italy, he would think I had a different motive for being there. 'I don't want to say goodbye, not anymore. Are you actually pleased to see me? I can't tell.'

His whole demeanour seemed to collapse in on itself. He went from solid and unyielding to fluid, releasing his shoulders and taut elbows as if letting out in one speechless exhale whatever had held him in check.

Then we touched each other and this time we didn't let go.

❖

Speaking in the dead of night was perhaps going to be our thing.

Light from the street streamed through the high, curtainless windows, which reminded me of a castle's embrasures with their pointed arches and tracery on the stonework. Up there, dancing beams highlighted the fault lines in the ceiling struts; down on the floor, we lay in the folds of darkness. The Old Chapel House with its seamless shadows and alien features didn't frighten me. I had no sense of its past, nor of the folk that once congregated inside. There was just me and Joseph, side by side, tucked up in his bed.

He fondled gently, and I let him, and now that we were relaxed and no longer excitable and feverish, we talked. We pieced together the misadventures of York, Spofforth and Conisbrough.

'Oh my God. The poor bloke was running after me with your note.' I slapped my forehead. 'I'm an idiot.'

Joseph laughed at the timings. 'And that old geezer, dressed like it was about to snow. I thought he was about to expire on me. I nearly painted him into the picture.'

'You kept painting and I kept taking photographs. Aren't we stubborn?' We weren't the only ones. It was time to reveal what I knew about Loretta's twinned projects.

He listened without interrupting, occasionally when I stuttered nervously, he stroked my bare arm with his fingertips. Even at the point that I revealed my patron was in fact a woman, not a man, he absorbed the news with only a small groan. He too had assumed the situation was being controlled by a man and neither of us had questioned it. It was when, after holding the detail back, I spoke Medici's real name that Joseph jerked and sat upright, his back facing away from me.

'Joseph?'

'Lora. Lora Di Matteo. Tony's mother,' he said. 'I stayed with them when I travelled back and forth to Greece.'

My suspicions were confirmed: the connection between us made concrete. 'Loretta. Lora. All the same person. My great-aunt, half a great-aunt, Loretta. How did you meet her?' I knelt next to him and, in the darkness, found his hands.

'An advertisement. They rent out this converted barn to visiting artists. But I didn't have enough money to stay long the first time. The second time, they invited me back for nothing.'

'Why?'

'Because Lora liked me, and Tony is kind.' He sighed.

'Can you tell me about Loretta?' I cupped his hands between

mine and they stilled.

'It's a shame your grandmother never met her. Her sister has this wonderful laugh. Really deep like from here.' Joseph touched my belly. 'And though she isn't always easy to understand, because of her speech impediment, her English is excellent.'

Has. Is. I realised I hadn't told Joseph what David had said in his message: Loretta was dead.

Appropriate words escaped me, so I procrastinated. 'Why castles? Did she share the same passions as me?' I asked.

Joseph shrugged. 'I saw no evidence of an interest in English ones. But she is a historian of architecture. She worked, before she retired, as a celebrated academic. She writes books now.'

David and Loretta both historians and writers of books. Of course, it made sense. Now I knew the purpose of my photographs.

'I wonder why she didn't tell us.'

He reached over and switched on the bedside lamp. I blinked several times before focusing on his pensive face.

'What?' I said, alarmed.

'I told her everything, Robyn. All about me. My family. She's easy to talk to, and Tony would wheel her around to the barn to watch me paint. They both said I had extraordinary talent. But I didn't believe them because where was my focus? I just moved from place to place, running away from my past.'

'So you told her about Jake and Ben?'

'Yes, especially how my father hadn't coped with them. They were wild, Robyn. Terrifying. When the police took them away, I knew they wouldn't be forgiven, even though they were kids. I blamed myself so much, especially because I knew Ben wasn't like normal kids. Jake, well, once he was fostered, he righted himself, and lived to regret that day. He's somewhere far away now, which is for the best, and he doesn't visit Dad. They adopted him, his new family.'

'And Ben?'

'In and out of prison. I nearly followed him what with all the harassment from vigilantes. Plus the press, documentary makers. I got close to going there. Drugs and gangs are very appealing when you don't belong. But Dad, to his credit, kept moving me, and I was never anywhere long enough to be tempted until we finally got a proper house.'

'With a garage.'

His smile broke through the melancholy, and he waved his arms around. 'And now I have this place.'

'And Loretta helped you by giving you a space to paint.' I wiped the lone tear from his cheek. 'Do you think she meant for us to meet?'

'Yes. I do now. I wasn't sure when you first told me about Medici's role, but now we know the links in the chain, it's plausible. I wish I knew what she's done with my paintings.'

'Mm. Camilla and David were sworn to secrecy.' I inhaled deeply. I couldn't hold back any longer. 'I'm sorry. I have to tell you bad news. David contacted me when I got back. He said Medici, Lora, had died very recently.'

Joseph's cheeks and shoulders sagged. But there were no more tears; he'd expected this news. He fingered the gold chain around his neck, the little pendant of a man carrying a small boy on his shoulders, taking him to a place of safety. I could ask him if Loretta had given him the St Christopher's charm, but I knew the answer lay in the caress of his fingers.

'She had this disability,' he said. 'I suppose it shortened her life.'

'I think she had cerebral palsy.'

'Probably. She never referred to it by name. If she was born like that, she didn't want to be judged by it.' Joseph puffed out his lips. 'Did David tell you any more?'

'No. I've been waiting for more information, but it probably doesn't matter now. I worked out who Medici is without his help. I don't know if David knows that she's my great-aunt.'

Joseph lay back, drawing me down with him. 'I would be surprised if he didn't know something. When you think about it, David found you, but it's Lora who considered Coalville important and that had to be because she knew there was family nearby. Kind of a coincidence David discovered you and not some other photographer. Good job, lucky man.' Joseph grinned briefly then his lips dropped. 'David didn't care about the photography so he had to be involved for a different reason, so I would have thought he had some clue as to why.'

'And you? Any regrets about those paintings? They're very good.'

He squeezed me tighter. 'I just wish I hadn't given them to Camilla, who I suppose knows Lora wanted them for her collection. That must be what she meant by the gift. It's a gift from me to an ailing Lora and kept secret so I wouldn't get upset at the thought of it. They've probably going to be sold. That would make sense. With Lora dead, her whole art gallery will be up for grabs. Tony wasn't into dealing.'

'Art gallery?' I eased myself up onto one elbow.

'Lora had a gallery in the town. She bought and sold local artwork. What?'

I rested my palm on his chest. His heartbeats were pounding as fast as mine. 'We're going to Italy.'

'Why?'

'To speak to David. I know where he is, and your paintings.'

PART SIX

'*How short a while all mortal joys endure,*
But not so soon doth memory pass away.'
Lorenzo de' Medici

FORTY-FOUR

Potenza, Italy

WE DECIDED TO CALL on Tony first before locating the art gallery. It seemed rude to go all the way to Southern Italy and not offer our condolences.

The car was hired in Naples airport. Unfortunately, with only a long weekend scheduled, the luxury of meandering from one end of Europe to the other wasn't on the cards. Joseph had held my hand during take-off and landing, murmuring sweet things that made me smile. He had softened, shaken off those cold mannerisms he wore like a shield, and let me in without fear. We had talked so much, I wondered if there was anything left to tell him about myself.

We had held hands as much as possible in the last week or so. Ever since our reunion, we'd continued the momentous task of carving out a future together, but mostly we planned our trip to Italy. My parents would have to wait, so would Yvette, to meet the man I intended to live with in London. I was keen to find David while I had a good inkling of where he might be.

On route to Potenza, I announced categorically that I was in love with Italy. The food, the perfect autumnal weather, the terracotta roofs, the golden fields, even the post-drought parched soil. Over the English summer I had toughened to warm weather and arid scenery. Joseph pointed out things an artist saw, the colours and textures, the rise and fall of the hills, the mountains. My fascination lay with the uniformity of buildings, especially in the older towns, and the narrow winding streets. We drove past Vesuvius and Pompei into the amber flows of the forests of the Apennines, then onto Potenza. We stopped for food at a roadside cafe, and I took photographs of the view with the digital camera, now my own.

'Should I mention to Tony we that we're related?' I asked Joseph.

He pursed his lips. 'I don't know.'

Neither did I. I would wait and see.

The art gallery was in Potenza, but the Di Matteo family home was located on the hills outside, isolated and accessed by a challenging, scary track. The car skidded a couple of times on the corners. The gates were open; we were expected, and Joseph had called ahead to announce our arrival time.

Perched on the hillside, stone built, three storeys and square, was the main house. The windows were shuttered like a fortress, but it emanated tranquillity and I wondered if my presence might fracture the serenity. Joseph parked the dusty car outside what he referred to as the barn. It wasn't a timber barn nor a corrugated monstrosity. The walls were crazed with stone and mortar in a delirious pattern, the roof tiled and the windows small, like arrow slits. This was where Joseph had painted?

He grinned. 'I know, from this side it's not much. On the other side is a wall of glass. You can see the mountains in the distance, the valley below. It's beautiful.'

We approached the main house. I wasn't so sure now. I might have been mistaken about Loretta. Perhaps the letters to Isabel were faked; the translations flawed. The connection to here suddenly felt tenuous and fanciful, as if I had imagined everything, which was feasible. I was perfectly capable of losing myself in fantasies.

Joseph squeezed my hand.

The door opened, anticipating us. The man, raven black hair tufted with grey, smiled at Joseph and spread his arms.

'Tony,' Joseph said, and welcomed the embrace of his friend, the kiss on both cheeks.

Loretta's son wasn't young, but neither was he my parent's age. Slightly rotund and short legged, Tony spoke quietly, inviting us in. I realised, very quickly, he was nervous, and his apprehension mirrored mine. He wanted to look at me, but glanced away each time I tried to make contact with his dark, flitting eyes.

He led us into a spacious living room, which was cool and dotted with elegant, yet simple furniture. However, my attention was drawn to another man in ash chinos and navy blue t-shirt. Still the epitome of smart casual, David Carmichael hadn't lost any of his suave. Where he differed were the rings around his eyes and the extra flecks of white in his thinning hair. He seemed much older than I remembered from six months ago.

'David,' I said, bluntly, and licked my lips. 'You've not met Joseph Smith, the artist I mentioned in my emails to you.'

It was hard not to add daggers to my tone.

David held out his hand and Joseph cautiously shook it. Meanwhile, Tony bustled, bringing over a tray of tumblers and a jug of water.

'Please sit.' David assumed the role of host. For the moment, my mind focused upon him. The questions I had brought with me were for him alone.

Joseph and I sat facing David. Tony had his hands pressed together as if in prayer, his eyes full of anxiety. I loosened, relieving my face of a stiffness that I had carried into the house; this man was my cousin, and I was behaving ungraciously, as if I was in enemy territory.

'It's beautiful here. I'm sorry we couldn't give you any more warning of our visit.'

Tony held up a hand. 'You are welcome to visit.' His English was heavily accented, used sparingly. When Joseph had stayed alone with the family, he had opened up to English-speaking Loretta, not Tony.

David cleared his throat. 'I knew Lora had instigated another project alongside yours, Robyn, but she kept me in the dark. I'm sorry. Neither did she explain her connection to you. I only found that out recently, when I returned to help her with the final stages of her book, which was when she told me I was to inherit her gallery. Tony spoke of your mutual friend Joseph, which led me to recall your email, and Tony reminded me of the connection to Coalville. It all fitted.'

'Did she see the last email I sent her about Joseph?' I asked.

'She was aware of it. She was frail and determined to put her affairs in order. By the time I got here, there was little for me to do. You should know, Lora gave me a description of a young woman whom she said I would meet at the Curzon.' David blushed. 'Not a painter, but a photographer. She had an uncanny ability to predict things. I thought it was highly unlikely I would find what she was looking for. I confess, I never had her faith in destiny.'

'I thought she was… the Medici name misled me,' I said, still bruised on the inside by David's complicity.

'I am sorry,' David repeated with feeling. 'It wasn't intentional. Only, later, it became convenient. Lora was bemused by your misconception, but asked me to maintain it. She meant no harm. Maybe she never anticipated you would work out who she was.'

'Didn't she?' I said sharply. 'There were letters, you see, from Loretta to my grandmother. Decades old. They were only discovered after I went back to Coalville.' I didn't want to mention Beryl's interference in front of Tony.

'Well, I would think she thought it unlikely.'

It probably was. Loretta's letters to my grandmother wouldn't have been discovered if Beryl hadn't died, and I suspected Loretta thought that they had been destroyed long ago. Without the letters, there was a slim chance I might have worked at the connection to Loretta through David and Joseph's mutual friendship with her. With hindsight, whether that friendship would have been sufficient to lead me here, I didn't know.

'In any case,' David said, 'If you hadn't come here, my instructions were to contact you and pass on her last request. I think her entire intention was not about dredging up her past. She hid her identity specifically to avoid—'

'No, not avoid. To ensure I was drawn to Joseph's story, not hers.'

David nodded, slowly.

I dare not look at Joseph, and instead I turned to face Tony. 'Do you know who I am?'

He lowered his eyes. 'Mamma's mother was English - Catherine. This I knew, we all knew. My grandfather married an Italian.' Tony laboured over the choice of words. 'He loved his wife much.

Mamma was happy in Italy.'

I didn't doubt that, and there was no indication in the letters I had read that Loretta was neglected by her father and stepmother, and they had educated her to a high standard.

'We are kind of cousins,' I said.

Tony nodded. 'Yes. Your mother is my cousin.'

'And it wasn't a secret that Loretta had a half-sister in England?'

Tony caught David's eye and said something in Italian.

David nodded. 'Tony says it was a secret for many years until his grandparents died. Lora had honoured her father's wishes not to speak out of respect for her step-mother, who raised her as her own. Only later did she speak of her mother in England, and her family in Coalville.'

Tony hadn't said all that.

'You knew then?' I asked David.

'Some of it. Lora and I have been friends for many years. I was her student. I studied in Naples where she worked as a professor for many years. She told me about Catherine, her mother. I didn't know about a half-sister.' David weaved his knuckles together, tempering something that nearly betrayed his emotions.

'Loretta wanted to find me? Or did she think her sister was still alive? Her name, by the way, is Isabel. Izzy.'

David offered an apologetic frown. 'She never mentioned Isabel. Lora was particular about finding a female photographer living near Coalville.'

Like her mother Catherine, but Loretta already knew she had died a long time ago. 'Izzy didn't know a thing about photography.' I glanced at Joseph, who maintained a neutral posture. He had his own questions, but he doubted David could help him explain Camilla's role.

'Then, we won't ever know,' David said, pointedly, his frustration mirroring my own. 'I'm sorry. She really could be a stubborn woman. She wanted photographs of these castles for a book she was writing—'

'I guessed that—'

'She wrote it as part of a series on the fortresses of Europe, and their historical significance. Academic and detailed, it won't be a best seller, I'm afraid. She finished the text, in Italian and English, and commissioned me to help her with the photographs. The book will go to the publishers. Your photographs will not be wasted, and you will receive credit for them. They are very good, by the way. I saw them before sending off the manuscript. I've been editing it; Lora was too ill by then, which was why I sent the message to you, but she saw the last batch you sent, I promise you, and she was happy. The memory sticks were forwarded to here. Only the last lot arrived too late.'

A glow of pleasure of warmed my heart. It was a silver lining to know some of the photographs reached Italy in time, and that my patron, for she had kept true to that part of the bargain, was pleased with them. As for the book, I didn't care about its prospects now that I had a job, but it would do my new career no harm. The gaps in the story were gradually filling. My mind raced, checking for holes.

'Why you?' I asked David. 'Castles aren't your speciality.'

'No. Obviously not. But I owed her my gratitude.' David retrieved something from his breast pocket. He held it out.

I took the faded photograph. It was of a couple, David and a startlingly attractive woman, seated next to a crooked woman propping herself up with walking sticks. I stared at my great-aunt, at her vast eyes and slanted jowls, as if she was permanently tilted to one side. Even in the static photo, she seemed to twitch. There was a definite grin on her parted lips, a sparkle of optimism in her vibrancy. She wasn't ashamed of her disability, and why should she have been? She had borne a child, no doubt proving many wrong that it was possible for one with her affliction. She was older than her companions, but not by much. The hair on David's head was thick, his face youthful and his jeans flared in a style I had seen in pictures of my teenage parents.

'Your wife?'

He smiled. 'Maggie. Magdalene. She was born in this valley. I came to Naples as an exchange student and Maggie was Lora's research assistant. She introduced us, and when Maggie's father resisted because I was not Catholic and considered a radical – I know, hard to believe, but this was the seventies and I got caught up with the communists and did some foolish things. Lora spoke up on our behalf. She helped us elope to England. It caused a scandal. Being a disabled woman was always a disadvantage. She lost her position at the university, which is how she came to be in Potenza, writing books, offering patronage to artists. And dealing in art.'

'She left you the art gallery?'

David nodded. 'I've retired, a little earlier than I anticipated. Maggie is excited to be returning to Italy. She's house hunting as we speak.'

Loretta's motives remained clouded though. She had used David to find me when she didn't even know I existed.

There was more. I spoke, breaking the temporary silence. 'Joseph was commissioned by a woman called Camilla Brooke.'

'Camilla!' Tony gaped. 'She is a cousin. Went to England years ago, married a horrible man. She left him.' He said something in a scathing tone. David didn't translate.

'She would have known Loretta.' I patted Joseph's knee. 'It's all fitting together.'

'Yes,' Joseph said, curtly. 'But I don't like being used. I painted those pictures in good faith, and now I don't know what has happened to them. If I could, I'd buy them back.'

David rose to his feet. 'I'm sorry, the paintings are not for sale. Lora insisted they were a gift. But I know where they are and what to do with them. Your arrival here is precipitous yet advantageous since it has saved me writing you a long email.' He nodded to Tony. 'They're in the atelier.'

The shadow under Joseph's brow deepened. The way his back stiffened told me what he was thinking.

He stood over David. 'What do you mean – you know what to do with them?'

David held up a placating hand. 'Please, come with me. It's not what you think. When Lora realised she was fading fast, she left me a message, a codicil to her will. She didn't trust Camilla with all the details; Tony says Camilla doesn't care much about anything that isn't money.'

Joseph guffawed. 'That I do know.' However, he followed David out of the house, and we all crossed the cobbled courtyard to the converted barn.

Inside, I gasped. It was like an undercroft with its vaulted ceiling and archways, but light and airy. The far end was the living quarters with a bed and kitchenette; most of the open space was given over to the atelier and there was plenty of room for whatever was needed, from sculpting to large canvas work. There was even a potter's wheel.

However, it was the back stone wall that snared both Joseph and my attention. Between the niches of the narrow windows hung paintings: watercolours. I recognised some, but not all. The earlier and later ones I hadn't seen him paint. The collection was framed, the styling identical, the layout from left to right a mirror of our conjoined journey: Bamburgh's windmill to Conisbrough's limestone keep.

David waited. He might have an idea of the flood of emotions that ripped through me as I embraced the joy of revisiting that eventful summer without fear of losing my mind or regretting my decision to leave Joseph. Each one told a different story, some of love, others of war and loss. I was familiar with their intricate histories and the details of their construction. Those ruined castles were free of the past, just like Joseph, and now I was no longer trapped and afraid to move on, I could love each place without regret.

'They're staying here?' I asked.

'That depends on you.' David said.

'Me?'

'Lora gifted them to you. She commissioned Joseph to paint a collection for you.'

'Me,' I repeated, aghast. 'She always intended me to have them?'

'Yes.'

Joseph drew me into his arms. 'Yours. The crafty old gal. She always liked to play games.'

Tony laughed, picking up some meaning in Joseph's remark.

'What will you do with them?' Joseph asked. 'I wanted to give them to you. That's why I wanted them back.' The shadow of uneasiness continued to lift from his face, leaving behind an expression of relief and delight.

I opened and shut my mouth, my eyes unfocused and blurry. Words failed me. I had one idea; I wasn't sure it was right, though.

David blew his nose on a handkerchief. 'She was a bloody romantic, Lora. Couldn't stop herself. Thought of herself as modern day Lorenzo de Medici, but really, she was more an idealist and philosopher with a good heart.'

'And a …' Tony chipped in an Italian word.

David nodded. 'Yes, that's true. She was a visionary.'

Joseph loosened his embrace. I lowered my arms from his shoulders. The choice of word was either deliberate or merely symbolic.

'Visionary.' I turned to the mild-mannered Tony. 'She had visions?'

David translated.

'Si,' Tony said, nodding. 'Like a dream. She dreamt of you, I think. She told me, I have seen a girl with …'

'Honey,' translated David. 'Honey-coloured hair. And English eyes.'

'English eyes?' I asked.

'Blue,' said Joseph.

'And where was I?'

Tony blushed and pointed at the paintings. He offered a diplomatic shrug of the shoulders. 'In them. She dreamed many times of you. But…' Tony's face screwed up as he translated, 'it was for my friend Joseph that she wished happiness.'

Something I already believed. 'Of course, Joseph—'

'Me?'

Our voices clashed.

Tony's filled with tears. 'She was very sad for you. She wanted you to be happy. You came and painted, and you told her a sad story. She thought that you needed a happy ending. So she gave you the girl with… honey hair.'

'Me,' Joseph said again. 'She commissioned me to paint these as a gift for Robyn? But she couldn't have known we would meet for sure, or that she was related. It's too improbable, it doesn't—'

I hushed him. 'Don't think too hard.' I grinned. 'Just go with it.'

Tony disappeared.

'Is he okay?' I asked David.

'He has gone to fetch something.' David said. 'He's been so excited at meeting you. Hard to imagine, I know, but he wanted to be sure you wouldn't be angry with him.'

'Angry?' I said, perplexed.

'Because your grandmother, Isabel, died without meeting Lora. Tony thinks Lora should have tried again to find her. He's very keen to meet your mother, too.'

'Oh, you see, Mum doesn't know why I'm here. She thinks I'm on holiday. There were letters that Loretta wrote to Izzy that she saw. I haven't told her everything that's in them.' I grimaced. 'Should I?'

'Maybe if she sees this,' Tony said. He was carrying two boards sandwiched together. He propped them on a nearby chair and removed the topmost one. Underneath was the canvas of an oil painting, an unsophisticated portrait of a young girl.

'My mother,' Tony said, proudly. 'Bambino.' He chuckled.

She was amongst the grass of a meadow in the halo of a sunbeam. The colours were a wash of buttercup yellows and spring grass, her face bronzed, eyes charcoal black, hair spiky and newly hatched, as if she was fresh out of her mother's womb. The bloom of her cheeks were dimpled, a little like Joseph's, and she had four tiny teeth. There were braces on her skinny legs.

Joseph crouched to inspect the brush strokes. 'It's signed.'

'Yes,' Tony said, pleased.

'By whom?' I asked.

Joseph squinted. 'Catherine Maynard.'

I covered my mouth before finding my tongue. 'Of course. She was a painter too. She left this behind; she didn't take it?'

Tony shook his head mournfully. 'No time. She was in danger. And Mamma was too young to travel. Too ... delicate. So Catherine left her with my grandfather; it broke her heart. The picture stayed. She could not carry it. They told her to go, just go.' He gestured animatedly to the door. 'Mussolini's men, like my grandfather's brothers. They wore black uniforms and marched into town.'

Joseph squeezed my shoulders. I hiccoughed, fighting back

tears. 'Poor Nana Catherine. She didn't live long enough to come back to find her.'

Tony reached behind the boards on the chair. 'These, my mother hid too.' He held out a bundle of familiar looking letters, the same blue tinged paper, but the stamps on these had the queen's head on them. They were the flip side of the correspondence between Isabel and Lora.

I clutched the letters to my chest.

'And this.' Tony held several sheets of paper, folded over once.

My name was written on the plain side. The printed text was small, the signature at the bottom just legible: Loretta Di Matteo.

'When did she write this?' I asked her son.

'I don't know.' Tony left, quietly.

I excused myself to one corner of the barn, and braced myself for a difficult read. I imagined my aunt Loretta, fading from this world, fighting the spasms as she typed. I sensed she might have written the letter in the atelier. I was almost there with her. I blinked several times, and refocused.

Dearest Robyn,

If you are reading this letter then you know my true identity. At the time of writing, David has told me that you have encountered Joseph and I am optimistic that your natural curiosity and the kind heart you inherited from your grandmother will encourage a friendship. Sadly, I will never have the delight of meeting you in person.

I must begin my story with a heartfelt apology. I am very sorry for the clandestine use of David, the lack of transparency, the secrecy I inflicted upon you. I had my reasons, and now that I am gone, and you hopefully have achieved part of your aspiration to travel and explore the past, I can explain my actions.

We are related and I was kept hidden from your mother's family. It was my mother's, Catherine, behest that Isabel was not told of the existence of a half-sister. She feared Isabel's future prospects would be damaged. Remember, during the war, Italians were the enemy of England, and not to be trusted. Here in Italy, she was ostracised by my father's despotic uncles, who pushed her away, insisting she was not capable of raising me. She was an artist without regular income and had no faith; religion played heavily in this sad tale. She suffered as a consequence of the politics of the era. The church wiped clean my father's sin. So simple an act.

Afraid for her life, hounded out of the country, she had no choice but to leave me behind. I was raised as if I never had a natural mother, although my step-mother and half-siblings have always shown me nothing but kindness and love. My failing was not the weakness of my body, but my illegitimacy. So the secrecy of my birth was maintained. Your grandmother, Isabel, was born in wedlock to Catherine, my mother, and neither of us were told of each other's existence. But I found out.

Before she left Italy, Catherine painted a portrait of me, a small, crippled child, but she was forced to leave it behind. She had been given no opportunity to take personal possessions. My father's family claimed everything. The painting was bound in cloth and stored in a disused barn.

I refused to be hindered by my affliction, and as a child I established the barn as my space, a sanctuary. It took years for me to learn to climb a ladder, then I finally found the boxes lying forgotten up in the attic. I uncovered the painting, unframed, and recognised myself. My angry questions led to recriminations – I was no longer a small child and I insisted on contacting my real mother. My father begrudgingly granted me access to my birth registration and adoption records – for he had ensured I was formally his. It took time. The last my father had heard was that my mother had a new family and a career as a photojournalist. I wrote many pleading letters to the last address near to Coalville, the last place my father had written to Catherine when he told her he had married.

But because Catherine was long dead, Isabel answered my letters. She retrieved them, unopened from her father's bureau, where they lay dusty and stuffed in the back of a drawer. I believe she was led to seek them out by a dream, perhaps of me or her mother. My half-sister took up the challenge and we corresponded for years. I taught her Italian, she improved my English, and we used code to hide our innermost thoughts, a request on her part as she didn't want her step-mother to know of our correspondence. I crafted the code for her. My tendency for cautious secrecy has its foundations in those few years when she was a curious teenager desperate for excitement.

She also told me tales. It became apparent her imagination was vivid and often blurred with reality, something of a family trait. While I might picture a future scene, Isabel was lost in alternative realities, places she should be, but was not able to visit.

Unfortunately, my letters with their Italian stamps were discovered by Isabel's step-sister, Beryl. They argued. Beryl wanted to tell their father Nigel. Isabel preferred secrecy. It drove a wedge between them that never should have been there. I suspect Isabel had to make a decision and chose to protect her life in England. One day the letters stopping arriving. Mine were returned unopened, the addressee not recognised.

I know little of what happened to Isabel next: she lived in Coalville, and she had mentioned an older man, who lived locally to her, so I assumed she married him and moved out of the family house. Why she never informed me of her fate, or stayed in contact, I do not know. From then on, my English connection was severed. Decades passed, and I had no expectation of ever meeting my half-sister.

As my body began to lose what little coordination and strength it still possessed, I decided to make one last effort. The man who inspired me was Joseph, a wandering artist who made use of the converted barn, now an atelier for the visiting artists I nurture. He painted landscapes by day and in the evening, we talked. The tragic events of our lives are markedly different, but during those summer weeks, I came to admire his determination to carve out his own future regardless of his brothers' mistakes.

His loneliness and humble origins struck me as unfortunate. My father's family were wealthy landowners, respected and frightfully aristocratic in their approach to life. Even with my disability, I was expected to aspire and achieve. I did – I became a distinguished architectural historian, a professor and author.

While he stayed with me, I felt an awakening, an awareness, not of my late mother, nor of my sister, Isabel, but you, Robyn. Your presence trickled into my thoughts. My hope was that you were one of Catherine's descendants and had inherited her love of photography or painting. This visionary ability is a gift for open-minded women in our family – Isabel, me, and you.

So I searched out a good friend in England and set him a task – find a photographer. David was incredulous of course, but willing to try. He is racked with guilt that instead of him, I had been blamed for the recriminations of his elopement. I had sent him to England with Magdalene and he had not suffered any direct consequences, unlike myself. I do not feel the same way in the slightest. It was my choice and I have no regrets. It was our friendship that I relied on, and he thankfully wished only to help me.

I had an inkling, from the flashes of images I saw in my head, that I had a good indication of your passions and your general features. I wanted to give you the chance to explore those passions we both share: history and castles. Although I only ever read of your English castles, I wanted to see them through your eyes, the same eyes as my mother, who also had a talent for creating pictures. I tasked David with a challenging requirement: a female photographer based in Coalville, the last location I had for Isabel, and I envisaged you as a young woman on the brink of a new adventure. When David told me how he had met you, his description matched what I had seen in my vision of you. He also provided me with details of the photographs of Ashby-de-la-Zouch. I knew I had found you, and that I could put in place the rest of my plan.

How was I so confident of finding you? A good question. You see whispers of the past, and Izzy was constantly transporting herself to other realities of the present – she "visited" me in Italy many times, but obviously not in person! I foresee things to come. I saw you, nameless and a little fuzzy, but only after I met Joseph, and from then on with increasing frequency. His first visit triggered a vision of you at Ashby-de-la-Zouch, where Izzy also liked to go. You were there taking photographs, like my mother. From there I saw you at Bamburgh by the windmill and at Dunstanburgh in a dark cave, which led me to research the stories and folktales associated with castles. Did you see other strange things as you walked among the ruins? I hope they did not scare you. In one of my premonitions, at Prudhoe, there was a shadow of a man nearby. He moved with you to Middleham, where on the ramparts you reached out, as if to grab something, and with you was his shadow once again.

I was certain that the figure at your side was my friend Joseph. He was the echo of a possible future that I hoped would become real. You faded a little as my body weakened. There was one vision, again and again, of you standing among a multitude of towers, each one the same, yet different. I recognised where you were and why. I recalled the Curzon Institute's annual exhibition. What art dealer doesn't know of its reputation? I placed my hope in finding you there.

But why, you might ask, did I not tell you, or reveal in our correspondence the true nature of our relationship? It is because Joseph was my motivation for this project. For if David had not met you, I would have to look elsewhere to find someone suitable for my young friend. I nearly ran out of time. However, I had put a plan in motion, and its outcome depended on the natural flow of events. Contrived, yes, but the sentiments invoked by my choreographed journey had to be genuinely, and spontaneously, discovered. I am still hopeful. But I also accept that my dreams might not be perfect realisations of what will happen, and that Joseph might still be alone in this world. If you have this letter, then it is likely Joseph is with you, his paintings in your possession, and I will be content in my resting place.

You are my gift to Joseph, the sad young man who took my paintbox and hopefully put it to better use than I with my twitching hands. I make no apologies for matchmaking. I dream of you together, a strong vision I first sensed in the barn where he had slept. I hoped in setting you to work in parallel that you would encounter him. Fifteen castles, fifteen opportunities. The precise route, the timings, they were a gamble that you might meet at least once or twice, and then it would be out of my hands, which is why I had to keep quiet and not interfere. I informed David I was indisposed, and he had his convenient vacation.

So if you have worked it all out, I admit I engineered Joseph's agenda to match yours. Although things began badly. He chose to start earlier in the spring when I knew you couldn't possibly be ready. I had to accept this change of plan as necessary given his explanation. Camilla told me she had received three paintings at Easter and the reason why. I feared, back then, that my goal was already doomed to failure. But my dreams of you include him and even with three less opportunities for you to meet, I must rely on both luck and faith in my premonitions. The vision of you together, which was just before your last email, is so strong. You're standing together in what appears to be a church, or so it seems from the windows. His face is illuminated this time with light, and yours with relief.

Joseph has an independent spirit that I cannot fault, and you will learn much from it. But I needed your imagination too. I prayed you would stick to the schedule, and above all else, persevere and breach Joseph's barriers, free him from isolation. I hid the reason from both of you. David and Camilla, a distant cousin on my step-mother's side, have no knowledge of each other. I put them both in an awkward position of trust.

The paintings and book are my gifts to you, my spiritual niece, and although we will never meet, I know you are as close to me as the daughter I never had.

David, I'm sure, will lick his wounds as he would detest the extravagant secrecy I inflicted upon him. He will be delighted to own a prestigious gallery and art dealership. Camilla will always enjoy the pleasures of money. As for Joseph, if my aspirations for you both come true, then I am truly at peace.

If you continue to "see" and "hear" your connection to the past, do not fear it. You are not ill or impaired like this disability I have. This innate ability is as commonplace as any other, and I likened it to reincarnation experiences. Perhaps, in combination with Joseph's skills, you can bring those visions to life in some way.

This letter I send with my portrait. You will note the signature on the canvas, and, I hope, you know that I am genuine in my affection for you.

Farewell, Lora Di Matteo.

Now I had the full circle of communication, which also meant I had the confidence I needed to approach my mother. There was no need for any more secrets. Beryl was gone, and if she had thwarted the siblings' chance of meeting, there would be no recriminations, only regrets, and what person never suffered those?

Later, after we'd dined with Tony's wife and children, enjoying the most delicious pasta bathed in olive oil, the fulsome flavours of wine, and the icy sparkle of Italian gelato, Joseph and I retired to the guest house, the atelier where Loretta had watched Joseph paint and lament his past.

'What will you do with the paintings?' Joseph asked, easing his body onto the bed. There, comfortably stretched, freshly showered and wearing only boxers, he rested his back against the headboard. I desired every inch of him with renewed hunger.

Crossing to the other side of the barn, I admired the castles of my dreams, the fifteen with which I had started my journey. They had also nearly ended it prematurely. I still wanted to continue the quest, but now I wasn't interested in exploring them with my mind. I was content to use my camera.

I smiled as I recalled how we had bumped into each other, wary at first, then curious. The amusing conversations regarding latrines, the technical ones about composition, light and shadow. At no point during their creation had I anticipated that these pictures would be mine. The choices Joseph had made for his paintings reflected his moods and sometimes his lack of interest in the subject matter, a contrast to my often overly enthusiastic approach. It dawned on me, standing in the warmth of the evening, what Loretta had planned with her gift to me: the purpose of the paintings wasn't to make them aesthetically pleasing, they were in fact a collection of memories, and in hindsight an artistic wooing. By watching the artist at work, and without realising it at the time, I had fallen in love with Joseph.

I wondered if he would paint other castles for me. Like Kenilworth, where I had mused over the courting of Elizabeth I, and Robert Dudley's opulent attempt at winning her heart. Fifteen paintings was mediocre in comparison, and hardly warranted an historical footnote, although for me, they were priceless. Moving them again seemed criminal, especially as the collection belonged to not just me. They existed because of my late patron's foresight.

I joined Joseph on the bed. 'If Tony doesn't mind, do you think we could leave them here, and now and again, when we feel restless and distracted by the real world, we could come back here to remember the summer when we met. I think they'll be therapeutic for both of us.'

He draped his long arm around my shoulders. 'Whatever you like. I don't think the chapel is suitable.'

The chapel house was a way station, convenient for now but without the comforts of a settled life. Joseph needed a proper home; we both did.

Recalling the chapel prompted me to show Loretta's letter to Joseph. He refused to read it at first, then I persuaded him that Loretta was really more part of his life than mine. I had never met her, nor formed a bond with her. If we had a connection, it was one way. Joseph read in silence, scratching his chin, as he did when thoughtful.

'The paintbox,' he said, and added a low groan of annoyance.

'What about it?'

'She carved her initials into it. LDM. Why hadn't I noticed that before when you told me about your Medici?'

'Ah, well, that was her idea, calling herself that, and I took it as good sign. It doesn't matter. David thinks the code in the letters can be broken. He's also going to translate the Italian in both sets, so when Mum reads them, she'll understand everything.'

'What will she think?'

'She'll not like what Beryl did. It will upset her. But I think it will help explain why Isabel had those phases of disorientation and confusion. She shouldn't have been labelled crazy.' A pang of regret gnawed inside. 'She was different, that's all.'

Joseph handed me the letter back and I put it safe with the other documents. Perching on the edge of the bed, I plucked at the stitching of the quilted duvet.

'What?' Joseph was too perceptive.

'Lora wrote I shouldn't be afraid of my visions. I pretty much decided they were at best a form of worthless self-indulgence and, at worst, harmful.'

He stroked the back of my hand and stilled it. 'That's a bit harsh. You said yourself it's about controlling them. Daydreaming is something we all do.'

'True.'

He kissed my palm. 'If you can help me with my fear of heights, I'm sure I can keep an eye on you, too.'

I laughed. 'Why, thank you, kind sir.' I flopped onto the bed. 'What now?'

'We've a day or two. Tony doesn't mind if we stay here.'

'We could go into Potenza…'

He grinned. 'See the art gallery.'

'Yes, and I could take photographs.'

'That's a given.'

'Then I could watch you paint the view out of that window.' I snuggled closer to him. 'I love watching you paint. I could imagine Lora here with us and see where that takes me.'

He sighed, lovingly, the exhale of a man deeply happy. 'I'd like that too. You can tell me what you see, then you'll have the best of both worlds, the past and present. And I'll paint it for you.'

EPILOGUE

A further extract from the Memoirs of Professor David Carmichael, Emeritus Professor of Art History, Charnwood University.

As I put the final words to paper, I raise a glass to absent friends and family. I'm not alone in commemorating the departed. Every year I am joined by Robyn and Joseph, and their two delightful daughters - Kate and Isabella. Today, while their mother balances a camera on the palm of her hand, the same now outdated digital camera Lora gave her, the two girls craft colourful posies using the flora of the terraced gardens on Tony's extensive estate. Robyn often laments that the idyllic summer can't be bottled and taken back to England. There hasn't been an English summer like that of 2003 in a while. Unperturbed by the heat, the little family find ways to capture their time here.

Robyn occasionally snaps a photograph, but mostly she uses the zoom as a telescope, scanning the valley far below for a bird of prey. In recent years she has shifted her allegiance somewhat from ruins to nature; her photographs often appear in prestigious publications. She has mastered the art of quiet confidence, too. I remember that feeling. There is nothing more satisfying than knowing you are riding the peak of your career without fear of failing anyone.

A palette of acrylic paints sits on a stand and next to it, perched on an overhanging outcrop, is Joseph, with his easel. He meticulously paints an amphitheatre from memory and injects what Robyn interprets, as if she was immersed in the same scene, but at a different time. Joseph doesn't let her wander for too long and draws her back with a kiss on her cheek.

Lora would be proud of her protege. And of the next generation to come.

Kate is energetic like Robyn, full of exuberance when excited, but also contemplative when drawn into conversations. Isabella is naturally introspective and thoughtful; she sketches for hours upon end. The Italian mingles fluidly with their native English; only the sisters' pale skin reminds me this isn't their permanent home, only a summer retreat.

My darling Maggie tells me nobody will read this memoir. She likes to tell me that I am, after all, merely a retired academic who makes a small living from the proceeds of a provincial art gallery. Nevertheless, I shall publish it in some form. She suggested a title for Lora and Robyn's chapter – "A Summer of Castles". I rather like the idea.

AUTHOR'S NOTE

This book would not be possible without the support and help of many people, especially my editor and her invaluable contribution.

Although this book isn't historical fiction, the historical aspects are largely accurate and taken from real guidebooks or official websites. As for the myths and ghostly tales associated with a few of the locations, these too have been recorded and I have borrowed them to embellish my own story.

The ghosts of Bamburgh and Spofforth castles are both apparitions that fell from the ramparts: one pink and one blue. The various happenings in Prudhoe Castle, including a bouncy ball, is one of many unexplained events. The verses of Sir Guy the Seeker were originally published in 1808 as part of Matthew Lewis's *Romantic Tales*. Lewis was a gothic novelist who liked to pen horror stories and wrote a play called *The Castle Spectre*. Lewis wrote his Sir Guy the Seeker poem based on a legend at Dunstanburgh Castle, the origins of which still remain unknown.

Whitby Abbey was bombed during the First World War by battleships and Rievaulx Abbey housed an ironworks. There is a windmill on the ramparts at Bamburgh Castle and a Gold Hole Tower at Richmond Castle, so called because it housed the latrines. Conscientious objectors were imprisoned at Richmond too, and some were transported to France to face possible firing squads. Their stories are told through the graffiti on the walls.

The Medici family were great patrons of the art. Lorenzo de' Medici, also known as The Magnificent, was born in 1449 in Florence. He sponsored many artists, including Botticelli and

Michelangelo by helping them to secure commissions. He also wrote poetry.

If you enjoy stories with historical or magical elements, please have a look at my other books.

Rachel Walkley also writes crime fiction under the pen name Rae Shaw.

RACHEL WALKLEY'S BOOKS

The Women of Heachley Hall

The house itself is almost a breathing entity with its own personality and I loved this about it. A cleverly written plot that drew me in and had me wandering the rooms of Heachley Hall along with Miriam. A story about love, regret and the secrets families keep. ~ Brooks Cottage Reviews

Only women can discover Heachley's secret.

The life of a freelance illustrator will never rake in the millions so when twenty-eight-year-old Miriam discovers she's the sole surviving heir to her great-aunt's fortune, she can't believe her luck. She dreams of selling her poky city flat and buying a studio.

But great fortune comes with an unbreakable contract. To earn her inheritance, Miriam must live a year and a day in the decaying Heachley Hall.

The fond memories of visiting the once grand Victorian mansion are all she has left of her parents and the million pound inheritance is enough of a temptation to encourage her to live there alone.

After all, a year's not that long. So with the help of a local handyman, she begins to transform the house.

But the mystery remains. Why would loving Aunt Felicity do this to her?

Alone in the hall with her old life miles away, Miriam is desperate to discover the truth behind Felicity's terms. Miriam believes the answer is hiding in her aunt's last possession: a lost box. But delving into Felicity and Heachley's long past is going to turn Miriam's view of the world upside down.

Does she dare keep searching, and if she does, what if she finds something she wasn't seeking?

Has something tragic happened at Heachley Hall?

Miriam has one year to uncover an unimaginable past.

The Last Thing She Said

It was a gripping story of family dealing with loss and love with an added sprinkle of magic for good luck! ~ Amazon Reviewer

A sister and her lover bring turmoil to a family.
Was her grandmother's prophetic warning heeded?

'Beware of a man named Frederick and his offer of marriage.'

Rose's granddaughters, Rebecca, Leia and Naomi, have never taken her prophecies seriously. But now that Rose is dead, and Naomi has a new man in her life, should they take heed of this mysterious warning?

Naomi needs to master the art of performing. Rebecca rarely ventures out of her house. She's afraid of what she might see. As for Rebecca's twin, everyone admires Leia's giant brain, but now the genius is on the verge of a breakdown.

Rebecca suspects Naomi's new boyfriend is hiding something. She begs Leia, now living in the US, to investigate.

Leia's search takes her to a remote farm in Ohio on the trail of the truth behind a tragic death.

Just who is Ethan? And what isn't he telling Naomi?

In a story full of drama and mystery, the sisters discover there is more that connects them than they realise, and that only together can they discover exactly what's behind Rose's prophecy.

Three sisters. Three gifts. One prophecy.

Beyond the Yew Tree

Absolutely stunning, all-encompassing read. ~ Devilishly Delicious
Book Reviews

Whispers in the courtroom.
Only one juror hears them.
Can Laura expose the truth before the trial ends?

In an old courtroom, a hissing voice distracts reluctant juror, Laura, and at night recurring nightmares transport her to a Victorian gaol and the company of a wretched woman.

Although burdened by her own secret guilt, and struggling to form meaningful relationships, Laura isn't one to give up easily when faced with an extraordinary situation.

The child-like whispers lead Laura to an old prison graveyard, where she teams up with enthusiastic museum curator, Sean. He believes a missing manuscript is the key to understanding her haunting dreams. But nobody knows if it actually exists.

Laura is confronted with the fate of two people – the man in the dock accused of defrauding a charity for the blind, and the restless spirit of a woman hanged over a century ago for murder.

If Sean is the companion she needs in her life, will he believe her when she realises that the two mysteries are converging around a long-forgotten child who only Laura can hear?

Ordinary women.
Extraordinary experiences.